Praise for Sandra I

THE UNMAKING OF El

'Ireland is fast becoming an exciting new voice in the psychological thriller genre. Her latest offering is darkly gothic and plunges us into the world of Ellie Rook' *Sunday Post*

'Sandra Ireland's third novel, *The Unmaking of Ellie Rook*, cements her place as the queen of Scottish folklore-inspired domestic noir . . . [her] writing of emotion is confident and assured' The Wee Review

'Darkly mesmerising with throbbing attitude and heart . . . a fabulous read' LoveReading

'A truly magical novel' Goodreads

BONE DEEP

'In themes that ripple through the ages, *Bone Deep* is a taut, contemporary psychological thriller about love, betrayal, female sibling rivalry and bone-grinding, blood-curdling murder' *Sunday Post*

'Gripping from the outset, an atmospheric, fluent book which kept me reading into the small hours' *Dundee Courier*, Scottish Book of the Week

'The final chapters take *Bone Deep* from being a beautifully written and thoughtful constructed psychological study into sheer gothic novel nightmare territory . . . a tremendous example of writing and plotting' *Scotland on Sunday*

'A psychological thriller drenched in suspense' *Sunday Herald*

'Atmospheric, with a delicious build-up of tension, and beautifully observed throughout' Michael J. Malone, author of *House of Spines*

'Captivating, compelling and infused with Sandra Ireland's evocative sense of place' Noelle Harrison, author of *The Gravity of Love*

BENEATH THE SKIN

'Ireland writes about powerful and troubling subjects and shows how the past can have devastating consequences' *Daily Mail*

'This debut novel is an exceptional calling card . . . an in-depth psychological thriller packed with suspense and loaded with eerie excitement' *Dundee Courier*

'A powerful exploration of PTSD from an astonishing new voice in fiction' Blackwell's Bookshops

A NOTE ON THE AUTHOR

Sandra Ireland was born in Yorkshire, lived for many years in Limerick, and is now based in Carnoustie. She began her writing career as a correspondent on a local newspaper but quickly realised that fiction is much more intriguing than fact. In 2013 Sandra was awarded a Carnegie-Cameron scholarship to study for an MLitt in Writing Practice and Study at the University of Dundee; she graduated with a distinction in 2014. Her work has appeared in various publications such as *New Writing Dundee* and *Furies*, an anthology of women's poetry. She is the author of *Beneath the Skin* (2016), *Bone Deep* (2018) and *The Unmaking of Ellie Rook* (2019), all published by Polygon. *Sight Unseen* is the first in a new series of thrillers featuring Sarah Sutherland.

Sight Unseen

A Sarah Sutherland Thriller

Sandra Ireland

First published in Great Britain in 2020 by Polygon,
an imprint of Birlinn Ltd.

West Newington House
10 Newington Road
Edinburgh
EH9 1QS

www.polygonbooks.co.uk

1

ISBN 978 1 84697 528 8
eBook ISBN 978 1 78885 281 4

British Library Cataloguing in Publication Data
A catalogue record for this book is available on request
from the British Library.

Typeset by 3btype.com, Edinburgh

To my late mother-out-law, Joan Ireland.
Raising an Irish coffee to you. *Sláinte*

Sarah

I don't know about you, but if things aren't in order I find it impossible to think straight.

My colleagues tease me, mock the neatness of my desk, the way everything has to be lined up symmetrically. But the alternative, as I keep telling them, is chaos, and I don't do chaos. I take a sip of cold tea from my china mug and check my phone. It's on silent, but it never leaves my sight. Chaos could be on the other end of a missed call.

Steeling myself, I hitch up the cuffs of my managerial jacket and clasp my hands in front of me on the desk. My palms are sweaty and my mouth is tinder dry; I hate confrontation. My favourite pen, an envelope and *the letter*, printed on our best quality headed stationery, are all in place. I will sign it in his presence. It will carry more weight that way, be more of a statement. Then, I will simply stuff it into the envelope marked *Mr Grant Tranter* and wave him goodbye.

Job done.

A sharp rap on the door is followed by the sight of Grant Tranter's short bouncy dreadlocks. His cocky grin is already in place. I'm about to knock that off, big style, and my heart sinks. I'm not the sort of person who enjoys destroying smiles.

'Come in, Grant. Take a seat.'

He settles himself in the chair on the opposite side of my desk. His teal-striped uniform shirt is unbuttoned more than is strictly advised, and he's doing that manspreading thing, taking up a ridiculous amount of space. I avert my gaze from his muscular thighs.

'Am I in trouble, boss?'

He's such an actor, Grant. I don't need to look at him to see the puppy dog expression, the melting eyes. He knows how to turn on the charm.

'What do you think, Grant?' I meet his gaze steadily, willing myself not to be intimidated by his youth, his boldness.

'Is it about me taking a ride on the warehouse door?' He can see from my face that this little nugget has escaped me, and he's happy to elaborate. 'It's a thing we do on night shift. You press the button and catch hold of the shutter handle and it scoots you upwards. Better than Alton Towers, although there's quite a drop. Usually we jump down onto a pile of rubbish sacks . . .'

I hold up a hand. 'Grant. Just stop. You're in enough trouble as it is. I'm afraid I'm going to have to give you a written and final warning.' I indicate the paper in front of me. 'Wisebuy Supermarkets is very clear about the consequences of any breach of its health and safety protocol, and to be honest, Grant, you have flouted the rules consistently since you came to us.'

The smile fades. I think he's realising he's not going to wriggle out of this one. 'That time I went AWOL was for perfectly legitimate reasons.'

I turn to the computer screen, where his employee file is open, and read. 'Your first verbal warning was received in January after you worked only two hours of an eight-hour shift, that being the first and last hour.' I gaze at him coldly. 'Basically, you clocked in, messed around, disappeared and returned an hour before the end of your shift to clock out.'

'I had family issues.'

I raise my eyebrows. 'Taking your cousin to the airport for her hen party weekend in Ibiza does not count as a legitimate reason for unauthorised absence. We've been through this, Grant.' I turn back to the screen. 'April the twenty-second. A second verbal warning for misuse of company property and a serious health and safety breach.'

Grant flicks his dreadlocks indignantly. 'That was crate-surfing. I invented that as a little morale booster for the lads on the Twilight Team.'

Despite the implications, I'd had to swallow my amusement when I'd replayed the CCTV footage of teams of my trusted and very sober employees hurtling through the warehouse tucked into crates loaded onto wheeled pallets. But, as always, Grant has gone too far. He is a maverick, a menace. Three strikes and you're out.

'And this time, Grant, we have—'

'Forklift scooter.'

'Forklift scooter.' I glare at him, but his expression remains impassive. I never know whether or not he's taking the piss, he hides it so well. He has a clever, beautiful face. He should be on a catwalk, or a movie set, not here in a small-town supermarket, and I reckon he knows it. I sigh and glance at the letter. Maybe I'll be doing him a favour. I pick up my pen.

'Forklift scooter,' I murmur. We have a small forklift in the warehouse, one of those hand-operated ones for stacking pallets. Grant thought it would be a good idea to ride it like a child's scooter. I believe the staff were holding races in the small hours, placing bets. I sign my name, *Sarah Sutherland, Store Manager*, and watch the ink dry. 'You know the rules, Grant. This is your final written warning. One more transgression and—'

He sits forward, unexpectedly, elbows on knees, gazing at me with a strange expression. A light has popped on behind his eyes. The dark gleam unsettles me, and under the cover of my desk I wipe my palms on my skirt.

'Is this about race, Sarah?'

'What?'

He leans back and waves an airy hand. 'It wouldn't be the first time.'

I grip the edge of my desk. 'Don't you dare try and play the race card with me, Grant Tranter. You're as Scottish as mince and tatties.'

'But am I, though? Am I?'

I will not be derailed. I fold the letter briskly into thirds, sensing the sudden upward flash of his eyes on me.

'Actually, I'm glad you called me in, Sarah,' he says, 'because I've been wanting a word.'

'Oh?'

'Yes. I wanted to tell you I'm leaving. I've got another job, you see, and I have to start immediately, so unfortunately I won't be able to work my notice. Hope that doesn't inconvenience you.' He gets casually to his feet and grins at me from his superior height. 'So, as for your written warning' – he goes to the door, pauses for effect – 'you can stick it up your arse.'

John

John came across the pen while searching for his chequebook. A big fat fountain pen, in a presentation box, inscribed with his name, John R. Milton, and the date of his retirement. That little torch of Sarah's had been a godsend, illuminating all the dark corners where things can hide. Old age is no joke. When the eyes start to go you might as well turn up your toes. Imagine, thirty years at the building society, and now he can't even see to find his own chequebook.

He's had a good rake through the top drawer in the sideboard, taken out some stuff and piled it on the dining table. So much *stuff*. Old address books with half the names scored out (that's the trouble with being ninety-odd – it's a lonely place), discarded batteries and a basket full of stationery supplies: rubber bands, a bulldog clip, a pencil sharpener. His fingertips touch the edges and corners of each object, trying to bring things into focus.

No sign of the chequebook, but the fountain pen has distracted him. It's heavy and smooth, a superior quality pen. He rolls it in his fingers like a fine cigar. He always used a fountain pen at the building society, in the old days, for signing documents, taking notes. No computers then, just reams of heavy paper. Words carry more weight on heavy paper. That flimsy stuff they use nowadays! From time to time, Sarah prints off Hannah's emails. Goodness knows where in the world Hannah is, but she always signs off with 'Love and hugs to Granddad! Xxx'. He pretends he can read the emails, but the words swim off the edge of the page like fish.

He has a bottle of Quink, somewhere. Probably in the same drawer. He renews his efforts, piling more bric-a-brac onto the table. When Marjorie was alive everything was shipshape, but he's letting things slip, and slipping makes him anxious. The ink hasn't been used in a good while and the cap is stuck fast. Despite his best efforts, it won't budge, and he becomes short of breath and has to sit down. With persistence, the cap finally gives and he chuckles in triumph.

He sniffs the ink. Its raw classroom whiff takes him back to his salad days. Scribbled notes in Latin class, wartime love letters. Without warning, the bottle slips from his grasp and drops onto the table.

'Oh, bugger!' He's always made a point of not swearing in front of his daughter, but luckily Sarah is at work. He can't see how far the ink has spread but he hopes it's been stemmed by the various piles of paper he's evacuated from the drawer. He makes his way into the kitchen and comes back with a towel. The torch reveals a small pool of midnight black seeping into a pile of gas bills, but hopefully the towel will soak up the worst of it before it can drip down onto the carpet. Sarah is a stickler for a clean carpet. She has one of those shampooing machines which she brings over at regular intervals. He hates the noise and busyness of it, all that moving of furniture when he just wants to listen to the radio, but Sarah is very determined and it's best to go along with it.

She's not going to like this. Helplessly he leaves the towel soaking up the ink and goes in search of the time. He can't see his watch very well now. The dining room and lounge are open plan, so it's just a few steps to his favourite easy chair. Amazing how your world shrinks as you age. He used to be able to see the wall clock perfectly from that chair. He could programme his day: breakfast radio, sandwich, lunchtime news, maybe an old Ealing comedy in the afternoon, but now the clock face is a blur.

He's been known to have his lunch at half eleven, because he's mistaken the position of the hands. Nowadays he has to go into the hall and through to his bedroom to check the digital clock radio. The numbers are large and illuminated, but even that isn't foolproof, because sometimes he presses the wrong button when he tries to change channels. Once he spent an entire weekend three hours ahead of the rest of the UK. He can't resist a little chuckle, remembering. Not so much GMT as Milton Mean Time.

Now, the digital format reads 15:00. That feels about right. Sarah won't be finished work for another hour or so. He remembers the ink and slumps down on the edge of the bed, exhausted. That's when he sees them. His stomach does a little flip. Voice trembling with false bravado, he calls out, 'I can see you, you know! Don't think you can hide from me.'

No answer, of course. They never reply. He's become accustomed to their silence, although every sighting of them puts the fear of God into him. He can never tell when they will appear. It's random, like a snowstorm or an earthquake. They're tall and thin and pale, like those elongated marble statues you see in churches that never look in proportion. He screws up his eyes and tries to see their faces, but they shift like smoke.

He calls out again. 'Away you go! My daughter will be here soon, and she won't be happy.'

He can't make out how many there are today. Sometimes they sit on the couch while he's watching TV and he forgets he's afraid of them; pretends he's talking to Sarah or Mrs

Chalmers from next door. He chats away, remonstrates with them, without ever expecting a reply. It's company.

He gets fed up of it being one-sided, though. It's not as if he's even invited them in. During the ad breaks he always asks them to leave, and sometimes they do, but then he gets anxious about where they've gone and what they might be doing. He has to get up and follow them. He loses the thread of his favourite TV programmes and it's exhausting, but he can't bear the thought of them going through his stuff.

He shouts at them again, cross now. 'Get out of my house! This minute, or I'll call the boys in blue!'

They don't like that. He blinks his eyes rapidly, and they're gone. Just like that.

Sarah

My cottage is a mixed-up affair, with the sitting room on top, and the rest of the rooms on the ground floor. It was once the home of a weaver, and the upstairs, which housed the loom, still bears the scars of industry. There are three narrow windows at the back to let in the light, old iron hooks in the beams, and a depression in the floor which I imagine is due to the heft and movement of the machinery. I've covered it with an old Persian rug, but the timber still squeaks if you don't watch your step.

The cottage has the kind of quaint frontage that tourists love to photograph. I've lost count of the times I've pulled back the curtain to see strangers with their phones out, snapping exterior shots. They are fascinated by the red pantiles and corbie-stepped gables, my three storybook windows and the outside stairs that slice diagonally across the front and lead up to my door. They love the iron railings and the deep scoop of each stone step, sometimes settling their backsides into the dips for the ultimate rustic selfie.

If I'm in a good mood I go out and explain about the roof and tell them what a corbie is – sometimes we get lucky and a crow alights on the chimney, right on cue – and then I draw their attention to the marriage lintel above the original downstairs entrance, now my kitchen window.

RW AG

♥

1648

Robert Webster married Alisoune Gowdie in the year before Charles I lost his head. Little did Alisoune know, as she shook out her wedding finery and closed the lid on her spinster life, that she too would meet a grisly end within the year. As stories go, it's a brilliant hook. While they're gasping and gawping, I press my business card into their hands. Not my official retail management one. Oh no.

This one says: *Sarah Sutherland, Storyteller.*

*

I've been standing under a steaming hot shower for ages. It's such a relief to flush away the earthy vegetable smell of the supermarket. It comes home with me at the end of my shift, an unwelcome reminder on my skin and on my hair. I step out of my clothes and leave my managerial self in a heap on the bathroom floor, before emerging twenty minutes later smelling of the spicy new shower gel I bought for these evenings. Wrapping myself in a fluffy white towel, I wander through to my bedroom.

The rear window overlooks a tiny courtyard, which can be accessed through the kitchen. The glass is speckled with an earlier drizzle. Here on the east coast, we're used to getting four seasons crammed into a single day. It confuses everything from my hot flushes to my herb garden. Even the wood pigeon which has set up home in the solitary tree has been enduring phantom pregnancies. Last year, she spent the entire autumn brooding on an empty nest. I feel sorry for her. I can identify with that pigeon and her empty nest. I'm a bit of a home bird too, which can be a problem for others, the ones who like to fly.

No sign of any pigeons tonight. I pull down the blind and settle myself at my antique dressing table. A sense of peace steals over me, although my reflection still appears pale and strained. I put it down to the Grant effect. I unzip my make-up bag and get to work with wipes and foundation. The retail manager is deftly erased and redefined. Just as I'm applying a third coat of mascara, my mobile vibrates, sending eye pencils shivering across the table surface. The word *Dad* appears on the screen. Sighing, I pick it up.

'Sarah? It's your father here.'

'I know.'

'I wasn't going to telephone, but I've had a bit of an accident.'

'Oh?'

'With some ink.'

My shoulders sag. 'Can it wait, Dad? It's Friday evening – I'm about to be really busy.'

A sigh, and the voice drops. 'I know, love. I'm really sorry. I know you're working. I didn't want to bother you and I'm sure it will be all right. It hasn't reached the carpet – yet.'

I look at myself in the mirror and take a deep breath. 'It's fine, Dad. Don't worry. I'll pop in before I start.'

'Thanks, love. You're an angel.'

'No problem. I'll be there in twenty minutes. Bye now.'

The connection breaks. I get on with applying a vampy pillarbox-red lipstick, but my hand is all jittery, and I end up with a smeared cupid's bow like Baby Jane. I have to wipe it off and start again. Tears come unexpectedly, threatening to leave black tracks on my face. I blot them with a tissue before they spill. *Don't you start feeling sorry for yourself. Don't you dare.*

But the truth is I'm not sure how long I can keep this up, juggling two jobs and my father. He's getting confused and frail, and I'm permanently on red alert. I'm never fully present, not for him, not for the shop. I'm never enough.

*

My father's house is within walking distance of mine. That's a bit of a double-edged sword, because I can be by his side in less than thirty minutes, and he knows it. He pretends not to understand modern technology, but he has me on speed-dial.

He lives in a modern bungalow, a five-minute trip in the car, but if I'm trying to reach my daily 10,000 steps I tend to walk. Walking takes you through the town centre, where everything is pretty and medieval and touristy, and then, squeezed between the newsagent and the museum, down the alleyway known as Butter Wynd. In another life, the museum was the old tolbooth, the town gaol, but I'll give you the tour later. I tell him he lives on the wrong side of the tracks, and he accuses me of living in another century. You have to have these little strategies when you're caring for someone. We have lots of little in-jokes and comedy riffs, mainly based on the old routines that Dad remembers as keenly as if he'd written the script himself. Humour keeps us sane. Almost.

The railway more or less dissects the town, but if you take the pedestrian bridge over the line you can stand on the top, a diesel wind blowing in your face, and observe the two ages of Kilgour: the medieval burgh where I live and the newer expansion to the east. Different centuries, different side of the tracks.

My father lives on a leafy estate where everyone knows which day to put out the correct bin. The kids playing in the gardens tend to be one generation removed; grandkids, mostly, and the friends of grandkids. They go home at teatime and the street falls silent and everyone is happy. If Cornhill Crescent was a person, it would be mild-mannered and discreet.

Since Mum died, I feel like I've worn a rut between our two houses, pounding out my grief on the pavements, as if I'm on one of those walking pilgrimages you can tackle abroad. The Camino de Santiago with added rain. I watched some celebrities do that once, as part of a reality show, but in my version there's less wailing and more anger. I didn't ask to be left with my dad. I had plans. A life of my own.

As I make tonight's pilgrimage, my heavy make-up and black cloak attract stares from everyone I encounter along the way. Those who know me nod and smile, and those who don't let their jaws drop for a millisecond as I pass. It doesn't faze me. Instead I let my mind drift back through the events of the day.

I never saw Grant Tranter again after his 'resignation'. I was relieved, if I'm honest. It was a clear-cut case, HR-wise, and I'd adhered to company policy, keeping meticulous records. I thought I'd handled the situation sensitively, and couldn't imagine any comeback, so why can't I shake off this feeling of misplaced guilt, as if I am, in some way, the offending party? The arrogance of his parting shot floored me, but he has a vulnerability which almost makes me feel sorry for him. He keeps that part of himself carefully hidden, of course, just like me. They say it takes one to know one.

When Grant Tranter walked out of my office, I think he kept right on going without clocking off. That would affect his final wage, but I get the impression he doesn't care. Has he really landed a new job, or is it all bravado? The encounter had left me slightly shaky and I'd taken my china mug in search of a refill. Peggy, who mans – or rather *womans* – the canteen, took one look at my face and produced a cream doughnut.

'They're from yesterday.' She shoved it on a plate and licked sugar and cream from her fingers. Peggy's fingers, like her face, are always red raw and puffy. I can never get her to wear Marigolds.

I accepted the plate. 'Have these been entered correctly as waste?'

She didn't reply, and I flopped down at one of the dull cafeteria tables and watched her make me a fresh cup of tea. Milk and half a sugar, just as I like it. Peggy is everyone's mum, and there's something about her that reminds me of my own. That unshowy sort of kindness. I accept the tea gratefully. She's looking for gossip.

'So Grant has jumped ship then.' It's not a question. More than once I've caught her listening at doors, like some kind of Edwardian parlour maid. Nothing gets past her. 'That mother of his, a bit of a wild one in her youth. I know her folks – very respectable they are. Churchgoers. She gave them a terrible time. Ran away from home in her teens and took up with a black man. Talk of the town.'

'Peggy! You can't say that.' If Wisebuy is the equivalent of the village well, Peggy is always first in line for her daily fix of tittle-tattle, casual racism and scandal.

'It's true!'

'Apart from the obvious objections, you know my views on shop gossip.'

She sniffed righteously before launching into another topic as I sipped my tea. 'This kitchen was a total state when I came in this morning. A total state.'

I made a mental note to schedule a cleaning audit. 'The new contract has only just been put into place. I expect there's been a few teething problems.'

'I bet we'll have foreigners like the last time.'

Peggy's attitudes echo those of my father, but I was too weary to call her out again. I gobbled up the doughnut, which really hit the spot. I decided to let her dubious adherence to waste monitoring procedures pass.

'That Polish girl we had did an excellent job.'

Peggy makes a reluctant concession. 'True. She didn't stay, though. The good ones never do. She was a bookkeeper, you know.'

I smiled at her surprise. 'Everyone has a story, a life away from work. I expect folk would be surprised to learn what I do on the side!'

My 'job on the side' was waiting for me. A quick visit to Dad and my evening would be my own. The supermarket, Grant Tranter, Peggy and the rubbish cleaner all faded away as excitement bubbled through me once again.

John

Sarah appears in the sitting room like a ghost. He must have dropped off in front of the telly again, and it takes him a moment to come around, to shake off the stupor that comes with a sudden awakening. There she is, in that awful frock, the black one with the lacy sleeves, and she's wearing the cape too. It takes him a second or two to register what she's saying.

'Where's the ink?'

Blinking, he struggles to sit upright. 'You look like that woman from the Addams Family.'

'Last time you called me a black widow,' Sarah says. 'I'm working, remember. What on earth were you doing with the ink?'

Belatedly he remembers why he'd called her and gets stiffly out of his armchair. 'I was looking for my chequebook.'

'What do you want with your chequebook? And why is this stuff all sitting on the table?'

Her sigh gusts around the room. She picks up a sheaf of bank statements and puts them down again.

'I – I can't remember now, but I found a fountain pen.'

'This one?' She holds up the evidence. 'This one takes cartridges, so there was no need to be messing about with ink.'

He hopes the ink hasn't reached the carpet. And then she's lifting the towel he'd put down and scowling at him. 'Where's the ink you spilled then?'

'On the table. A lake of it. I'm sorry, Sarah. I know you have enough to do.'

She's shaking her head at him sadly. 'There's nothing here, Dad. That old inkpot is all dried up. I'll chuck it out.'

'But there was a pool of it. I saw it shining on the table – that's why I put down the towel.'

She hands him the clean dry towel. 'I think you imagined it.'

Anger prickles inside him. 'I didn't imagine it.' His voice grows stronger. 'You think I'm losing the plot, don't you?'

Sarah sighs again, but it's a sad sigh. 'I don't think anything of the sort. Probably a trick of the light.'

'I'm sorry, lass. Will you stay for a cuppa, now you've come out of your way?'

She touches his shoulder. The contact is warm. He misses human contact. 'I can't. I start in thirty minutes. Just enough time to get back to the Black Bull and then – showtime!' She twirls her sleeves.

'Oh well, you just get going, love. I'll put that stuff back in the drawer tomorrow, save you a job.'

Her eyes soften. He doesn't like all that muck she wears on her face at night. She's a bonny fresh-faced girl and all that sooty stuff around her eyes makes her look older, bolder. He doesn't think it's a good idea, walking the streets looking like that, but he would never say so. It's her life.

She perches on the edge of the couch with her arms on her knees, like she's preparing to fly. He likes it better when she lets herself relax, and they can have a coffee and reminisce. Her memory is so much sharper than his, and she remembers the good times better than he can. It makes him sad, forgetting all those holidays by the sea, and the day trips in the old Austin. Marjorie loved to get away.

And then he spots it, sitting beside Sarah on the couch. Not Marjorie, but one of *them*, one of the Figures, just watching, waiting. His heart starts to flutter in his throat. There's a roaring in his ears, so when Sarah asks him a question, he can't answer. His eyes are fixed on the Figure, and he can't look away. *What do they want from him?*

'What are you looking at, Dad?' She glances at the cushions beside her.

He pulls his gaze back to her face. He can't tell her. He can't even explain it to himself.

'I was just looking out of the window. I hope the rain stays off for you.'

Sarah looks out of the window too. Her expression is a blur, but he knows her well enough to imagine her anxious frown.

Sarah

I reach the door of the Black Bull with a jolt of surprise. My walk back was short, consumed with thoughts of Dad. What was all that about the disappearing ink? Only last week he'd warned me not to slip on some nonexistent water on the kitchen floor. I'm anxious about the muddle on his dining table and the muddle in his mind. I've been pushing away thoughts of dementia for some time now, but perhaps it's time to face up to it. I need to make some phone calls. Get help.

My head is still in the little bungalow across the railway, so when I push open the mock Tudor door of the pub, the warm reek of stale beer and soot from the open fire is like a wake-up call – like switching on the radio and getting sucked into a cheesy old tune. Heat and laughter and the clinking of bottles momentarily disorientate me. The interior is artfully rustic – lots of low lighting and black wood and brass that would gleam if someone could be bothered to give it a rub. Maybe the Black Bull has the same cleaning contractor as Wisebuy. The old boys at the L-shaped bar swivel in their seats at the scent of fresh blood, but it's only me. They turn back to their pints and resume their banter.

Time to pull myself together, put on my professional hat. I've never liked going into bars on my own. It's fifteen years since Ian Sutherland decided to take a hike, so you'd think I'd be used to it by now. We were a total mismatch. He liked his 'nights out with the boys' while I preferred my 'nights in with a book'. I guess you're either one way or the other. The only thing we have in common is Hannah. Our daughter has inherited not only his party genes but his itchy feet too.

My fist tightens on the handle of my holdall. It's a vintage leather Gladstone bag I picked up on eBay. The seller assured me it had appeared on TV, in some costume drama, but I'd taken that with a pinch of salt. It does, however, have enough scuff marks and spills to hint at an intriguing provenance. It's carefully packed with the tools of my trade: needles, watercress, red thread, some bent coins and a set of thumbscrews.

'You've got a nice wee bunch tonight.' The barman lifts a wine glass up to the light and squints at it. 'They're all in the snug. An American couple too – they love that sort of thing.'

That sort of thing. Once I'd had a drink with the very same barman after hours. I'd drunkenly tried to explain about the hold the past has over me. It captivates me more than the future, I'd slurred. Maybe because I can't envisage my future. I'm like a book with the pages stuck together. He'd ended up describing the entire plots of all three *Back to the Future* movies. He didn't get history. He didn't get me. We never progressed to a nightcap back at mine, which says all you need to know about the state of my love life.

At the bar, the old boys go into some routine about Yanks and start talking like John Wayne. I take a deep breath, find my game face and pin on a smile.

'I've been doing a bit more research over the last few weeks and I've got some interesting titbits up my sleeve!' I make a dramatic gesture with my own gothic cuffs, but I lost the barman at 'research'. He's gone back to cleaning glasses.

I'm about to head for the snug when I get the distinct

feeling I'm being watched. Across the far side of the bar, Grant Tranter is sipping trendy blonde lager from a bottle. For a split second, our eyes meet, and I think he's about to salute me with his beer, in typical cocky Grant fashion, but his gaze slides away as he turns back to his mates, who are noisily holding court around the fire. Again, that vulnerability. I push away the notion. He should look embarrassed, after what he said to me. Indignantly I square my shoulders and turn away.

The snug has a little brass plaque on the door engraved with its name and a scattering of horse brasses on the walls. There's also an A4 poster depicting a lamp-lit cobbled alley and a lone cloaked figure in the distance. I know the text by heart:

MRS SUTHERLAND'S MAGICAL WITCH WALKS
Time travel into Kilgour's sinister past. Uncover the fascinating truth behind our darkest stories. Thrill to tales of witches and warlocks, cauldrons and curses. Follow in the footsteps of our gloriously gruesome ancestors!
Dress warmly.

I brace myself, push open the door.

*

'So how do you recognise a witch?'

Having prised my punters from the warm embrace of the snug, I'm making them stand in the chill shadow of the mercat cross. As a starting point, the cross is suitably impressive – lofty, enigmatic, like a nameless gunslinger in a spaghetti western. The tumbleweed isn't quite blowing across the town square, but it feels like a lonely place tonight, the cobbles bathed in yellow light from reproduction gas lamps. It's more of a triangle than a square, a vestige of what might once have been here, revamped for the twenty-first century, with designer benches and a dog poo bin. It's Friday night. Everyone's either at home watching *Gogglebox*, or in the pub. The kids hang out in the play park, drinking and getting off their heads on stuff they've bought off the internet. The square is all mine.

The couple from New Jersey zip their windcheaters over thin golfing sweaters and comment on the unseasonable weather. 'It's May,' says an older woman, dressed from head to toe in navy waterproofs. 'Ne'er cast a clout.' The Americans look at me in bemusement. They have that well-nourished, naturally tanned appearance that stands out a mile in a place like Kilgour. Our default setting is overcast. Even if the sun does make an appearance, we don't trust it.

They're a mixed bunch. In addition to the Americans and the waterproofed hiker, there's a couple of phone-checking teenage girls and their mother, plus two middle-aged guys in jeans and smart jackets who could be a couple. For ages I've toyed with the idea of a singles-only tour. Sixty minutes of creepy alleyways and macabre tales on a dark night would surely be enough to drive singletons into each other's arms. And then there's the inevitable bonding session in the pub afterwards. Yes, it could be a big hit, and I like the notion of playing matchmaker, even if I'm a big failure in the couples department myself. One of the guys is wearing a Hogwarts scarf, looped artfully around his neck in the sort of way I can never achieve. Add scarf envy to my list of flaws.

When no one jumps in with an answer I repeat my question with more drama. 'How do you recognise a witch?'

'Black pointy hats,' jokes the American guy.

I chuckle as if I've never heard that one before. 'Yes, and broomsticks and black cats!'

The teenagers are still heads down, fingers scrolling, and then one of them looks up at the cross. A light has come on in her face. 'Isn't this the cross where they filmed *Lowlander*?'

She starts namedropping various actors, and her sister joins in, heads together, whispering. My shoulders sag. Use a place as a film set and everyone's a history buff. But they don't know the real stories of real people. That's where I come in.

'In the sixteenth and seventeenth centuries, everyone knew how to spot a witch! A witch was typically female. She lived alone, had hairs on her chin and was fond of cursing folk.'

'Sounds like every menopausal woman I ever knew,' pipes up the woman in waterproofs.

I smile. I haven't heard that one a million times either. 'Which is exactly the point. Your mother, your sister, your eccentric auntie or your reclusive neighbour – just about anyone was fair game when the witchfinders came calling. All it took was a spiteful comment in the right ear for a person to be arrested.' I think of Peggy and her wayward tongue. 'The Kirk took a very dim view of witchcraft, sorcery and necromancy, and somewhere along the line it moved from being a sin to being a crime, punishable by the worst death imaginable. "Thou shalt not suffer a witch to live": Exodus, chapter twenty-two.'

As I begin to lead them away from the cross I catch the American man's eye. He's now looking very serious.

'One other thing,' I murmur. 'A witch will not look a man straight in the eye.'

I deliberately slide my gaze from his. As we move on I can't resist a grin.

John

He's not sure when it started. He'd been watching *Rip Off Britain* – you can't be too careful these days – and he thought he might have heard a noise in the hall. The sitting-room door was closed, but instead of its usual glossy white surface, there seemed to be a rosy tint about it, down at the base. A trick of the light? He'd switched on the reading lamp behind his armchair, but when he looked back at the door, the angry glow was still there. He couldn't work it out.

If it hadn't been for the noise in the hall, he might never have noticed. The Figures usually don't make a sound, but he definitely heard something. He was just about to get up to investigate, and there it was: a pinkish hue around the bottom of the door, which grew deeper as he watched. And started to waver. He recognised it suddenly, with a dull thumping horror. Surely not? Tongues of flame were licking at the bottom of the door.

They must have done it. That was the noise he'd heard earlier. They'd let themselves in and set a fire in his hallway. You hear about it all the time on the news – young hoodlums sticking petrol-soaked rags through the letterbox. Molotov cocktails.

Oh no. Oh no. He hauls himself to his feet. Maybe he can beat back the flames, but you must never open a door where there's a fire. Keep it contained. Don't give it oxygen. He knows all about fire safety from the war. Incendiary devices everywhere. No. Best call the experts. He reaches for the telephone.

Sarah

'So, did they burn them all at the stake?' the American asks.
His name is Frank, and his wife is Pearl, that much I've
learned. I don't answer. The tour takes sixty minutes, and
I want to keep my powder dry, ramp up the tension.

'To your left, you can see the museum, which is housed in
what used to be the tolbooth, or gaol. Prisoners were held in
the room upstairs' – we all look up to a dusty mullion –
'where their confessions were . . . *extracted*. And yes, it was as
painful as it sounds.'

Between the tolbooth and the newsagent lies Butter Wynd,
the walking route to my father's house. My Camino de
Santiago. Actually, it's more of an ancient furred artery of
weathered cobbles and hulking stone walls. It once led up
from the outskirts of town to the butter market in the square,
but nowadays people are more intent on heading in the opposite
direction, heads down, scrolling for train times. It's also a
handy shortcut to the big new supermarket behind the station.
You can see the cars whizzing past the lower end of it, but
I tend to block them out and let the past rise up to meet me.

Those great walls on either side are more than just walls.
I have a forensic interest in them – all that recycled stone, the
blocked-up windows and sagging lintels. They are the
vestiges of dwellings and workshops clinging to the present
like the last few teeth in an old skull. I lead my merry band
down the passageway in single file. There are a few oohs and
aahs as they peek through archways into private courtyards

that were once pantries and parlours. Most of the houses in Kilgour are an odd shape. They've been added to and meddled with. Every age brings new needs: taller chimneys, bigger windows, more space. It's all about space. Money buys you space. The rich folks have tons of it, while the have-nots are squashed into corners.

Halfway down, on the same side as the tolbooth, we come to Lumsdain House. It's a conundrum. Grey and imposing, with a grand stone portico and a courtyard which is now a car park, it's a nursery these days, with gaudily painted signs and flowers planted in cute little wellies. There are butterflies and ladybirds taped to the windows. Some days, you see the little ones with their noses pressed to the glass, as if longing for freedom. It gives me a momentary thrill of fear I can't explain. Lumsdain is reputed to have a dark past, but I suppose the same can be said for most buildings. Every generation has its share of hard luck stories.

One of the teenagers yawns. I decide to let Lumsdain House keep its secrets for now.

Sarah

There is another house to see. You'd mistake this one for a lock-up, an old byre maybe, that no one can decide what to do with. It has sedum growing in the cracks in the harling and ferns sprouting from the gutters. What paint is left is the colour of dull yellow lichen. An old horse-drawn grass rake is positioned out front as a nod to its rural roots. Various plans have been mooted. The Kilgour Development Trust want to raise funds to turn it into a heritage centre. The Council prefer the cheaper option of demolition. Its fate is uncertain, but it too is hanging on.

This other house is a short walk away, along Butter Wynd and down the steps to the main road. Don't cross the road but stay on the pavement and turn sharp right. Keep walking until you come to the park, the haunt of dog walkers, teenage lovers and underage drinkers. The grass is kept short, the borders neat and the dog bins empty. It's all very civilised, except . . . except if you keep walking you come to a wood. The wood isn't quite so civilised. The house I want to tell you about is in the wood.

*

'Oh my,' says Pearl. 'Is that what you call a bothy?'

'The bothies are all out on the hills and in the farms,' says Waterproofs Woman with some authority. I just bet she's a member of every heritage charity going.

'This is reputed to be the home of Alie Gowdie, the town's most notorious witch.'

Gasp. One of the girls checks her phone – probably cross-referencing me with Google – and I resist the urge to grab the bloody thing off her. 'Alie – according to the records she's Alison, spelled A.L.I.S.O.U.N.E. – was a young woman who lived here with her father and younger siblings. Her father was a souter, or shoemaker, and Alie looked after the younger children, because her mother had died in childbirth, an occupational hazard for women in those days.'

'So what did she do?' The girl slips her phone into her jeans pocket, giving me a little surge of hope. 'Did she cast spells?'

The guy with the Hogwarts scarf shuffles closer.

'Of all the witches, and there are several associated with this town, Alie is my favourite, not least because when she married she and her husband used to live in my house.'

As always at this point, I can feel the interest shift to me, to my personal life. What sort of house do I live in? Is it haunted? Have I ever seen anything spooky? The questions spring up thick and fast, but I deftly turn the focus back to Alie. That's why we're here.

'I suppose I feel I've come to know her over the years. Her husband, Robert, was a weaver, producing linen for the export market. In my back garden Alie would've grown plants for dying the cloth, such as woad and madder. Upstairs, the floorboards were warped by the weight of the loom. They creak when I walk on them and every time they do I think of Alie and the wrong that was done to her. She *was* wronged. Every time I do this tour, I try and put the wrong right, as best as I can.'

It's not the whole truth, of course. I don't think of Alie every time my floor squeaks – that would be bizarre – but you have to ramp it up for the punters, give them a bit of drama, a bit of pathos. That's the art of storytelling. Once I'm sure of their attention, I set the scene.

'One day, Alie took one of her siblings to the town well . . . I'll show you where that is in a minute. I suppose he was a bit cross and making a fuss, and Alie had to ask one of the other women to hold him while she drew water from the well. That's when it started.' I look around the circle of faces. They've forgotten about the appearance of the place. They are already with Alie as she tries to juggle the screaming infant and her wooden pail. 'The woman who helped her reported to her neighbour that the child's hair smelled of brimstone.'

'Hah, the Devil!' says Waterproofs Woman, as if she knows him personally.

I nod. 'It only takes a little bit of gossip in a small town to spread a story like wildfire. And Alie had form. A few weeks earlier, a butcher of this parish, one Archibald Donald, had asked for Alie's hand in marriage. She'd refused, probably because she couldn't leave her father with all these kids, or maybe she already had her eye on her future husband, or maybe she just didn't fancy him. Anyway, Archibald went to see a local cunning woman.'

'Isn't that the same as a witch?' The teenagers' mum thinks she's being short-changed, that maybe I don't know what I'm talking about.

'There's a very fine line between old ways and witchcraft. The authorities turned a blind eye to cunning folk and what was termed natural magic. Holy wells and plant remedies were fine. Calling up dark entities was not. That was *maleficium*, evil-doing, and I'll tell you about that soon. The woman told Archibald to bring her some combings from Alie's hairbrush.'

'Yuck.' One of the girls makes a face. 'What was she going to do with that?'

'Concoct a charm that would make Archibald irresistible to Alie. Archibald bribed one of the kids to bring him the combings, but Alie found out and snipped off some of the hair from a cow's tail and substituted that instead. Apparently, at church that Sunday, a heifer made its way up the aisle and stood mooing beside Archibald's pew. It found him utterly irresistible!' There's a ripple of amusement. 'Unfortunately, it made him a laughing stock, and he was not amused. He swore he'd get even with Alie Gowdie.'

*

I used to end the tour with Witch's Knowe, but despite what happened there it's a little underwhelming. They've all paid a hefty sum online for the privilege of having me shunt them along medieval wynds and through the woods; I don't want any stroppy customers looking for a refund. No, nowadays I end back where I started, at the mercat cross, because that too has a tale to tell.

You can get to the Knowe quite easily from Alie's dwelling. You take the footpath through the woods – it peters out a little in the summer when the grass is in full growth, but it's now the last week in May and the beaten earth of the track is clearly visible. Watch out for nettles and briars, and if it's been raining it can be a bit muddy in places, where underground springs threaten to wash everything clean. But there's no cleaning up this place.

The trees thin out and the air goes quiet. The path ascends steeply and encircles the summit like a belt. A stone cairn marks the spot where people died in agony, and a modest plaque sanitises it all by using words such as 'purports' and 'said to be'. Cop-out words. But, as I say, it can be a bit of an anticlimax. Some people lack my imagination. They stand passively, unsmiling, and don't ask questions. Some people are happier remaining in ignorance. I can always tell which ones.

My current gang are easily pleased, though. They're a little in awe of the place. It's not yet nine, but the breeze has turned sharp and twilight is looming. The space under the trees has a dull dark emptiness that may or may not be brimming with something they can't see. Frank jumps at the distant toot of the 20:40 train to Edinburgh, and when the tolbooth clock chimes the quarter hour the two girls burst into nervous giggles. As always up here, I can feel the sough of Alie's voice on my neck.

The girls are first to ask. That surprises me. I thought it would be Waterproofs Woman. She's been nodding and anticipating every word out of my mouth since we began. A proper little know-it-all. So, I wasn't expecting the million-dollar question from the girls. They want to know how it was done. They ask it in a whisper, as if the perpetrators are still lurking behind the stones. How do you burn a witch?

We stand in a tight knot and I explain to them about the burning of 'unruly' women, how 'ruly' was an archaic term for 'amenable to order'.

'They tortured them first to extract the confession, so that was an ordeal in itself. Then, the witch had to be killed first. Very few were burned alive – that's a myth. Alie was sentenced to be "wiried" at the stake. She was tied to a garrotte or strangling-pole, and the executioner wound a cord about her neck, tightening it with a stick.' I scan their faces. Expressions range from revulsion to pity. Stories never have a shelf life; they always have relevance. 'Maybe your ancestors met the

31

same fate. Just because we didn't witness something doesn't make it any less real. When the victim was dead, they'd leave her tied to the stake, or stand her in a tar barrel, and let the body burn. That's what happened to Alie.'

'Did they burn all of them?' one of the guys wants to know.

I shake my head. 'There was certainly a bit of a frenzy, but most offenders got off with a token fine or imprisonment.'

The girls make faces like they've found something disgusting on their designer footwear.

'Did they burn Alie just for the cow prank?'

'The cow prank seriously upset Mr Donald. He wanted to get revenge. But first, let's go and see the well where the rumours started.'

I can see they've forgotten about the well and the brimstone baby. That's the best bit about storytelling. Manipulate the tension. Rise and fall, rise and fall and *bam*. Lull them into a false sense of security and then hit them with the trump card.

*

I usher them back into Butter Wynd, up the steps and towards town. This is the direction the country people would have come to market, laden with baskets of produce to sell: kale and beans, and butter wrapped in muslin and still dripping with whey. I imagine it leaving a trail on the cobbles, like a burst carton of milk in the supermarket. There's a door set into the wall about halfway up on the left-hand side. The paint is peeling and the latch is an old Bakelite handle salvaged from somewhere else.

The door is so warped I have to shoulder it open. I'm never sure what people are expecting at this point, but they always seem shocked to see a neat acre of allotments, so close to the town centre. There's always a collective gasp of appreciation, which I find quite amusing. Who knew veg plots could capture the imagination?

I let them admire the scene for a moment or two, the creosoted sheds and the dark soil, canes and netting, burgeoning shrubs and birdsong. The inevitable robin sitting on the handle of a garden fork. All we need is Peter Rabbit stealing carrots. But this is not why we're here. I lead them to a sheltered spot in the far corner where there's a collection of galvanised buckets and watering cans.

'See this?'

'It's a faucet?' Frank turns to his wife. 'It's a regular outside faucet.'

I twist the tap and ice-cold water trickles into a barrel. 'This is spring water. This used to be the well meadow, where the townsfolk – and Alie – would come to get their water. This is where the neighbour smelled brimstone on the child.'

'Is it a wishing well?' Pearl peers into the depths of the barrel.

Waterproofs Woman grunts. 'It looks like a barrel to me.'

I open my leather bag. 'Traditionally people throw coins into a well for luck, but long ago villagers would toss in new pins.' I produce a small tin, full of pins. They all take one and solemnly toss them into the tub. I like to create these little rituals on the tour.

As I'm leading them back out onto the wynd, my phone, which I've chucked in the bottom of the Gladstone bag, begins to ring. Regretting my choice of ringtone – 'That Old Black Magic' – I let it ring until the caller gives up. Guiltily, I plunge into the bag to check the screen. Missed call from Dad. What on earth could be wrong with him? I only just saw him an hour ago, and he was perfectly okay. I decide to ignore it and continue, back to the mercat cross and my grand finale. They have been in the company of Alie and the other witches for over an hour, got to know them a little. Plus, they're beginning to unwind, chattering among themselves. The Americans and the guy with the scarf are talking about Harry Potter as if he's a real person, and the teenagers are wading in with endless movie references. It transpires that the hot star of *Lowlander* began his career with a bit part in the Potter franchise. There's a lot of bonding going on, but I can feel Alie being nudged to one side. Not on my watch. She is the star of the show.

'So we were talking about Archibald Donald, and how he wanted his revenge.'

All eyes are on me again. 'He reported to the Kirk Session that she'd been talking to the Little People in the wood. She could describe them in great detail – a fairy host. He accused her of using sorcery to summon the fairy folk, and worse. He said he saw her dancing with the Devil.'

A gasp from the audience. The Devil is always the trump card.

'Where?' They all want to know. 'Where did she dance?'

I smile. 'Follow me.'

*

Once you mention the Devil, you can feel the energy in a group begin to shift. People draw closer together. They look over their shoulders and imagine the air just got a few degrees colder. The timid ones quicken their pace, so they don't have to be the last in line. As they follow me through the town, on the last leg of our tour, I can feel someone breathing down my neck. I suspect it's Frank, rather than Old Nick.

This is more exciting than a cairn. Maybe they will see something too! We all think that, don't we? If someone tells you a place is haunted, you always *hope* that you'll be the one to see something.

I know just where to take them, to reveal all those ancient scribbles in the landscape that modern folk can't read. We're all incomers, flitting across the surface of what's gone before. At certain judicious points I produce the artefacts from my bag: watercress, used to bewitch the best of the milk from the cow, red thread for binding spells, rowan for protection. Just in case. And, of course, a genuine set of pilniewinks, thumb-screws, for extracting those confessions.

I leave the best till last. The burgh square, the mercat cross, where in 1648 Alisoune Gowdie, the young wife who used to live in my cottage, was accused of dancing with the Devil.

*

Alie's dancing is the stuff of legend, whispered around the fire with the curtains drawn and shapes shifting on the ceiling. From that simple source, the yarn has been spun by a handful of local historians into something firm, authoritative, but the truth is, we don't know the truth. Nothing of Alie's experience survives. She didn't leave a diary, or a letter, or anything that might give us a clue. I've decorated my house from top to bottom, hoping to find scribblings under the wallpaper, hidden papers, anything that might fill in the gaps, but it's been fruitless.

When people ask me if I've ever experienced anything in my house, Alie and Robert's house, I always laugh it off and say no, but that's not strictly true, either. One morning, I woke too early, five o'clock or thereabouts. Maybe I had a day off or maybe I was tired. Anyway, I let myself drift back to sleep, and I saw her.

I saw Alisoune Gowdie dressed in a fine gown. The fabric was bright, much brighter than you'd imagine, but maybe that's the upside of marrying a weaver. A specially designed dusky pink plaid. Was it a Fair Day, or a holiday? In my dream, she gazed right at me, the incomer. It was a business-like appraisal, as if I were a bale of flax or a laying hen. I remember thinking she'd drive a hard bargain in the market place. As happens in dreams, the questions all stuck fast to the roof of my mouth, and maybe she felt the same.

In the dream, I'm outside. I'm in the market square in my pyjamas, and the cobbles ripple beneath my bare feet as if someone is shaking the dust from a rug. I lose track of what is sleeping and what is waking, who is living and who is dead. The cobbles turn to gravestones and the gravestones into gargoyles, the weird faces you see high up in church, all reptilian, repulsive, with stone wrinkles and snake tongues. And horns.

Alie is there. She's dancing with one of the Horned Ones. Is there just the one? I am so terrified I wake up. Do I tell this to my walkers? No. It isn't fact, is it? I stick to what we know of as the truth. Archibald Donald saw Alisoune Gowdie dancing with a dark stranger around the mercat cross. The man had the face of a demon, with red eyes and horns like a ram.

*

As my clients approach the door of the Black Bull, I like to think I've left them slightly altered. The teenagers have pocketed their mobiles and are sporting sprigs of rowan in their hair. Pearl has shed her windcheater, despite the chill, and the two guys are surreptitiously holding hands, more out of fear, I suspect, than affection. My job is done.

'Oh wow, that was just terrific!' Frank rubs his hands together. 'So much history for such a little place. Can we buy you a drink? *A wee dram!*'

His attempt at a Scottish accent is amusing and the offer kind, but I hesitate. That missed call has been haunting me since Butter Wynd. My phone is ticking away at the bottom of my Gladstone bag like an unexploded bomb.

'I have to make a quick call. You go on ahead. You've been a brilliant bunch, thanks – you all deserve a wee dram!'

I acknowledge the praise and the handshakes as they file into the pub. A cold glass of Pinot Grigio would go down very nicely, but I'm left alone in the night air scrabbling for my mobile. Squinting at the screen I realise with a sick lurch that there's a voicemail from my father too. Something is amiss. Why would he want to get in touch with me so urgently when I've just visited him? My brain downloads possibilities as I stab out the numbers for my voicemail. Maybe he found the ink spill, or his chequebook. Or maybe he remembered why he needed his chequebook, and I've forgotten to pay one of his bills? Impatiently I listen to the familiar recording: *You have one new message . . . For your messages press two.* A crackle of white noise and then Dad's voice breaks in. 'Sarah? It's your father here. Spot of bother at this end, but the firemen are here now.'

*

The best of my running days are over, but I manage to do a ragged, panicky trot back the way I've just come. I should have left the bag at the pub. Who, except a doctor, would attempt a mercy dash with a bloody Gladstone bag? I should have thought that through, but it's too late now. I scuttle across the town square, past the mercat cross, down Butter Wynd, leaning for a moment against the familiar bowed walls to catch my breath and redial my father's number. It goes straight to voicemail and the noose in my stomach tightens another notch. Best just to keep going.

I pound down the steps at the end of the lane, wait for the traffic to pass. Some joker can't resist howling out of the window, 'Forgotten your broomstick, hen?' I long to flick him the finger, but instead my grip tightens fiercely on the Gladstone bag and I limit myself to a hard stare.

The rail bridge is within reach. I take the worn steps two at a time, pausing to regroup at the top. Normally I enjoy this bird's-eye view of my father's estate – all the neat bungalows sewn into a seam of trees, and the older cottages beyond – but today I'm sniffing the air for the taint of burning and a telltale glow. There's nothing. No smoke, no commotion, but it's no comfort. Don't they call fire the silent killer? I plough on, lungs fit to burst.

It takes a lot to stir things up in Cornhill Crescent. It's an orderly mix of semi-detached bungalows and more spacious dwellings with rock gardens and double garages. Residents venture out in an orderly fashion, to medical appointments, coffee mornings and bowling matches. Golf on Saturday, church on Sunday. Mostly they're invisible, but tonight the conspicuous presence of a fire appliance outside number 8 has lured a small band of Neighbourhood Watch types away from their soaps. They're monitoring proceedings from a safe distance, observing the communal policy of *don't get involved*. All eyes swivel towards me as I steam into view, and

I experience a spurt of anger that they're on the opposite pavement. My dad would have been first into a burning building to help any of them.

But the building is not burning. The fire crew are standing around in their dun-coloured overalls, enjoying a bit of banter. Nothing to see here. No smoke, no flames. My breathing starts up again. One of the group, presumably the one in charge, detaches himself when he sees my face.

'You're the daughter? He said he'd phoned you. False alarm. Nothing to worry about. My colleague is with him now.'

'So what happened? Did he smell smoke? Was he making toast again?' I rack my brains for the last time I replaced the batteries in the smoke alarm, already preparing to hug the blame squarely to my labouring chest.

'Nothing to worry about,' the guy repeats. He gestures towards the front door and falls into step beside me. 'He thought he saw flames, but probably just a—'

'Trick of the light. Right.'

On entering the sitting room, I see a female crew member crouching down beside my father's chair. Someone's made him a cup of tea and he's in full-on old-fashioned charm mode. The young woman isn't much older than Hannah, with dark hair swept up in a knot and a keen, no-nonsense gaze, but even she seems to have fallen under his spell.

She rises to her feet and grins. 'He's a wee gem, isn't he? Don't you worry. He did the right thing.' She pats his shoulder. 'We're only a phone call away, John, if ever you're anxious.'

My father beams up at her, loving every minute. This has brightened up a dull evening no end, and I'm sure to get a blow-by-blow account as soon as they're gone. The adrenaline that's been flooding through my system dissipates like steam and I drop down onto the couch.

'So what happened, exactly?'

'Oh, he thought he saw flames, right there at the bottom of the door, but we've done a thorough check. No sign of any heat anywhere, and all the alarms are working. We reckon maybe he dropped off to sleep in front of the box and got a bit confused. Been watching too many thrillers, eh, John?'

As she smiles down at him his face blooms like a flower with the sun on it. The firefighters troop out, and I watch from the door as they squeeze into the cab of the tender. With no real drama on offer, the Neighbourhood Watch gang have given up and gone back to the latest reality show, without even asking how we are. Sighing, I close the door quietly.

Sarah

'He said he saw flames – licking round the bottom of the door.'

'Nooo!' Hannah's face lights up my tablet screen. She loves a bit of drama, even from halfway across the world. I settle myself into the couch and kick off my slippers, tucking my feet under me and taking a much anticipated slurp of chilled wine. My eyes drift to my own image in the little square at the top of the screen, and I see myself as she must see me, face scrubbed of make-up, tired eyes, my magenta rinse growing out at the roots. I pull my fleecy robe tighter.

Predictably Hannah widens her eyes when she spots my glass. 'You know what they say about wine-o-clock mums.'

'Who are *they*? People who've never been mums, probably.'

'It gets to be a habit, that's all.'

'It's not a habit. I've had a busy and trying day.' I do a quick recap in my head: Grant Tranter, Dad duties and a Witch Walk, not to mention the unexplained 'fire'. If anyone deserves a drink, it's me. 'I can't believe I'm getting grief from someone who's sitting in a bar!'

Her indignant laugh makes me smile. 'It's not a bar! It's six in the morning here, and this is the best hostel in Phnom Penh.' She pans her camera around and I get a vivid glimpse of her life: pale green walls, sellotaped posters and utility furniture. Two guys playing pool somewhere in the background. The thwack of a ball and a distinctly male epithet and she swings the picture back to herself.

'Someone's starting early then.'

She sniggers. 'I don't think these guys have even been to bed!'

I try to quash my alarm. I don't want to think of her surrounded by drunken males. I drink in her surroundings through the screen, refresh my knowledge of her. It's been so long. Is she staying safe, not drinking too much or going off on her own? I hope she's not skipping meals, she's rake thin as it is. 'So tell me, how do you like Cambodia? How's Katie?'

In my humble opinion, Katie is the sensible one. Even when they were at school Katie was the one who got things done. Hannah was the follower, the dreamer, content to fall into someone else's plans. That's more or less what happened with the gap year. It was Katie's gap year. Hannah had been happy in her marketing job. Still, it was a fantastic chance to broaden her horizons, and as long as she's happy . . . She is happy, isn't she?

I take a sip of wine and listen to her tales of temples and tuk-tuks, taking the opportunity to peer more closely at the screen. She looks the same as she did when she left, a curious mix of maturity and schoolgirl softness. She has a few more freckles and a bit of a tan, and the upward flick of her fringe in that one spot – a cow's lick, my mother used to call it. Is it my imagination, or is there a new wariness about her expression, the beginnings of frown lines when she drops her guard?

'Katie's met someone,' she finishes abruptly.

My heart fills steadily with all that that might mean. I feel suddenly queasy. 'Oh. Is it serious?'

Hannah shrugs. Off camera the pool players applaud a good shot and there's a bit of leg-pulling and laughter. 'She's in *love*. A guy from Sweden.'

My heart fills up and sinks. I gulp more wine to stop the inevitable questions. Has she gone off with him? Are you alone? Have you made other friends? I can't voice any of this because I know Hannah. She'll shut down and make some excuse to end the call. I want to hold on to her, even if it's only in cyberspace. Without warning, her face falls. Are those tears in her eyes? I sit up straighter and put down my wine, cradle the tablet closer.

'Are you okay, darling? You know, you don't have to stay. You can—'

'Mum!' If there were tears, she dashes them away with the back of her hand. 'It's all good. I love it, and we've applied for visas for India. I'm travelling with this girl I met in Siem Reap. Aisling. She's Irish.'

'Irish?' Well, that was all right, wasn't it? The Irish are a friendly bunch. Kind. 'Oh, that sounds nice. What does she do when she's not backpacking?'

Hannah shakes her head at me. The tears have been replaced by an impish twinkle. 'Oh, Mum. You mean what's her family background and is she trustworthy!' She gives a hoot of laughter.

'I meant nothing of the sort! I just . . .' I let out my breath, unable to vocalise what I want to say. I can feel my own eyes growing moist and I pray she won't notice. Any schmaltzy emotion on my part makes her bristle. We're alike that way. 'So is Katie not going with you? Whereabouts in India? Where are you going to stay? What about vaccinations?'

'I don't know, Mum, depends on the budget. Look, I have to go but don't worry. I'm fine, honest – safe and well.' She looks directly into the camera, but is it my imagination or does her gaze flicker for a millisecond. It's a little betrayal which will stop me falling asleep tonight. 'Gotta go, Ma.

Give Grandpa a big hug from me and tell him to stop watching scary films. No wonder he's having weird dreams! Byeee!'

She does that cute flappy-fingered wave she did as a child and blows a kiss at the screen and then she's gone.

*

I stay up too late and drink too much wine. I find myself watching that movie where Maggie Smith ends up living in a campervan on someone's drive. I'm not really taking it in. Instead, my brain is insisting on regurgitating undigested strands of conversation – all the odd little snatches that don't necessarily register first time around but suddenly take on a whole new dimension close to bedtime. *I don't know, Mum, depends on the budget.* Is Hannah running out of money, and would she tell me if she was? She knows I can't afford to support her, so she might not admit to it and be forced to stay in the seediest hostels. Her father gave her money for her birthday, but I never knew how much. She could hardly contain her excitement, whether because of the amount or because it came from Ian I've no idea. The more he distances himself from us, the more she idolises him.

Under the influence of alcohol, my mind steals out to the sort of places I refuse to let it go to in the daytime: all those stories I've tried to resist reading in the press of young female backpackers beaten and raped and abducted. What about that case of the girl who was trussed up and driven around in the boot of that guy's car for two months? Or the one who was stabbed at the hostel in Queensland?

In an effort to clear my head, I haul myself from the couch and stumble down the rickety interior staircase to the kitchen.

The bottom floor doesn't get much light, so it's cool, like a basement. I grab the chilled bottle from the fridge door to pour another glass. There's barely a measure left in it. Shit, this will never do. What if Dad calls again tonight? I believe he definitely saw something, and it's not the first time. He told me recently that there was a man on the roof of Mrs Chalmers' house, but it's been vacant for months. I actually went out into the back garden, stood on the stack of broken paving slabs and peered over the back wall, but the house was locked up and deserted. I suppose he's lonely, and making things up gets him some attention.

We're all bloody lonely. I upend the bottle over the sink and watch the remaining few mouthfuls glug away down the drain. *You know what they say about wine o'clock mums.* One more thing I have to get to grips with.

I make a cup of Earl Grey and carry it up to my eyrie, where Alan Bennett is pushing Maggie Smith in a wheelchair with a Union Jack on the back. I realise I haven't got a clue what's going on and switch it off. The sudden silence is huge and engulfing. Without the constant backing track of the TV I can hear the night-time settling of the house, the timbers flexing like someone cracking their knuckles. I take myself off to bed, tea in one hand, phone in the other. Another snatch of conversation comes back to me. Dad, this time. *I thought it was them. I heard them out in the hallway, before the fire started.* The thought of a 'they' in my father's house sends a chill all the way to the roots of my hair.

We can't go on like this. One of us needs help.

Sarah

I have three hagstones on my bedroom windowsill. Grey and gritty, each one is full of holes the size of a child's finger. They're not tactile and pretty like moonstone or quartz, but in the tales of old wives they are a protection against evil: bad spells, harm and ill health. Common sense tells me that the holes are a result of the continual pounding of the elements on the stone's weakest point. Do I believe they can ward off bad things? I believe we're all in danger of being ground down at our weakest point. Perhaps that's why I keep them on my windowsill. I found them in the garden, and it seemed prudent to keep them.

On the morning Hannah left to go travelling, she presented me with a hagstone pendant. She'd had it specially made, a tiny version of the garden specimens strung on a leather thong.

'I know what you're like, Mum, so I got you this to cheer you up.'

She handed over a black velvet pouch. I didn't want to look inside. It was her last day before she flew. Before she flew the nest. I'd taken the day off work and spent it inventing new ways to be sad. Everything had turned into a ritual. This is the last time I'll make her porridge. This is the last time I'll pick her towel off the bathroom floor. There's a gap where her toothbrush should be. A gap in my heart. I couldn't imagine how anything in a black velvet pouch would improve my mood, so I took refuge in a bit of sass.

'Is this so you don't have to buy me a birthday present?'

'Mum! Open it.'

She was laughing, so excited. Her laden rucksack took up half the room. It was bigger than she was. She was wearing shorts even though it was only thirteen degrees in Kilgour. I loosened the neck of the pouch and tipped the contents into my palm. I couldn't speak for a moment. Hannah took the little stone from me and looped the leather thong around my neck.

I looked her in the eye as the charm settled into place. The truth between us was frightening.

'Wear it every day, Mum. It'll connect us through time and space!'

I knew she was joking, kidding me along, but I'm a bit superstitious and I took to wearing it all the time, because it was the next best thing to never letting her go. I came to believe that while I was wearing it no harm could befall her. I swore I'd never take it off, in case she somehow slipped through the cracks.

*

Saturday morning finds me shoving the stones roughly aside to throw open the window. I suck in a great gulp of fresh air, cringing at the amount of booze I put away the night before. My head and tongue are thick with it. There's a noise in the tree, a rustling of feathers or leaves, it's hard to tell, and the wood pigeon starts up with her cooing.

'Look at you. You have a great bloody life. Nothing to do but survive.'

She shuffles enigmatically on her branch.

Why had I slugged nearly a whole bottle of Pinot when

I'd volunteered to do an early shift? I don't usually open up at the weekend – Rosie, who is young, keen and willing, gets that pleasure – but after Forklift Scooter I thought it would be judicious to throw in a few surprise visits. It's almost half five and I'm already beginning to regret that decision. I could text Rosie and go back to bed, but that wouldn't look good. 'Lead by example' is one of Dad's favourite sayings, and of course he's right.

I get to Wisebuy just before six, and Rosie has already opened up. The early bird staff are going about their business with varying degrees of cheerfulness, unpacking newspapers, clearing away boxes, checking the fruit and veg. You can sort the larks from the owls in one glance. The owls are white-faced and scowling, huddled in fleeces and stinking of last night's kebabs. One of them deliberately turns away from me when I bid him good morning.

'You're wearing trainers,' I point out. 'I could send you home.' The lad tosses an aubergine from hand to hand like it's a grenade. He'd love to lob it at me and run for the hills, follow Grant into the great blue yonder. No more stacking shelves, just endless fun-filled days of crate surfing and scaring old ladies. 'Regulation shoes tomorrow, please.'

He grunts and turns back to his green plastic trays. Beneath my own regulation suit, my heart is tripping along like a goat on a shaky bridge. I have a sinking feeling that the ghost of Grant Tranter will not disappear easily. He was a slant of sunlight in a high window.

At six fifteen, Rosie comes looking for the keys to the locked bond, so she can restock the cigarette kiosk. I've known Rosie since she was five. She started school the same day as Hannah and was one of those kids who had to be prised from her mother's hand, who always ended up crying at parties. Now she's taller than me and engaged to the local plumber. Part of me wishes Hannah could be so content. I hand over the key but she hesitates. She clearly has something on her mind.

'Heard about Grant. What a tool.'

I shrug. 'He won't be missed. He told me to shove the job up my arse.'

She giggles. 'I heard that too.'

I don't dare ask how. 'Grant was not a team player.'

She laughs again, as if she's suddenly remembered something. 'You know he asked me out last year? He was going to take me to Nando's.'

'Did you go?'

She shakes her head. 'No. I told him I don't eat chicken, I'm a vegetarian, and *he* says it's your lucky night then, I've got fruit-flavoured condoms. Oh my God! *So* Grant.'

I make a face. 'Yup. *So* Grant. Anyway, he's gone, so can we get on with the work, please?'

As I head back to the warehouse, I notice there's a new and unfamiliar gleam to the shop floor, telltale stripes of freshly mopped brightness. I inhale the crisp tang of lemons. Excellent – a new cleaner. Grant slips to the back of my mind.

John

She looks so like her mother, perched on the edge of his couch. Marjorie always sat like that, elbows on knees, knees pressed together, feet apart. Like a coiled spring, he always thought, ready for the off. Get a cushion behind you, lass, he used to say to Marjorie. Relax, for goodness' sake. The world will wait. She must have passed on the coiled-spring gene, because even young Hannah has it now, convinced the world won't wait until she's seen it all.

Sarah is on a mission this evening, even more so than usual. Still in that grim work suit. He prefers her in sunny florals, but she never dresses up much now – the only bit of colour about her is the dyed hair. It reminds him of Red Cedar fence paint. She's taken off the dark jacket and folded it neatly beside her. From this angle it looks like a black collie dog with its head lolling on the arm of the couch.

She must have a lot on her mind because she hasn't even put the kettle on, which is usually her first job when she arrives. He suspects a lecture is imminent, about his close shave with the fire brigade. It was an honest mistake. They happen all the time, false alarms, and that young lady had told him better safe than sorry. But now Sarah's here like a black cloud about to rain on that particular parade.

Maybe she'll make a cuppa after she's had her say. He's fair parched, because he didn't make his usual brew after his breakfast toast. The humble hot beverage has become something of a gamble lately. Only last week, he scalded himself. Goodness knows how it happened – one minute he was pouring the boiling water onto his teabag and the next it was all over the counter. Third-rate kettle, he reckons. They don't make spouts the same as they used to. His mother had an old tin kettle she kept on the stove all day, so you had hot water any time you needed it. Not just for drinks, but for washing dishes and kids too. It whistled like a canary, that kettle. He hadn't told Sarah about the scalding incident. She'd have a fit if she knew, and anyway, the long shirt sleeve hides the red mark. He realises she's talking at him but he must have drifted off.

'Dad. Are you listening to me?' Sarah's voice cuts into his thoughts, but he's so focused on the thing sitting next to Sarah on the couch that he can't even blink. Difficult to say whether it's male or female because the features are all blurred, but at a stretch it looks a little like his mother. Imagine, Sarah and his mum on the same couch.

'Dad!'

He lets his gaze drift back to his daughter and that's enough to break the spell. The second figure vanishes like a puff of smoke.

'I was just saying, I think we should get the doctor to check you out. I'm going to phone the surgery on Monday and ask to speak to her.'

He eyes his daughter steadily. 'Is this about the fire?'

'There was no fire.'

'There were folk in my hallway. I heard them.'

'No one can get in, Dad. I have the only key. No one can get in, unless you let them in.'

Had he let someone in? He's normally so particular, and those fly-by-nights who come to the door, they don't fool him. Mrs Chalmers had a very bad business last year, got scammed out of a lot of money by rogue traders. They said her roof was dodgy and she parted with a pile of cash. That's why her son – a rough chap who likes a drink – put her into a home. He doesn't want that to happen to him. He has a hard-backed notebook on the table beside his chair in which he scribbles down all the helpline numbers from the TV: *Crimestoppers*, *Whistleblowers*, the Silver Line. You just never know when one of them might come in handy.

He decides to play the game. 'You're right. Just my ears playing tricks. And the fire, I must have dreamt it.'

Sarah smiles a little sadly. 'These things happen, Dad. Don't worry about it. I think we should get everything checked out, though, just to be on the safe side. I'll be here when the doctor comes. Don't worry. It'll all be fine.'

Of course she'll want to be here, to discuss him out of earshot. His ears aren't that decrepit; they'll manage to pick up the sort of phrases and words that will make him all cold inside. *Frail ... Impaired ... Imagining things ... DEMENTIA.*

Things discussed out of earshot are seldom fine.

Sarah

Mum died of a heart attack. Boom, just like that. Dad found her sitting on the couch in the wee small hours, barely conscious. They say heart failure is worse between the hours of midnight and four because your oxygen levels drop and anxiety strikes. You experience a sense of impending doom.

I wonder if that's what it had been like for Mum, at the end. I can picture her climbing out of bed in the middle of the night so as not to wake Dad. They were like that, the two of them, always protecting each other. He never let her see the bills; she never bothered him with her worries. She makes her way to the lounge, sits there in the dark, sagging against the cushions in a way she never did in life. Mum always sat bolt upright, ready to jump if anyone needed sustenance. She liked to nurture people. She should have been mum to a big brood, not just me, a late baby when they were both in their forties.

Dad says she was trying to say something when he found her. Her side of the bed was cold when he'd woken up some time later and he'd immediately feared the worst and found it. He tried to rub warmth into her frozen hands, offering words, any words, to bring her back, and she seemed to return, for a second. Her blue lips moved, but he couldn't catch what she was saying. Even with his ear to her face and her breath moist against his unshaven cheek, he lost it. Her last words remain a puzzle.

Dad has always been a capable man, a clever man. Not being able to understand his wife in her last moments must have been torture. He called the ambulance and then he called me. We arrived about the same time. The paramedics did all they could, but there was no fanfare of blue lights accompanying us to hospital, just a slow procession of grief.

I sometimes think we're still going through it. One of us will say something, recall a memory, and the eyes will mist and we'll pause for a moment. Usually it's me who changes the subject. Dad's only allowed a few brief seconds of grief when I'm there. The show must go on. There's no point in dwelling on the things we don't understand: puzzling words, death. Imaginary folk.

I scoot around with the vacuum before the doctor comes. The surgery had kept me on hold for ages on Monday morning. I'd had to answer my emails with my mobile jammed against my ear, listening to Pavarotti. Eventually the receptionist granted me an audience with one of the GPs, a woman whose name I didn't catch, and she'd agreed to pop into Dad's on Tuesday when she was making her house calls. She sounded kind but distant, and now I'm in what my mother would have called a 'tizzy'. I find myself doing what she would have done, making everything presentable, as if the orderliness of the home might somehow ward off bad news. To my parents, doctors are godlike creatures, and I keep up the pretence, like an agnostic in church. Just in case. But my palms are sweating long before the doctor arrives.

She's far from godlike, just a rather ordinary older woman with an old-fashioned iron-grey up do and a lilac blouse with an elaborate pussy bow. I shake her cool hand and position one of the upright dining chairs beside Dad's easy chair, and then stand guard behind it as the introductions are made.

Like her blouse, the doctor is pale and shimmery and unthreatening. She is the Mary Berry of family medicine.

She listens politely as I launch into a list of Dad's issues, completely omitting the real reason she's been called. The Figures. She does all the usual comforting things that you see on daytime soaps – chest, heart, blood pressure – and makes a little murmur, *hmmm*, deep in her throat, which doesn't really give anything away. When she mentions blood tests, I try to catch her eye.

'Is there anything else bothering you both?'

She's quick. I nod, Dad shakes his head, and we both speak in unison.

'I'm hale and hearty for ninety.'

'I think he's confused.'

Dad glares at me.

The doctor takes off her stethoscope and lays it across her lap. 'Sometimes a urinary infection can—'

'It's more than that.' Dad glares at me again but I rush on. 'He's seeing things.'

Dad sits back with an angry *flump* against his cushions and raises a hand. 'Just talk about me as if I'm not here, why don't you?'

'We have to sort this out!'

The doctor breaks in firmly. 'If you're worried, we can do a simple test.'

'Yes, please do.'

'Fine.'

Dad and I trade glances like wary bullocks. Tension is making me snappy, and I'm aware that my arms are clamped around my midriff. I take a deep breath and subside onto the couch. The doctor perches on her dining chair and takes out a notepad.

'Mr Milton, can you tell me what day it is today?'

Dad raises his eyebrows. 'Tuesday.'

'And the date?'

He tells her, and the infantilising questions proceed. Dad names the Prime Minister, the First Minister and then delivers a diatribe against the Transport Secretary and the state of the railways. I wish fervently that I'd never started this and left his imaginary friends in peace.

'Could you draw a circle on this piece of paper, Mr Milton?' The doctor hands over the pad, and he takes the pen. I notice for the first time how shaky his hand is, how unsure. An old man's hands now, knobbly knuckles and blue veins. The hand that had held mine and fixed punctures and broken toys, signed off on thousands of pounds' worth of loans with the stroke of a fountain pen. He makes the first arc of the circle, takes the pen from the paper, rests for a few seconds to refocus. And then tries to draw the second half. We all stare at the interrupted shape. Two halves of a whole. A game of two halves and the game is up.

'I wonder if you have a vision problem.' Speaking half to herself, the doctor looks up suddenly. 'Nothing at all wrong mentally.'

Dad grins up at me, vindicated. She pats his shoulder, promising to pop in again, and then she steers me out into the hall.

'Tell me honestly,' says the doctor, 'how are you coping, really?'

Her attention is fixed on me. I don't know what to say, and when I open my mouth nothing comes out. Tears form and fall, and I can't swallow the lump in my throat.

'Carers are always the last people to admit they need care.'

Suddenly I'm sobbing against her pussycat bow. She eases me gently away from her and looks me in the eye. 'I'm going to get in touch with Social Services. Let's get something sorted out for you. I bet you're doing everything – running around with the hoover, the whole works.'

She glances at the hall carpet and I can feel myself go red, an embarrassed child who's failed a spelling test. 'Maybe a home help, or something. How's he coping with personal care?'

I've never broached the subject with my father. He's a proud man, independent, and I tell her so.

She just smiles, like she's heard it all before. 'The time comes when we all need extra help.'

It's her final word on the topic. She goes back in to say goodbye to her patient and I'm left dithering in the hall. I feel like things are being taken out of my hands but instead of being grateful I'm bristling. How dare they? We've always managed. I'm sure that was what my mother was trying to say at the end: *Sarah will look after you.*

John

It was a relief to see the back of them. Sarah could be hard work when she was in that organising frame of mind, and she'd managed to get the doctor alone. Muttered words in the hall. Try as he might, he couldn't get a hint of what had been said, but when the doctor breezed back in she was going on about getting extra help, handrails and a fancy seat for the bath. He told her in no uncertain terms that they were fine. Just fine. He could make his own meals and all that stuff. He didn't mention his difficulties with the kettle – it was none of her business. She was writing things down, but he couldn't read it. It just looked like barbed wire looping across the page.

After the doctor left, Sarah made him a cuppa – thank goodness. They didn't speak about what had happened although she seemed keen to get him an optician's appointment and started checking the calendar. Empty white squares stretched through the year, punctuated by things he couldn't decipher. Sarah's handwriting was as poor as the doctor's, and he hoped they weren't important.

Off she went, after that, to see to her own housework. She always made a big thing about the cleaning, Sarah. She never said anything out loud but there's always a lot of sighing and eye-rolling when she has to get out the dusters. Leave it, he'd snapped on one occasion. I'm well able to do it myself, you know. But she'd tutted some more and brought up the subject of a home help. He hadn't taken her up on it. All the cleaners nowadays were foreign, according to Mrs Chalmers, and he didn't want foreign folk in his house. That was the start of her decline, poor soul. Mrs Chalmers' son, the one with the drink problem, hired a foreign cleaner and the next thing you know all her jewellery was missing, wedding ring and all. Sarah said ten to one the son had taken it to Cash Converters, but no good can come of letting strangers into your house. That's the trouble. Once you let in the medical bods, they start interfering.

He lingers in the hall after Sarah leaves, caught in that funny nowhere place. An anticlimax, that's what it feels like. Maybe dementia or one of those other horrid things might go some way towards explaining what's happening to him, but he's been left in the dark. Literally. The hall bulb has blown again and it's very dim out here. They get through so many lightbulbs he's beginning to think the Figures have a hand in it, but he can't mention that to Sarah. She hates replacing the lightbulbs because she doesn't do heights. Hates even standing on a chair, and as for flying, she hasn't been in a plane since before Hannah was born. It's the height.

There's a kind of peace in the dimness, though. Everything so quiet and cocooned, like being in a museum. He likes it, likes his own company after all his years of managing people. Of course, he misses dear Marjorie, and Mrs Chalmers, if truth be told. He used to speak with Mrs Chalmers every day across the back garden wall, him standing on a couple of paving slabs and she on a plastic step. The wall was so high he could only ever see her blue eyes and the white wisps of her hair – and even that had become a blur, latterly. But it was company. He'd looked forward to their little chats, just about the weather, or what was on the telly, or what they were having for lunch. Mrs Chalmers was partial to a Cheddar cheese and chutney sandwich. He'd got Sarah to buy some of that special homemade chutney at the farm shop, but the next day Mrs Chalmers had been carted off in an ambulance and he'd never seen her again. Sarah said she'd find out what care home she was in and visit her with the chutney, but she'd never had time.

As he turns to go into the sitting room, a movement catches his eye. Two Figures in his bedroom. He can't see their faces, but one of them is gliding towards the dressing table where Marjorie's jewellery box still sits. A primitive fear grips him, a fight-or-flight panic, and his old heart starts chugging in his chest at such a rate of knots he fears it will do damage. He can't flee. This is his home. He can't have this in his own home, and Marjorie's jewellery box! It hasn't been opened since Marjorie passed. Sarah's always hinting that she'd like something of her mother's, for sentimental reasons, but she's never got round to it. And now this.

He clears his throat, piles all his strength into two words: 'Hey, you!'

It comes out as a growl, but the Figures don't react. He repeats the challenge, but the effort makes him cough. He must confront them. Call the police. Perhaps they slipped in while he was seeing Sarah out. Had he locked the front door? She usually reminds him to lock it after her, to put the chain on, but today she didn't. Today he forgot. He must check, as quickly as he can, loth as he is to turn his back on the intruders. The Yale is closed, as he'd expected, but also he can see that the chain is firmly in place. He takes a moment to think about that. There was no gap between Sarah leaving and him putting on the security chain. No chink in time for anyone to slip through.

But they're here. He saw them, in his bedroom. He'll call

999, that's what to do. The handset is on the wee table beside his chair. He'll just go back into the lounge and . . . He glances through the open door of his bedroom as he passes.

There is no sign of anyone. Puffing with anxiety, he makes his way into the room, cautiously, in case they might be hiding. He checks behind the door and under the bed. Nothing. Marjorie's jewellery box remains intact, unopened.

The intruders have vanished into thin air.

Sarah

In the staff canteen, there's a red stripe on the wall that runs at shoulder height all the way around. It pisses me off on three counts. First, the contractor, a man of magnolia habits, had taken it upon himself to add a little pizzazz with a job lot of red paint; second, it's squint; and third, I hate myself for not confronting the guy over it.

The morning he completed it, I found him swooshing his bristles in a jar of turps with the air of one who'd done a great job. He stood back to appraise his own handiwork and said the words: something snazzy for the kids. The kids? What kids? You mean the likes of Grant Tranter? Yes, it's really going to alleviate their hangovers, especially the *squint* bit. Yes, there is a definite downward slope between the two windows.

I should have said all of that, let rip at him and enjoyed a satisfactory outburst. But I didn't. I squashed it down and signed his job sheet, and now every time I go into the canteen the damn stripe taunts me like a crooked painting.

My grip tightens involuntarily on the mug in front of me. Stress does this to me. I need order and symmetry and lines that are on nodding terms with a spirit level. I sigh so loudly Peggy casts a wry glance in my direction.

'That says it all.' She's attacking the inside of our ancient coffee machine with a Brillo pad, her ginger curls bouncing vigorously.

'It's my dad.'

'What's he been up to now?'

'I think he sees dead people.'

She pops up from her task, fingers dripping pink suds, her mouth a slack 'O'. 'Come again?'

I giggle despite myself and take a sip of coffee. It's strong and bitter. Peggy's made it with Instant on account of the cleaning task list – she always cleans the coffee machine on a Wednesday – and I make a mental note to make my own in future. 'Not dead people. Imaginary people, and fires that aren't there.'

Her eyebrows shoot up to her hairline. She tends to pencil them in with a very dark crayon until they bear no relation to the colour and shape of her normal brows.

'I think it's all in his head. He's lonely, imagining things, but the doctor says he's fine. She suggested I should take him to the optician.'

Peggy snorts and goes back to her scrubbing. 'What do they know? Keep you waiting weeks for an appointment and then don't give you any answers. Last doctor I saw was a slip of a lad. Asked me what I thought was wrong with me! I said if I knew that I wouldn't be here.'

She tosses her scourer into a basin and wipes her forehead, smudging one eyebrow and leaving a jaunty slash of suds.

I push the coffee away. The bitter taste of it lingers in my mouth. 'I got a bit upset. She's sending in the cavalry.'

'Not the bloody Social Services people?' Peggy's standing beside me now. I can smell her Red Door perfume. Even though my gaze is fixed on the table, I'm aware of the flip-flap of a tea towel as she wipes her hands. My throat is closing up; I can hear the rattle of it in my ears. I've never cried in this place. Never. I can't trust my voice, but it doesn't matter.

Without waiting for me to speak, Peggy goes off on

another rant about her deceased mother and how the carers came around at the crack of dawn to get her up. 'I said to them, in what world is it okay to haul an old lady out of her bed before the spuggies are even coughing? You wouldn't do it to your own mother, would you? I said it to her face, that woman from the Social Services, and do you know what she said to me?'

I didn't really want to know. I should never have confided in Peggy. The whole motherly thing gets to me at times, making me open up against my will, and then Peggy hijacks the issue and makes it all about herself and I'm no better off, no closer to any kind of comfort.

On the table my phone beeps. Something shrinks inside me, but it isn't my father or the fire brigade or any kind of emergency. It's a text from my friend Charlotte at the museum.

Hey! You'll never believe what we've just found.

I answer immediately. *What???*

Something of interest, hidden in a box of old books rescued from an attic.

And?

You'd better come and see for yourself.

As I stare at the screen, something surges in the region of my heart, electricity powering through jaded circuits. Even my thumbs are tingling as I fire off a reply.

Can I see it?

I've put it aside in the research room. I'll be working late if you want to pop over.

You're a star.

You owe me a wine xx

I glance up to find Peggy gaping at me with naked curiosity. She thinks it's a man. The idea amuses me so much I shoot her a grin as I drop the phone into my bag.

'Hot date tonight? What's he like?'

'Oh, you know. A little crinkly but sure to keep me out of mischief for a couple of hours.'

Her lewd cackle follows me out into the corridor.

*

You always gravitate towards your own tribe. When it comes to kindred spirits, we have an inner knowing. Bookworms curl up with other bookworms and petrolheads sniff out fellow petrolheads. It's a sort of unwritten law. I felt it when I first laid eyes on Ian.

We met in a nightclub in Edinburgh, I can't remember which one. I was drunk and dancing to the Manic Street Preachers. I saw this guy – quiet but not shy – just watching me. He was rocking the look back then, in a checked flannel shirt and dark hair in sleek curtains that fell across his eyes. He smiled. I flicked my hair in response. It was the start of something. Within thirty minutes I was doing everything you're not supposed to do. I ditched my girlfriends and we went to ground in a back street pub. An old man's pub, we dubbed it then. A bit like the Black Bull, I guess, with a jukebox in the corner and a selection of old worthies at the bar to cast an eye over newcomers.

We got to know each other, chatting over pints of cider. There was stiff competition from the clack of pool balls and a heavy rock soundtrack, forcing us to lean in close. I could never have imagined a time when we wouldn't want to lean in close.

We were both students. I was studying archaeology – a degree I was never to complete – and enjoying spending my summers covered in mud and midgie bites. I had big dreams of unearthing Pictish stones and discarded treasure but never excavated anything more exciting than bottle tops and minuscule shards of Victorian pottery. No Skara Brae, no new Vindolanda. Not that it mattered. It took a lot to dent my dreams back then. Ian was involved in a different kind of digging, forensics. We quickly found some common ground but lost it along the way.

For months after our break-up I had a bleak aversion to the past. All that sad summer, when Hannah was eight, I lived in waterproofs and wellies, trying to lose myself in the outdoors. Anything was better than being home. I couldn't look at our wedding photos or theatre tickets or listen to certain songs. The discovery of a discarded sock in the laundry basket reduced me to a blubbering mess. I had to forensically sift through the remains of Ian and remove him from my head. Bits of him remain, embedded like those invisible barbed thorns that don't hurt until you rub them. The good things we shared, like Hannah, sometimes seem very far away.

That common ground, I felt it with Charlotte too. A recognition. Not the same as the spark I felt for Ian, but maybe a different kind of flame. We've never really discussed it, but I guess she feels the same as me, that we're united by our passion for the past. We meet sporadically for lattes or a cheeky wine – girl stuff. She's younger than me, and her partner, Sophie, is a vegan cook. Their apartment is minimalist with a shiny white kitchen, and if you're invited for drinks you can be sure you'll also get rye crackers with three types of homemade hummus. Overexposure to Charlotte can sometimes make me feel a bit inadequate.

However, she gives me the run of the museum after hours and lets me sit at a dusty table and pore through old books.

My tours are the result of painstaking research, but even if I didn't pass on my pearls of wisdom to the visitors, I'd still yearn to spend my spare time with ancient handwriting for company.

*

When I finish work, the Tolbooth Museum is closed for business, but there's a light burning in the upstairs window. Knowing its history, I have mixed feelings about the place. I can admire its architecture, the weathered sandstone, the three steps up to an imposing arched entrance. If you were designing a gaol, it ticks all the boxes. The heavy iron yett, or portcullis, suspended above the front door like a guillotine, bars on the windows, a fierce arrangement of turrets at the roofline, and the later addition of a clock tower. But what went on in that place haunts me. I can almost see the candles guttering in that upstairs window, hear the frightened screams of torture victims.

The front entrance is now closed to the public, so I have to go around the back, slipping down Butter Wynd and through the door in the wall. When I press the doorbell a buzzer echoes through the silent building. It's a brown municipal-style door, with four panes of frosted glass at the top. They glow amber by the light of a single outside lantern. A progression of noises trickles down through the building like water: a slammed door, high up, hurrying footsteps on stone steps, the rapid release of a series of bolts and finally a muffled curse as Charlotte prises open the door. In the tower high above my head, the clock chimes the half hour, making me jump.

'Bloody security. Advance, friend, and be recognised!'

She does her best *Dad's Army* impression before giving me a bear hug. Charlotte is a hugger; myself, not so much, but I submit happily enough and allow myself to be led into the bowels of the building. The bits the visitors don't see are a depressing mix of corporate utility and neglected history. The winding staircase is dank, with exposed cabling and bulkhead lights like bugs' eyes bolted to sixteenth-century masonry.

Even down here in the nether regions that peculiar museum whiff hits me. I like to think of it as ghost smells hiding in the mortar, manifesting as a mixture of second-hand clothes and lavender and damp old books.

Today, there's an overlay of modern detergent. When we reach the first-floor landing, the linoleum has been freshly swabbed, the mop still propped in a tin bucket of steaming water. Even the bucket looks vintage. I realise I'd forgotten to ask Peggy if the new cleaner is up to scratch. I'm still smarting at the disbelief in her snigger as I left the canteen. It was hurtful. I could easily find myself a date, if I could be bothered. She was just itching to broadcast my fake news. The blue touchpaper of gossip had been well and truly lit.

'I'll get Robbie to make us a coffee. Although you can't drink it in the research room.'

Charlotte shoulders open a door and pokes her head around it, exchanging words with her unseen colleague. I'm sure Robbie will be thrilled to have coffee-making added to his responsibilities, but I've met him once or twice and he seems an enthusiastic sort. Unlike me, Charlotte has a natural authority about her. She expects to have her wishes carried out. It's like an entitlement she wears along with her snazzy museum lanyard. I feel like a schoolgirl in comparison, tiptoeing through a minefield of unwillingness and resentment. I think of Grant Tranter, who's probably badmouthing me in the pub right about now, and Peggy, telling everyone I've hooked up with someone new *at last*. I bet Robbie doesn't gossip.

I follow Charlotte through another door into the upstairs chamber. Visitors access it by a stone turnpike from the downstairs gift shop. Some of the artefacts are roped off: a silk eighteenth-century dress with a tiny waist and a man's frock coat and britches; little curiosities in glass cases such as snuff boxes, vintage handbags, apothecary bottles, instruments of torture.

Charlotte looks at me pointedly. 'Are your hands clean?'

I stifle a laugh. She's serious. I wave them like jazz hands. 'Squeaky clean.'

Charlotte always looks freshly scrubbed in little black tops and neat grey trousers. She has a runner's physique, lean and tiny, and jogs home every evening, does triathlons for fun at the weekends.

'Good. Clean hands do less damage than gloves, I always think.'

The research room is through yet another door on the left, which Charlotte swings open with a kind of reverence we both understand. The interior is sepulchral. Light streams in through a high window and tall display cases line the walls. Gilt-inscribed spines glint tantalisingly behind glass doors. I can't resist doing that strange library walk, a sideways shuffle with my neck craning this way and that, reading the titles: plays, parish records, old novels, dog-eared covers and yellowing pages.

Charlotte goes to one of the cabinets and unlocks a drawer. She lifts out a battered book – even from a distance I can tell it's battered – its pages frilled, a bit like my grandmother's old recipe book. She brings it to the central table and I sit eagerly in the chair. My fingers are itching to leaf through the pages.

'Be *very* careful. It's pretty fragile. Robbie took a call from the new minister. She's just moved into the manse and decided to explore the attic, as you do. The usual stuff, but she came across a cardboard box full of papers. She reckoned some of it was really old, so she handed it in to us for safekeeping. I expect there will be some discussion about it all, but for now we are the custodians! So, what do you know about the Kirk, at the time of the witch hunt?'

I'm still distracted by the book. 'Erm . . . well, the minister at the time had a hand in it, didn't he? Bit over-zealous. What was his name? Wilkie, I think.'

Charlotte grins. She's enjoying this. 'He was assigned to Kilgour in 1648—'

'The year of the worst trials in the town's history.'

'And he kept a journal . . .' She waggles the book, very gently. 'No!'

'There were six volumes in the box, dated 1643 to 1648. The earlier ones seem to be from his previous incumbency, but we know he was transferred to Kilgour in 1648, before being moved on the following year, after the witch trials, for being . . . over-zealous. This is the final one, beginning in January 1648, which I think may be of interest to you.'

'I can't believe it.' I sit, stunned, as she places the diary on the foam rest with as much care as a mother placing her newborn on the scales for the first time. Something pokes me in the gut – excitement blended with disbelief. This is an eye-witness account of an event that's always been part of my adult life. I only ever left Kilgour to go to university, and then moved back with Ian. Alie's story is part of the fabric of our town. It's part of me.

Opening the book releases the smell of mouldy trees. I breathe it in like an addict. The pages are as stiff as starched laundry. I think of all the things that were happening in Scotland in 1648. I slip on my reading glasses. There on the title page I come face-to-face with Alie's chief tormentor.

This being the narrative and journall of Rev. William Wilkie, Minister of the Kirk and Parish of Kilgour. A thankfull observation of divine providence and goodness towards me and a summary view of my life.

I glance up at Charlotte, remembering to breathe. 'This is incredible. What are the chances?'

She laughs. 'Chance is the way we find most of our treasures. When I realised what we had, I did a bit more digging and found a letter from a well-wisher to the bishop, a kind of reference from his previous parish.'

She pulls a sheet of paper from a filing cabinet drawer. I can see it's a facsimile. After clearing her throat, she reads out a paragraph. '"This man, the Reverend Wilkie, is worthy of being recommended by all on account of his admirable character both in his life and in his sound judgement. Shepherd to a multitude of brethren, not a beggar was ever to be seen in our parish, nor did any citizen dare violate the Sabbath." There are papers from other landowners and prominent families promising money towards the upkeep of a hospital which Wilkie is proposing for Kilgour.'

'The hospital?'

'More of an alms house, to provide accommodation for paupers. We think it must be Lumsdain House, but I'll check with the burgh architect.'

I settle down to read. The writing is spidery and faded to brown, like dried blood, and the language is tricky, even for a history buff. Conscious of Charlotte's eagle eyes, I resist the urge to trail my finger under the words as I read haltingly.

'"January tenth – AD 1648. The Lord in his Mercy has seen fit to bring me to this sinful place, to do His Work and to save the Godly. I have in the last month settled myself into the Manse and . . . furnished myself with one Mistress . . ." Telfer? It's spelled funny. "One Mistress Telfer who is slatternly at keeping house, but a prodigious cook."'

We both burst out laughing. I read on: '"Yet while my chambers go undusted, I sit down to a wondrous potage." Bloody hell! A man that thinks of his belly, obviously!'

'What else?'

'Let's see . . . "If the Lord sees fit I will scribe events of note within this book, and record the ridding of this Parish of all those . . . profane Offenders of God's Law. There will be no swearing or blasphemy or . . . filthy speeches. No lewd acts or singing of bawdy songs" – aw, William, you killjoy – "No foul drunkenness or night-walking or keeping open house. There will be no kissing on the causeway, no carousing, no playing of cards or dice. No surrendering to the *lusts* of the flesh."' I gawp at Charlotte over my specs and pull a face. '"No fornicating or adultery. We will not suffer bloodshed, or slaughter, or . . . witchcraft. We will not suffer a witch to live."'

I raise my head and pull off my glasses. 'I can see where this is going.'

John

A carer! He hadn't really been expecting that. Sarah had mentioned it before and he'd fobbed her off, but since the doctor visit she'd been determined. He doesn't want someone strange coming in, telling him how to live his life.

He's seen those documentaries on the telly, the ones that investigate the murky side of the care industry and it *is* an industry now. Processing old people – that's what it's all about. He imagines a clutch of Mrs Chalmers end to end on a conveyor belt, all worsted stockings and kirby grips. A merciless roller of doom. In at one end of the system, hale and hearty, and out the other in a pine box. In between, a regime of tea and biscuits and increased meds.

When Sarah had asked him if he would like to visit Mrs Chalmers in the care home, he'd said no, sensing a trap. There was no way he'd consider it. They wouldn't get one brown penny out of him, for the privilege of eating stale sandwiches and listening to an accordion player on a Sunday afternoon in the TV lounge. No, he's staying in his own home to the bitter end. He can look after himself and he's no burden to anyone. Sarah raises her eyebrows at him when he says that.

A woman from her work – Peg, he thought her name was – had given her some literature about a private agency that supplies carers and home helps to old people who can no longer look after themselves. Private, if you don't mind!

'That's going to cost an arm and a leg,' he'd protested.

'Let's start small. Maybe an hour once or twice a week,' Sarah had argued. 'You just need someone to help you get washed and—'

'No!' He'd washed himself since he was five. He wasn't about to have some young lassie coming at him with a flannel.

'What about the cleaning then? We could get someone to come and tidy up and make a cup of tea for you.'

'Isn't that what you do?'

Aye, there's the rub. Sarah was opting out. She wouldn't need to visit so often, and he'd be left, like that old boy in the next street. That old man had three kids and none of them ever crossed the threshold. They'd found him dead behind the door and everyone said they didn't know how it happened. A dark empty space opens up in his bowels.

She doesn't understand. He cannot leave his home or the Figures will take over. Lately he's begun to see their faces, as if a veil has been lifted and they've decided to show themselves. They have horrible gargoyle faces, pitted like stone, with alien eyes. Deep wrinkles and ears that look like horns. They come into sharp focus just for a second and then, just as quickly, like changing channel on the TV, they vanish.

Sarah

I take a deep, cleansing breath of night air. Seventeenth-century dust tickles the inside of my nostrils and I imagine the Reverend Wilkie breathing in the same air as he scratched laboriously with his quill. Charlotte has sent Robbie home and is locking up for the night. I wander into the square, stare up at the mercat cross outlined against the sky. We're a few weeks away from the Summer Solstice and even on dull days the sky stays stubbornly bright, as if it doesn't want to give up the ghost. I think of Hannah, under the same sky, about to wake up to a new day. She's already living in tomorrow. We are all separated by layers of time and space and dust: Hannah, the Reverend Wilkie, Alie Gowdie.

I sit on the top step of the mercat cross, lay my hand on its base, as if on the shoulder of an old friend. It sings beneath my skin. I can hear Charlotte marching across the cobbles, but I don't jerk away. I know she'll understand. I've never had a conversation with her about this, but I reckon she would think the same as me, that history is a whisper away, an insistent hiss below the cobbles. Maybe my passion goes deeper than hers. On moonlit nights at the end of a tour when the punters are in the pub and I'm all alone – on those nights I stand in the market square like this and the tug of the past is so strong I am consumed by it. I can feel it fizzing under my feet like some kind of seismic ripple. Old stones have a voice that only I can hear. They tell me about love and loss and living and dying, and how it's all happened time after time, and it will keep on happening. It's a kind of comfort.

Charlotte's hand rests briefly on my shoulder. 'You shouldn't sit on cold stone, you'll get piles.'

I smile up at her. 'Old wives' tale.'

'Let's go and drink to old wives.'

'Let's.' I take her outstretched hand and she pulls me upright. I slap the dust from my backside. Her hand is very hot in mine, and I realise how chilly it's become. The thought of wine and conversation and good company warms me.

*

It's Sunday before I think about calling Hannah. I'm sitting out in my little walled garden after work. The space is two-tiered: a sunken stone-slabbed patio with three steps up to a gravel square. The table and chairs, smart dark wickerwork, were my choice, but the stone lions that guard the steps were not. Ian brought them home from a car boot sale when we first moved in, and I seem to be stuck with them, just as I'm stuck with his choice of wife. The lions have identical mean expressions, and in my head I refer to them as Ian and Janine. It gives me a little inner smile.

I've only met Dr Janine Lawrence a couple of times in person. Dr Janine's speciality is cist burials. She gets to excavate ancient mounds and investigate beads and brooches that were last touched by the hands of the Picts. She's shorter than she looks on TV, hair scraped back, heavy black-rimmed spectacles. Much more the academic in real life, but still with that media gloss that made it difficult for me to have a meaningful conversation with her. I was so used to seeing her in various documentaries, I probably came across as a bit starstruck when we met in person. We should have loads in common: a fascination with what secrets the earth can give up, a passion for history. Ian. My daughter.

The first time Hannah stayed the night with Ian and Janine I didn't sleep. I stayed on red alert, convinced she wouldn't settle, all ready to fire up the car and bring her home. How cruel it is to expect children to shift their loyalties. Whatever our shortcomings, Ian and I were good together as parents, a strong family unit. I thought it would always be like that. I allowed Hannah to think that too. She used to ask me, at seven years old, 'Mummy, will you and Daddy be together for ever?' and I would laugh and ruffle her hair and assure her that we would be. Of course we would. Maybe she sensed something I didn't, a shift in the Sutherland tectonic plate.

At what point did Ian feel 'suffocated'? At what point did I realise he was drifting away? Actually, Hannah was fine that first night, and all the other nights. Dr Janine played reruns of a children's archaeology series she did for the BBC (think *Time Team* with more shouting) and Hannah became her biggest fan. It was a twisty little sore point, a Pictish cloak-pin jabbing me in the heart. Soon, I began to feel I was the one drifting way, let loose on my own miserable little land mass.

On one occasion, a teenage Hannah appeared with a newspaper praising Janine's achievements. Something about an old pot. I made a big thing of feigning disinterest, until Hannah snatched up the paper and waltzed off to her room in the huff. Part of me is incensed that my daughter remains a neutral island in our break-up, while the other part is mortified that, even now, I'm still thinking in terms of sides.

Hannah accuses me of being jealous, but I'm not jealous in the way she thinks. I don't shrink inside when I catch sight of Ian and Janine together. I feel a certain sadness. I mourn the loss of our togetherness: the long walks, the cosy evenings, the shared parenting. I feel like I've lost a friend. All those little things you chat about at the end of the day Ian's now sharing with Janine whereas my thoughts are all in my head, racing around like ferrets with no hope of release.

If I am jealous it's because Dr Janine Lawrence is the woman I might have become, if I hadn't got pregnant at 21. I abandoned my studies without a backward glance; all my passion suddenly focused on one tiny scrap of humanity. With a little more drive, a tad more confidence over the years, I might have been able to do it all: mother, wife, academic. So when Janine gives an interview on the news, when I see her latest publication in the bookshop – yes, I'm jealous. But, at heart, I'm not a bitter person. Whenever I catch myself thinking along these lines, I pull myself up short and remind myself that I have something she doesn't. I have a beautiful daughter, and no one can take her away from me, not even Janine.

So in my garden, it's just me and the stone lions, Ian and Janine. It's a rare warm spell and nothing is moving or making a sound, no birds, no traffic. Just for a second, time is suspended. Only a shallow dip in the weathered sandstone window ledges suggests a time before, a time when Alie Gowdie went about her business as a newly married housewife, washing, cooking, gathering fuel, marketing the cloth produced in the room that's now my sitting room. Sometimes I place my hand in the stone dip, coarse as salt beneath my palm. I like to imagine *she* might have placed her hand here once, and for a nanosecond we are connected, skin to skin.

I repeat the gesture with my mobile, curling my fingers around it, anticipating that connection with Hannah, thousands of miles away. She'd messaged her flight times to Kolkata, and I'd quickly googled the time difference. GMT + 5.30. So, if it's five o'clock here, I should just catch her before she goes to bed. There's a rather prim pot of tea sitting on the patio table, along with my paperback and my mobile. A large tumbler of rhubarb gin with ice would have really hit the spot, but as ever I crave my daughter's approval. I'm not sure how that started. Maybe it's an unconscious thing, a yearning to be a friend rather than a mother, as if that might be the better deal. Mothering is tough and thankless.

I allow myself a moment to dispel the tension that always builds before I call my girl. I can't explain it. It's a foreboding, as if I'm already anticipating all the things that could go wrong over there. I tell myself to snap out of it. I wish I wasn't such a worrier. Was Alie a worrier? Did she laugh off her accusers or was she filled with dread about what might happen? I never realised I was, until Ian labelled me as such. You're such a worrier, he used to say, when the infant Hannah screamed all evening with colic. *You're making her like that.* My anxiety was the cause of our every misadventure, according to Ian. He had to go down the pub, when she screamed like that, and, later, he had to take refuge with Janine.

Suddenly my mobile shrills into life. The 'Old Black Magic' melody catches my breath as I see Hannah's name light up the screen. I wasn't expecting her to call me. I grab the phone and jab the little green icon.

'Hannah? Are you okay? Is everything all right?'

'Mum!' A throaty chuckle. 'I was just calling to find out how it went with Granddad. I was worried.'

'Aw! You don't need to worry. He's fine. It's not dementia.'

'What's this? Are you outside? Is it warm?'

'It's lovely. Fifteen degrees!' I make a face at the screen and raise my china teacup.

I hear Hannah laughing and the sound warms me.

'No wine tonight, Mum?'

'Early start tomorrow. Checking up on the cleaner. Honestly, whoever she is, she's like a ghost. All I've seen of her so far are wet streaks and the smell of lemons!'

'Boring.'

'Sorry – back to Granddad. The doctor thinks he might have a vision problem, and that's why he's seeing all this weird stuff.'

'Oh, poor Granddad. I miss him. I miss you too.'

I sit to attention and put down my cup. Hannah looks washed out, but it could be the camera, or the light. As always I find myself checking the backdrop for clues as to how she's living. She's somewhere gloomy with a lot of background chatter.

'I'm in a hotel with Aisling,' she supplies helpfully. 'We've just eaten.'

Good. At least she's eating, even if not at regular times. I'm about to ask after the mysterious Aisling when Hannah pans the lens around, and there is the new friend, mugging to camera, all fresh-faced and daft, as they are at that age. She ripples her fingers in a wave, the way Hannah does.

'How's it goin', Mrs Sutherland? Jesus, that's a grand name! Is that for real?'

I assure her it's very real. Aisling has creamy skin, bee-stung lips and flowers in her sun-bleached hair. She is a festival babe, a free spirit, and not as much of a threat as I'd feared. I knew she'd be fine. Hannah is a good judge of character. The picture swings back to my daughter.

'So I had a job interview today, via Skype!'

'Really? Are you okay for money, sweetheart?'

'Stop it, Mother! I'm fine!'

'Well, let me know how you get on. What kind of . . .'

But her attention is claimed by something off-screen. Friends turning up, perhaps, or maybe the waiter with the bill. Whatever it is, I've lost her to that other world. She waves at the screen.

'Have to go now, Ma. Love to Granddad!' She blows kisses, and Aisling crowds in to join her. The call disconnects with a two-second freeze frame of their giggling faces. I blow a kiss at the blank screen and sip my tea. I feel better now.

*

As I said to Hannah on the phone, the new cleaner is a bit of a mystery. I've yet to meet her face-to-face, even though we've certainly been in the building at the same time. You'll like her, Peggy keeps saying. She's an asset. I'm inclined to agree, but so far all I've got to go on is circumstantial evidence.

The last cleaner, a wiry wee woman who smelled of gin, quit after two months. People only notice the cleaner when the place isn't clean, she'd complained, and she did have a point. I've become so used to going around looking for faults, I now find myself slightly blindsided. This new girl is one step ahead of me. Nowadays, as I do my store walkabout, the shop floor is drying nicely and the staff loos smell like an orchard. The tiles gleam and the toilet water foams a brisk Mediterranean blue. There's an abundance of fresh paper towels, and we no longer run out of loo roll every five minutes. Each waste bin in the place stands empty and ready for action like a well-disciplined soldier.

I arrive at work on Monday just before six. Alastair, the lad with the wrong shoes, and Peggy are already waiting at the back door. I squint down at the boy's feet, but he must have received a tip-off. His footwear is black and squeaky clean. Like the condemned man, Peggy has been puffing hungrily on a last fag before the doors clang shut. She tosses the butt to the ground and crushes it with the heel of her navy loafer.

'You'd better not let the cleaner see you doing that!'

As I haul the big bunch of keys from my bag, Peggy looks round furtively. 'No, she wouldn't like it,' she mutters. 'You know she sweeps all around the outside? Yesterday she was polishing the car-park sign. What an asset. A total asset.'

I check my watch. 'Well, I hope she's going to turn up.'

'She doesn't speak much English,' says Peggy as I man-handle the door open and set about deactivating the alarm. The warning *beep-beep-beep* always sets my nerves on edge.

'She speaks in the language of flowers,' I say, punching in numbers. 'The place smells like a rose garden.'

It's so unlike me to wax lyrical about the staff, I can feel their surprised gazes behind me. 'She even does that pointy thing with the loo roll.'

Peggy makes an appreciative face – a wee smile and a nod of the head. 'Aye. Just like that posh hotel Dave and I went to for our anniversary. The lavvy seat was sealed with tape and you had to break the seal to have a wee.'

Alastair utters an unidentifiable sound and disappears into the dark bowels of the warehouse to turn on the lights.

I check my watch again. A lone trolley with a crow perched on it sits beside the perimeter fence of the deserted car park. 'We can't get too attached. The good ones never stay.'

Right on cue, a black van motors into view and slows at the car-park entrance.

'Here she is,' Peggy whispers. 'Her husband always gives her a lift.'

The van looks expensive and sleek, with blacked-out windows. I'm hopeless with brands, but it may be a Mercedes. Its smart appearance is marred by a thin film of dust. It backs smartly into the entrance and I notice that someone has drawn an incongruous heart shape in the dust on the back door. As we watch, the passenger door opens and a tiny figure scrambles out. She is dwarfed by the van. There is no chat, no goodbyes. She shuts the door and the van immediately pulls away with a screech of tyres.

It's a bit odd that the girl's husband didn't pull into the car park, drop her off at the door. Instead, she has to make her way across the tarmac, walking in that self-conscious, hunched-up way you do when you know people are watching you. As she gets nearer, she doesn't seem to get any bigger. She's dressed in skinny jeans and a navy polo shirt embroidered with the logo of the new cleaning contractor.

Up close, she's a very pretty girl, South Asian perhaps, with dark eyes that don't make contact and long silky brown hair. She's bundling it into a scrunchie as she walks.

I stick out a hand as she reaches the door. 'Good morning. I'm Sarah, the manager. Welcome to Wisebuy.'

She bobs her head and hesitates before accepting my hand. Hers is surprisingly soft, for someone who's dealing with soapy water and cleaning chemicals.

'Mai,' she murmurs.

'So where are you from?'

But she's already gone, scurrying away to the janitor's room, which has been transformed from a stale, stinking hellhole of dirty mops to an ordered repository. She's even scoured the sink, turning it from tannin brown to porcelain white. It's like a commercial for those denture-cleaning tablets.

'Vietnam,' Peggy supplies as we climb the stairs to the canteen.

'Why the hell would you leave Vietnam to scrub floors in a Scottish supermarket?'

It's a bit of a rhetorical question, really, and as we go about our various duties neither Peggy nor I remember it long enough to try to find an answer.

John

Sarah insists on buying wholemeal bread, the real rough stuff with bird seed in it. She says it's good for his bowels, but he reckons his bowels are working just fine without her help. There's only one use for it. He struggles to identify the correct keys nowadays, so it takes him several attempts and at least ten minutes to let himself out into the back garden. The air is unusually warm and heavy with the scent of roses. A drop or two of rain speckle his skin, but it will probably come to nothing.

The wall calendar is already on June. He's not sure of the exact date but he's noted that Sarah has marked up one square in red felt tip so that even he can read it. CARER STARTS. Bloody hell. He reckons that's next week. Some woman in a purple tracksuit came around to the house a while ago – he can't remember her name or what the upshot was, but things seemed to move very swiftly after that. One minute Sarah's whispering with the doctor in the hall and the next he's getting a 'carer'. It's a slippery slope, as far as he can see.

Grumbling, he takes the torn-up crusts outside and dispenses them like a farmer distributing seed. He doesn't much care about birds one way or the other, but Marjorie always fed the little blighters and he feels obliged to keep it up. If Sarah twigged that this was where her precious bread was going there'd be hell to pay, but the birds seem to enjoy it. Even now, there's a pair of blackbirds faffing about on top of the shed, waiting their turn.

'You'd better look lively,' he warns them, 'or the crows will beat you to it. Or those bloody great seagulls. You don't want to mess with those boys.'

Great white ghosts, looming out of the sky. He sees them gliding past the windows sometimes, and he thinks its *them*, the Figures, lurking just out of sight.

'Hmmm.' He wanders over to the back wall, leaving a trail of breadcrumbs. The broken paving slabs are still there, and with a pang he realises how much he still misses Mrs Chalmers. Before they carted her off Sarah had suggested he invite his neighbour over for afternoon tea. She'd offered to set everything out and make cucumber sandwiches and open a box of Mr Kipling's, but he'd declined. What if he poured tea into Mrs Chalmers' lap? Or dropped the sandwich plate? No. Far better to live with the fantasy, the wisps of white hair glimpsed over the garden wall, the occasional flash of blue eyes if she stood on tiptoe.

She was a very genteel lady, Mrs Chalmers. They had their own little codes and ways of working. If he was in the back garden, like now, he'd move the wrought iron garden chairs around on the patio. The scraping would alert his neighbour, and she would give a discreet cough, a little *ahem*, and that was his cue to scale the paving slabs and bid her good day. It was like a little blind date every time. He frowns at the irony of that. Even if they had met up, her expression would have been a blur, and without the sight cues people take for granted it was bound to be a social disaster. Sarah should have understood that. Maybe he didn't explain it very well, and she thought he was just being awkward.

He regards the paving slabs with a heavy heart and turns his back on them to call down the blackbirds.

Sarah

When I wake up the following weekend, sun is streaming through the curtains, turning my bedroom walls the colour of butter. There's nothing quite like a lazy Saturday. It has a whole different feel to any other day of the week, and I've managed to wangle a whole weekend off. Two days to myself! I savour that feeling of luxury. My toes find a nice cool spot beneath the duvet and I stretch with pleasure, like a cat, feeling the muscles in my belly and calves let go. Sometimes I think my body has forgotten how to un-clench itself.

I scratch my head and yawn. My hair feels like wool. I could jump straight in the shower, or I could slob around in my PJs for a bit and take a cup of tea out to the garden. Or I could start that new romance I bought a month ago and haven't opened yet. Or check my emails? But there might be work-related stuff and that would eat up my time and then I'd end up checking my social media and . . .

Good grief. I massage my eyes. Having too much time is as stressful as having too little. The pressure is on to use it wisely, not to fritter it away. I never used to feel like this, but sometimes I look at my father and I wonder what it must be like to be able to tot up the remainder of your years on the fingers of one hand. How fragile would that make you feel?

When I was a kid the days spun out like dropped spools of thread unravelling. As a teenager I frittered time away, sleeping too long, being bored for too long. I spent way too much time waiting for the wrong boys to fancy me. When I was with Ian, in that brief time before Hannah, we would just take off up the hills, lose ourselves in the landscape, or hole up in a dark pub. I never had to make a choice. We just *did* things. Selfish things, I suppose. I don't remember prioritising anyone else in our schedule, until the baby came along.

Then, time took over my life. I had to plan, stick to a routine. The random spooling out of days returned too, but in a different way. I had a grown-up job to do. I was the time-keeper, as if my sticking to a rigid plan would somehow keep her safe.

Anyone who's ever had a baby will tell you this: you fret when your kid doesn't sleep and you fret when they do. I remember the first time Hannah slept through the night. We were living in a tiny student flat; I remember the original cornices and the mice under the sink, but the details aren't important. She was a poor sleeper. Even when she zonked out she never truly relaxed. You could see her eyeballs jittering beneath her pale closed lids and her little fists jerking, as if she'd suddenly let go of something. One morning, a morning like this with the sun streaming in, I woke up at half seven and realised that she'd missed her two o'clock feed. She was a hungry baby; she never missed a feed.

The fear was instant and heart-stopping. I still remember it. I didn't wake Ian, snoring softly beside me. I was in such a mother-shaped, all-consuming bubble of dread, I clambered over him to get to the door. It was a two-second sprint across the hallway to the nursery, but time was playing tricks, giving me just enough thread to imagine everything from a broken baby monitor to full-scale abduction.

And there she was, lying in her cot, eyes open and gurgling away to herself. She looked sleepy and relaxed, as if she'd been somewhere really nice in her dreams and only just got back. She clocked this crazy anxious woman coming at her and frowned. The Hannah frown, a deep furrow of puzzlement between her eyebrows. She still does it when she thinks I'm overreacting.

The importance of using this weekend wisely suddenly consumes me. I really want to go to the museum, pick up where I left off with the Reverend Wilkie, but there are other, possibly more pressing things to attend to, like washing Dad's windows and cleaning the bath before his carer starts on Monday.

It's a dilemma.

*

The museum wins.

It wasn't going to be any other way, was it? My personal narrative is firmly stuck in the reflective trough. It's safer that way. So I messaged Charlotte while I was having my breakfast. I'd thrown caution to the winds and had a full-on fry-up with black pudding and scrambled eggs. She'd replied with a smiley face and asked me to join her for coffee at the Pantry at ten fifteen. The museum opens for business at eleven.

I take one look at the cakes on offer in the Pantry and wish I hadn't had such a big breakfast. The counter is laden with domed glass platters crammed with scones and macarons and the fruit slices we used to call 'fly cemeteries'. I went to school in this town, but I don't remember hanging around posh places like this. I think there was an Italian ice-cream parlour in the square, with an Italian ice-cream man called Joe, who shouted at you if you overstayed your welcome. *No ice cream, no seat!* This place is full of earnest young professionals on laptops.

We settle for pancakes and I have a skinny flat white, just to offset the damage. Charlotte has a full-fat latte which she'll no doubt work off in the gym. I feel the usual twinge of envy, and instantly regret it. I'm turning into someone who begrudges things. It's not attractive.

'So, just to recap,' says Charlotte, who has recapping down to a fine art, 'the minister's diary is really a mixture of personal and parish business.'

'With added food.' I cut my pancake in two.

Charlotte unfolds her serviette. For a moment, I think she's going to jot down bullet points on it. 'Getting past the food. We've discovered that Wilkie set up a hospital for the poor.'

'Did you speak to anyone about that?'

'I did. I emailed my contact on the council, and he confirms that Lumsdain House was originally a paupers' hospital, although few records survive for the building in that era. In the 1800s, it was used to house orphans who worked in the weaving trade. They used to take them from the workhouse.'

I make a face. 'I've heard that. It's awful. I've always thought about mentioning it in my tour, but it seems . . .'

'Gratuitous.' Charlotte sips her latte, watching me over the rim of her tall glass. I know she finds me curious, an oddity. She deals with history in an entirely different way.

'I don't like that word. I do juice things up, I admit, but not at the expense of real people. I never let the punters forget that "witches" were real people. Child exploitation seems a step too far.'

Charlotte appears satisfied. She puts her glass down on its

saucer with a little click. 'We're both custodians, in different ways. I'm under a bit of pressure to send that diary to the archives, so—'

'I'm on it! I've cleared the whole day. No deviations, no distractions.' I drain my own coffee, making a mental note not to check my phone. 'Let me get this.'

I fish my purse from my bag. On impulse I buy two fly cemeteries for Dad. The assistant drops them into a brown paper bag. I was going to pay my usual visit this afternoon, but a day off should be a proper day off. They'll keep until tomorrow.

*

On Sunday morning, I get up early, buzzing with anticipation. There are loads of things I should be doing – I haven't vacuumed for over a week and my bedroom is a tip (my need for order doesn't extend to my own house) – but today is going to be just about me. Me and the Reverend Wilkie.

The museum is closed on a Sunday, so Charlotte has photocopied a dozen pages of the journal for me to take home. It will probably take me all day to decipher and transcribe the Reverend's spidery hand. Being holed up with a three centuries-old piece of the past may not be the average person's idea of fun, but I can't wait and there's only one thing stopping me. Before I do anything else I pick up my car keys and the brown paper bag from the kitchen counter.

I'm about to let myself into Dad's house, but he beats me to it. As the door swings wide, I make a bit of a joke. 'Ha! You were watching out for me.'

Dad just turns away with a snort, but not before I've clocked the mulish expression on his face. Oh dear. I close the door and follow him to the kitchen, where I decant the fly cemeteries onto a plate. Even they don't produce a smile.

'You and Mum used to love them, don't you remember?'

Eyeing up the plate, he makes no move to take one. 'Of course I remember. I'm not senile.'

It feels like a slap in the face, and I find myself wishing I hadn't bothered. I try to start up a conversation while I wait for the kettle to boil, telling him about Wilkie's journal and how it fits in with the Kilgour witch trials.

'It's an amazing find. It should shed more light on what happened to Alie Gowdie.'

I make tea in a pot – he prefers it that way – and give it a stir.

'You shouldn't stir it,' he snaps. 'Spoils the flavour.'

I bite my lip. 'Do you know what came up? Lumsdain House. You worked there for a while, didn't you?'

His natural eagerness to remember the past struggles with his bad mood. I can see the war flickering across his face.

'The building society rented the ground floor for a while in the sixties,' he says. 'It was a very old building, even then. Lots of stories about it. They used to house kids there, you know. Took the little orphans from the workhouse and made them work in the textile industry. It wasn't right. Nothing more than slave labour on our own doorstep.'

'I knew about that. Wasn't that in the 1800s? According to the Reverend's diary, he started it up as a home for pauper children back in the 1640s.'

'It wasn't right what they did with the kids back then. They never saw the light of day, you know. Marched out to work the looms, and marched back again. Bit of porridge, no doubt, and up to bed with them.'

I realise he's still talking about the Victorian era. 'Did you ever hear any stories about what the building was like before that time?'

'They even drew pictures on the walls, the bairns, to amuse themselves.'

My curiosity prickles, but just as I'm going to dig a little deeper Dad goes off on a work-related rant about how they relocated the building society to the High Street in 1971 and it's now a vegan café called the Bean Counter. He fails to see any humour in the name and I heave a sigh. I'm now itching to get away. I'm vaguely disappointed too, but did I really expect him to be enthusiastic about my interests?

Our relationship is coloured by disappointment, probably on both sides, but just for today I reserve the right to feel disillusioned. It's all so one-sided, like I'm doing all the giving and he's doing all the taking. It's exhausting. That's why he's in such a sour mood today, because I dared to put myself first, to take a day off to do my own thing. This is why he's sulking. Fine.

I pour tea into a single mug.

'Aren't you stopping?'

'Nope. I've got things to do.' I can feel his disappointment, but it will do him good to realise I have a life. He's selfish, and I need a bit of space.

'Fine,' he says.

'Fine.'

'You're far too hung up on the past,' he calls after me as I leave. 'You need to get out into the present and meet someone nice. You'll be old and lonely before your time.'

I slam the front door, cutting him off. I think I may have broken the speed limit on the way home. In the rear-view mirror, I catch sight of myself. It's not pretty; a wedge of resentment and ruffled feathers. How bloody dare he? But, if I'm honest, he's hit the nail on the head. *This* is why I'm fuming. *This* is why his words have disturbed me so much. When I look at my dad, I see myself, my destiny. A long time in the future, perhaps, but it's there all the same – a slow descent into old age and dependency. I can't imagine Hannah will display the sort of patience and sacrifice that I do. I'll probably end up like Mrs Chalmers, spirited away to a care home, leaving nothing behind but an empty house and possessions that no one wants.

Back home, I try to put Dad out of my mind, set aside the self-pity and reclaim the buzz I felt this morning. I make coffee in my favourite mug and stick on some woolly bed socks. The stone floors here suck out body heat faster than Ben Nevis in November. I've a long day ahead – best to be prepared. I climb the stairs.

The sitting room is bisected by a two-seater sofa. Together with a mismatched armchair, it forms a cosy group around a woodburning stove. The other half of the room is what I optimistically term my office space. I should really have an antique mahogany desk, with a green leather blotter and numerous drawers filled with stationery. But I actually have a Swedish pine excuse for a desk which arrived as a flatpack and still has some vital screws missing. It sits in the back corner beneath the high, narrow windows which were designed to shed some light on the weavers. You have to do a little skip as you sit down to avoid the squeaky dip in the floor. I try to avoid the dodgy floorboard, in case it suddenly gives and I end up with an expensive repair job on my hands. I really should get the joists checked, but I quite like the irregularities of this place, the angles and clefts and creaky hollows.

I have to shift piles of books and papers to clear the desk surface. Transcribing is a serious business that needs space and peace. I made a good start in the museum and I feel I'm beginning to get somewhere. I select a nice sharp pencil, and when everything is perfect – mug on coaster, lamp angled just right, mobile switched to silent – I sit down to begin today's stint.

> Februarii, 17, anno D. 1648. I was roused from business early by one of the Kirk Elders desirous of speech with me. Mrs. T. did shew him into the parlour, where he fell about me and praised the Lord for sending me to turn the brethren from the Path of Syn. He did informit me that in sum distant pairts the evill custom of Yule be observed with pyping, dansing, drinking and disordour. In the name of God and Session we can suffer nocht the lyke. They say of this place that you can startle Satan in every loan, as you would a hare, but the Horned One will not best me.

The Horned One? Was this the same Devil Alie was seen dancing with? No prizes for guessing who's been pointing the finger. One Archibald Donald, butcher. But as Charlotte would say, in her methodical way, don't jump to conclusions.

> Februarii 21, anno. D. 1648. This day three men came before the Session to confess that they did play at the futball and other pastyme on the Sabbath and the forth man, a tailor from St Androis, wud not confess bot was seen rinnin through the toun under silence of nycht in a lewd and drunken stayt. His punishmente is to sit on the cutty-stool in sack-clothe on Friday and Sabbath.

I can't resist a giggle at the 'lewd and drunken state'. He should see Kilgour at the weekend. I try to imagine the glowering Reverend stalking the park in his long black cloak, calling down the wrath of God on the kids shouting abuse from the swings.

They have one of those penitent stools in the museum. For all my years of mentioning it in my patter, I've never actually paid it too much attention. I've always thought it would be a handy addition to my kitchen, perfect for reaching the high shelves. It's tall, with a wee step up, crafted from stout oak burnished by generations of repentant bottoms. There's a rather sanctimonious label beneath it listing lax morals, brawling and defamation as the sort of sins guaranteed to put you in the hot seat. A very public shaming, and a visible deterrent to anyone who didn't toe the line. No room for dissent or doubt in the Reverend's world. I sip my coffee, imagining a conversation between the pair of us.

'What blasphemy is this? You don't believe in God?'

'It's not that I don't believe, exactly. I just need more proof. Maybe if I really came up against it in life, if I was visited by a catastrophe, I'd believe. But until then, I can take it or leave it.'

'But I am the Word of God. Believe in me, and you believe in Him.'

'Nah, not in my world, sunshine. In my world, you're just a crazy man in a black cloak.'

The conversation fades. What did Alie think about it all? Did anyone ask her, and if they did, would she have revealed her true thoughts? Would you, with the Reverend Wilkie on your case?

As always, history throws up more questions than answers. I top up my coffee and plough on.

March 1, anno. D. 1648. This day Alisoune Gowdie did confess to slandering Mr Archibald Donald of this Parish. Master Donald swears that she did tell him that she had once seen the Little People dansing on the Knowe behind her cottage and did follow them and watch them for sum tyme.

> When Master Donald did alert the Kirk Elder, Mistress
> Gowdie did call him a gowk what fornicated with Cattle.

My first reaction is to splutter into my drink. Alie is spirited
and strong. Archibald Donald is a spiteful lech. He probably
made up the whole heifer spell thing too, just because she
wouldn't give in to his questionable charms. I have an image
of a bullish red-faced hulk, reeking of onions and offal,
dangling his money pouch in front of her. At least Alie had
the balls to fight back, but at what cost? I don't have to read
much further to find out.

> She did spit upon him in the Mercat Place and was
> summoned before the Session. Despite the petitioning of
> her new husbande, Mistress Gowdie was ordained to stand
> at the Kirk door, bare heddit and bare footit ilk preaching
> day from the first bell to sermon to the last and then sit
> upon the penitent stool theiraifter until the sermon and
> blessing be given and until the Kirk be satisfied.

Oh, Alie. After all the fuss and finery of your wedding day
you're now dressed in a sack, being jeered at by your wedding
guests. It's preposterous. I'm not sure when the wedding
took place. I know from my door lintel that they must have
moved into this house in 1648, but brides didn't necessarily
take their husband's name. It sounds like Robert put up a
fight for her, but where is Alie's father, the shoemaker, at this
point? When I did the whole white wedding thing with Ian,
my father was a rock. In the wedding car, he nervously
adjusted his tie and told me I looked beautiful and how
proud of me he was. He's never said that to me since, but if
I were hauled up for some misdemeanour he certainly
wouldn't rest until he got me off the hook.

I want to reach into the pages and pull Alie out of there,

dust her down. Give her a hug, pour her a hefty gin and tonic and tell her how little any of this matters. The spells, the cow, God. But who am I to judge? Different mores, different times. Suddenly I need a break. The Reverend's handwriting is dancing before my eyes, the letters reforming into poisonous little thorns. I push the pages away from me and get to my feet.

I had to stop anyway as the photocopies ran out on page twenty-three. By then we'd got to May, and not even the promise of a bit of warm weather could perk up that misery of a man. He kept banging on about the endless cold and the price of oats. No more mention of Alie, just a dry commentary on the everyday life of a country minister. Not dry as in acerbic or witty – this man had zero sense of humour – but dry as in prosaic and dull. Maybe that was it: no more secrets waiting to be revealed, no further mention of Alie Gowdie.

Transcription over, I'd put down my pencil and rubbed my tired eyes, asking myself for the hundredth time what exactly I was hoping to find. Why am I so obsessed with this story of a dead girl? Some people just reach out and touch you for no obvious reason. You make a connection, across miles, across cultures. Even across centuries. The story of the Kilgour witches has been part of our consciousness around here for as long as I can remember. We have streets named after the main players, cafés and pubs. People have written books about them and there's even a permanent exhibition in the museum, with some very dodgy costumed waxworks and a fake pyre.

Mrs Sutherland's Magical Witch Walks were the result of one of those tipsy post-divorce conversations you have with your mates. Somewhere around the middle of the second bottle of Shiraz you feel the need to redefine yourself. I think it was Charlotte who planted the seed, and my other two conspirators, Janey and Pam, couldn't come up with a valid objection in time. I love history, I cried. I have a creepy black dress. I'll do it!

My new venture took a little bit of thought and lots of research. The first time I led a group around town I was so nervous I'd felt physically sick for days beforehand. But I've discovered as much about myself as about the woman who died on Witch's Knowe three hundred years before I was born. When I get into costume, I am no longer me. Or perhaps I am a version of me that is deeply buried. I am fearless. I am an avenger, putting Alie Gowdie and her companions on the map. I'm giving her a voice.

Or perhaps it's the other way around.

*

A week later, I've rota'd myself for an early shift. Dad's carer is due to start, and I want to be there. I arrive at the store at three minutes to six. We've had no rain for a week, but it's now drizzling and Peggy, Rosie and Mai are sheltering under a giant golfing umbrella at the back door. I feel I should be present to greet 'the carer'. Dad's quotes, not mine. He intones the phrase with a mixture of deference and fear, as if he's expecting a cross between the Terminator and Sister Julienne from *Call the Midwife*. I don't know what he's expecting, to be honest.

As I greet everyone and struggle with the door and the alarm, my thoughts drift back to the perfectly pleasant phone call I'd had with the woman from the social work department. She seemed intent, in the nicest possible way, on providing my father with a 'team' who would shower him in five minutes flat in the morning and return to put him to bed at six.

That was obviously a non-starter, and it was so far from what we actually required I didn't even relay the details to my father. The woman suggested we might do better with an agency. She didn't have any colleagues to provide the sort of services we wanted, which was basically to run around with a duster, keep an eye on things and make tea. Actually, she sounded a bit relieved to be saying no. The word 'overstretched' came up a lot, in a perfectly legitimate way. I was left in no doubt that we were on our own, so I'd ended up calling the number on Peggy's friend's card.

NIGHTINGALE HOMECARE
Care at home and domiciliary provision
Our carers care so you don't have to.

Despite misgivings about the tagline, I found myself in the capable hands of a woman called Louisa, who gave me paperwork and advice and called my father Dad. I'm not sure what he thought about that, because I deliberately didn't make eye contact with him for the entire visit.

'I'm doing this month's rotas right now, so I can't give you a name just yet' – I noticed a slight flicker in her eyelid, as if rotas were her least favourite thing in the world – 'but I'll email you beforehand so Dad knows exactly who he'll be getting through the door. And of course we all wear our rather smart ID badges!'

She held out her lilac lanyard. My father's gaze remained stubbornly on the blank screen of his TV. We'd agreed to engage a home help for a two-hour slot per week, with the option to increase the time further down the line. Amazingly, this unnamed person could be asked to do whatever you required – laundry, dusting, lunch-making – unlike the council operatives who were not allowed to switch on a stranger's kettle in case it electrocuted them. I've never come across a case of an electrocuted home help, ever, but I suppose someone has looked into it.

I'd checked my emails this morning, but there was still nothing from Louisa to advise on the name of our new helper. Despite that, I was confident that the woman would be a sort of Angela Lansbury type who would transform our lives, lightening my load and cheering us up with wise adages and lashings of apple pie that she made at home out of the goodness of her heart. I confide as much to Peggy as we climb the stairs to the canteen, hoping she'll snap me out of it with a pithy comment, but her face takes on an expression of wonder.

'My friend's mother had an Australian. Lovely girl. She could play the piano too, little bit of Glenn Miller after she'd tidied up.'

'Oh, that sounds amazing.' I sigh with relief and lay my handbag on one of the tables. The red stripe around the walls looks oddly straight today, but that may be something to do with my mood. I'm more optimistic than I've felt in a long time. 'I should've stood my ground and done this ages ago. I really needed help.'

Peggy is clattering around in the kitchen and raises her voice to be heard above her own noise. 'You should have! You're entitled to a life of your own, especially now.'

'Especially now?'

'That you've met someone.'

'Someone?' It takes me a second to realise she's referring to my text messages, to the story she's concocted from such spurious evidence. I'm about to put her right when Mai walks in with a handful of black bags. Peggy watches her intently as she cleans the bins, replaces the liners and hurries away with a full bag of rubbish banging her ankles.

'Did you see that?'

'What? I see someone keen to get on with their work.' I pick up my bag pointedly.

'Black eye.' She mouths the words as if the cleaner is standing right outside the door listening. 'A shiner.'

'Really?' I glance at the closed door.

I hadn't even noticed. Despite my thoughts on mystical connections down the ages, I hadn't spared a glance at this young woman. I should have. It's my job to see these things, to ensure that everything is shipshape instore. I'm annoyed with myself, but Rosie's voice crackling over the tannoy interrupts my thoughts.

'Store manager to kiosk, please. Store manager. Repeat, store manager.'

I sigh. It's going to be one of those days.

*

I can't believe it. Today of all days, and I'm running late. I said I'd be there to greet the carer and agree a plan, and now I'm going to be delayed and Dad will go ballistic. He'll probably put the brakes on the whole thing. I can hear him now, the Prophet of Doom: *I told you it was a bad idea. No good can ever come of letting strangers in your house.*

All because of a legless bloody chicken.

Naturally, we had to have an inquest into the missing leg. It wasn't the first incident of this kind, apparently.

'What do you mean, it isn't the first time?'

'There was a man. Last week.' Rosie's wearing her

apologetic face, which never bodes well. 'He'd been making up a picnic for him and his girlfriend. He bought a cooked chicken, took it home and discovered the missing leg. Or rather the space where the leg should be. He said this is no good to me, I wanted two drumsticks, I was going to propose—'

'Yes, yes, I get the picture.' I shoot Rosie a let-me-think look. 'So the same thing this morning?'

'This lady brought back a cooked chicken. Garlic and herb.' Rosie peers at the receipt. 'She bought it yesterday at 11.04.'

'Okay, so maybe we've received an *abnormal* batch. Who was on the hot chicken counter yesterday? Wasn't it Nikki? I'll see what she has to say about it.'

Nikki arrived at half nine. There were tears.

I decide to soften my stance. 'Look. I'm not blaming you, Nikki. All I'm saying is that you have to make sure you check the chickens before you bag them. It could be that they've been delivered like that, and I know all chickens look the same and you're probably not examining them very closely, but . . .'

Nikki sobs into a tissue. I send her to Peggy for a cup of tea. I phone both customers with an apology and an offer of promotional coupons. The man can see the funny side, even though he had to buy pork pies instead. The woman is a bit sniffy and mentions Head Office. I take great pains to agree with her; that the very least one can expect from Wisebuy is a chicken with all its limbs intact.

By the time I come off the phone, I'm giggling like mad. The last time this happened at work I was viewing the CCTV footage of Grant crate surfing. This is not a good look for a store manager. I wipe my eyes, and when I look at the clock I realise it's already after ten. *Oh shit*.

Flinging open Dad's front door I call my usual greeting, but there seems to be no one around. I check the sitting room for signs of an Angela Lansbury-type visitation: a diaphanous scarf draped elegantly over a chair back, a neat patent hand-bag with a silver clasp. All I can see is a battered old rucksack languishing on the couch. My senses start to prickle.

Then I hear voices coming from the bathroom.

Dad's first: 'They put it in a few weeks ago – a seat for when you're having a bath. Great invention. You press this button to go down into the water, and this one to come up again. What will they think of next?'

And then the reply: 'Ah, sweet! I could have great sport with that, Mr M. If we took it out the bath and set it up on the lawn, we could—'

My blood runs cold. I may even have sworn. Several seconds of shocked silence follow, and then a head pops around the bathroom door. I don't even need to look. Dreadlocks, cocky grin. Eyes alight with mischief.

'No! Don't tell me!' He steps into the hall, followed by my father wearing a confused frown. Grant looks from me to Dad and back again, mugging it up, putting two and two together with pantomime gestures.

'You? Your dad? What are the bloody chances!' He proffers his ID on its snazzy lilac lanyard. 'Nightingale Homecare, at your service!'

Sarah

My phone screen quivers a few times before starting to bleep like an NHS monitor. I'd put off calling: six o'clock here is about half eleven in India. I watch the video camera icon hopefully. The bleeping mutates into words: *connecting . . . connecting . . .*

I'm desperate to connect, that's the problem. You can bury yourself as much as you like, in work, in books, in bars. You can tell yourself you're doing fine, but every so often the need to connect with someone is overwhelming. I don't particularly want to offload stuff onto my daughter, and I hope she doesn't catch sight of the very large gin and tonic I've just put together. The first gulp has me wincing at the strength of the measure.

No, what I really want, right now – what I *need* – is a physical presence to talk to, someone to take this glass off me and kiss me, laugh at me and tell me I'm overreacting. Yes, I'm over-fucking-reacting. I've waited months for someone to come along and lighten the load – for Dad to agree to have some help in the first place – and then who shows up but my nemesis. The guy who's been leading me a merry dance for months, undermining my authority and chipping away at my self-esteem. He sees right through my assured retail manager act. When I set eyes on Grant Tranter I'm a kid in maths class again, all sweaty palms and nausea.

My phone flatlines. *Failure to connect.*

I take another huge gulp of my drink, swallow with a shudder. I haven't had any food. This is not going to end well. I curl up on the couch and aim the remote at the TV, flicking through the channels. I end up lip-reading some over-the-top quiz show host for several minutes before I realise it's on mute. He has a bold toothpaste-ad smile that reminds me of Grant Tranter. I jab the off button. If only it was that simple.

I could text Charlotte and see if she wants to meet for a drink, but no doubt she'll be cosied up with Sophie, tossing an edamame bean salad in their high-tech kitchen, and anyway, it's Monday. Zero units of alcohol generally pass her lips on weekdays. I feel utterly alone. Taking another sip of my gin and tonic, I pick up my phone and redial Hannah. The last time I did this she was really grumpy, and it hadn't been a good phone call. But a bad phone call when your child is abroad is worse than no phone call at all.

The sudden connection makes me almost drop the phone. My screen is filled with honey blonde hair and enormous eyes. I hear words – 'one second now, love' – and a bit of crackling and then: ''Tis yourself! How's it goin', Mrs Sunderland?'

The girl arranges herself on a green couch. I see brown knees poking out of ripped jeans and a friendly grin. Instinctively I check out the backdrop. Neutral wallpaper, the edge of a bedside cabinet.

'Sutherland, actually. Aisling? How's Kolkata? Where's Hannah?'

'She's asleep! Sssh . . .' She makes an exaggerated shushing noise like waves on a beach. She has a single braid in her hair and a ruby stud in her nose. She beams at me, and I'm suddenly lost for words. 'Sure, look at you wit' the ol' G&T! Had a shit day?'

I lower my glass with a rattle of ice cubes. Bloody cheek. 'Look, Aisling. Can I have a quick word with Hannah?'

'She's gone to bed, love.'

Love? Anger makes my breath catch. 'Can't you take *her* phone into her?' I hope she'll catch my inflection and feel a bit guilty, but Aisling doesn't look like she's on nodding terms with guilt.

'I'll tell her to call youse first thing tomorrow, Mrs S. *Ciao!*'

And with that the phone goes dead, leaving me in a limbo of irritation and fear.

*

By Wednesday, Louisa from Nightingale Homecare makes contact to tell me the name of my father's carer. Bit bloody late, Louisa. If I'd known in advance, would I have demanded a substitute? Damn right I would, but the weird thing is, after Grant left, Dad was looking livelier than I'd seen him in a long time.

'That Trant Granter – we've settled on a Wednesday morning. He's bringing me in some Caribbean coconut tart next time. His mum makes it. His dad is from Jamaica, you know.'

'He *thinks* his dad is from Jamaica.'

'And you know different?' My father looked at me in a way that made me stutter to a stop.

'His mother was a bit wild, back in the day,' I'd mumbled.

'Tittle tattle,' Dad pronounced.

He was right, of course. Grant has had a difficult upbringing: one parent, no security and small-town prejudice to overcome. Now, suffering the drip of Louisa's patronising office-speak in my ear, I climb down off my high horse. I tell her it's fine, we've made our introductions. Grant Tranter seems to be working out fine, and yes, he's due back next week at half ten.

I can't wait.

John

The young man returns the following Wednesday. John thought Sarah might have come along to supervise – he's still a bit doubtful about sharing his space with a stranger – but she doesn't turn up. Sarah isn't as hands-on as she used to be. He's a bit worried that she's taken a step back since the doctor's visit. He wants to say to her that just because he doesn't have dementia don't think everything is fine. It's not. It's not an easy conversation to have; he doesn't have the words to express to her how he feels. All that touchy-feely nonsense gets his goat. Back in the day, you just got on with things. And if you did have a worry no one listened anyway – they were all too busy with their own.

Not that he expects Sarah to be at his beck and call, but she did promise to make an appointment with the optician, and she hasn't mentioned it since. There are no more red squares marked up on the calendar. He just feels it would be nice to be consulted from time to time. And also he misses the company. The human contact.

She doesn't understand how alone he feels. He's constantly afraid in his own home; reluctant to go into the hall, into the bedroom, in case the Figures are waiting. In a way, he's glad poor Marjorie isn't here to witness all this. He can't imagine what she would say about it all. Would she have been able to see what he's seeing, or is it all in his mind? He doesn't know what's real and what isn't any more, but he has a horrible sense of foreboding. He doesn't know what they might be capable of.

So, in a way, it's good to have the carer here. And to give the lad his due he has a way about him. True, he could do with a short back and sides, but he makes a cracking cup of tea, nice and strong with an extra spoonful of sugar. That first morning had been a bit of a car crash, if truth be told. It soon became obvious that Sarah and the carer had been previously acquainted.

'What the hell are you doing here?' she'd snapped.

'I lost my job, remember?' the young man had replied. 'Now I'm a carer.'

'Not here, you're not. You can't be *our* carer.'

'I'm not *your* carer. I'm your dad's carer, but if you want a carer, I could—'

'I don't want a carer!'

They'd been eyeball to eyeball; Sarah breathing hard and looking murderous. In fact, he hadn't seen her looking so furious since one of the neighbours complained about her parking on the pavement.

John had tried to smooth things over by offering to make them all some tea, but Sarah had rounded on *him*, saying absolutely not, that's what the carer's getting paid for. The young man – Grant? Trant? Trant Granter? It was a funny name – slapped a palm to his brow and backed towards the kitchen like a cartoon villain.

'You're right. In here, is it, Mr M?' he'd said. 'I'll just stick the kettle on.'

It was all very tense. John had felt a bit sorry for the young man, although he seemed undaunted. He had a nice way about him, cheerful and breezy, a real whirlwind actually. Sarah wore her best scowl and refused to be won over – until the subject of Lumsdain House came up. John had mentioned it deliberately, as a way of cutting through the ice.

'Sarah, you know you were asking me about the Lumsdain place? I remembered a few more things, if you're interested.'

He could see that she was, the way the light went on behind her eyes. Not that brittle angry light, but a soft flicker, like a candle flame. She always loved a good story, Sarah, right from being a wee girl. She devoured books. If ever Sarah went missing, you knew she'd be up in her room, reading a book. Her mother called it an escape, although they'd given her the perfect childhood, with nothing to escape from. He was relieved to see her begin to thaw a little.

'Tea? Milk and just a wee bit sugar, if I remember correctly?' The boy had sidled a cup under her nose, and there was another stand-off, until eventually Sarah accepted the tea.

'Yes, always was a creepy old place, Lumsdain House. Your mother used to come and meet me from work sometimes, before you were born. She never wanted to hang around. The place gave her the shivers.'

'Lumsdain House? You interested in that?' Grant had piped up. 'My mum works there. I can get you in for a visit if you like.'

John had to smile. The lad had a smart noggin beneath his crazy mop.

Now, Grant interrupts his thoughts, entering the lounge with a feather duster under his arm and a tin of spray polish.

'This is how you do it, John.' He winks. 'Send the dust flying, squirt a bit of polish around. The bosses think you're doing a grand job. Learned that from a cleaner at Wisebuy.'

'Did you indeed?' John can't resist a chuckle.

'Yeah, she got the bullet for hiding bottles of gin among the loo rolls.'

'Maybe don't take her advice then, son.' John takes a sip of his tea and smacks his lips. 'Don't you tell my daughter you're giving me three spoons of sugar in my tea!'

It was much better than he thought it would be, relaxing in his chair watching the lad go about his work. He enjoyed the banter. Grant does an exaggerated mock salute and marches off with the feather duster tucked under his arm like a sergeant major's baton. John can't stop chuckling.

The following Wednesday, Grant suggests they sit outside. John would never have thought of it, and it's a wee bit airy, but Grant dusts off the patio chairs and brings out a blanket from the bedroom for John's old knees. He wonders if Grant caught sight of anything untoward in the bedroom, but it's probably a mistake to mention the Figures so soon. He doesn't want the lad thinking he's going bonkers. The Figures don't come around when Grant is here. Maybe his natural exuberance keeps them away.

Grant tips his face to the sky with a satisfied sigh. 'You gotta look at the sky at least once every day, boss. Make sure it's still there.'

Grant closes his eyes for a second, and then opens them, as if he's really checking. To John, his features are a blur, but a pleasant blur. Soft and undemanding. The sky is certainly big enough for John to see. It's a pale duck-egg blue, cloudless and uncomplicated, with no little details to muddle it up. He can relax.

At first Grant hadn't wanted to take a cuppa himself. He'd better get on with the dishes, or the vacuuming, he'd insisted. John wondered if he was a bit scared of Sarah, although it seemed unlikely after what she'd told him. She'd explained the circumstances of Grant's dismissal, but there's two sides to every story, so John said nothing. Least said, soonest mended was Marjorie's motto. Having been a manager himself, he's firmly in his daughter's camp, of course. Regulations are regulations, and you can't have employees flouting the rules. But still, there's usually a reason behind bad behaviour.

Eventually, Grant capitulated and now joins him for a cuppa.

'When I worked in the supermarket I took regular fag breaks so I could get out and look at the sky.'

'Are you a smoker then, Trant?'

He laughs. 'Nah. Not ciggies, anyway.'

John nods slowly, a little confused. Maybe he smokes cigars.

'They make people work in these huge warehouses like battery hens,' Grant continues, warming to his theme. 'You can do an eight-hour shift and never see daylight, but if you smoke you can nip out into the fresh air and they turn a blind eye. And they say smoking is bad for you!'

John makes a face. He has a point. 'So you pretend you're a smoker?'

Grant inclines his head. 'You gotta stay one step ahead of them, boss.'

John studies Grant from across the table. That sudden grin is like a lightning strike. It ignites the world for a split second, and dies, leaving you all the better for it.

'Do you like fly cemeteries, Trant?'

'Oh, you mean those hard little cake things? Not so much. Hate the flies.'

'Sarah got me some a couple of weeks back. They reminded me a bit of the bird seed bread she buys. Too tough for my old teeth but the crows like them.'

'Did you eat them?'

'No, but I'll tell you what I did, Trant. I thought I'd better get rid of the evidence. Sarah doesn't miss a bloody trick. So I came out here, and the birds were on the shed roof as usual. Greedy little buggers. I was trying to juggle the walking stick and the cakes so I placed the plate on the patio table – right here – but as I was doing that I scraped back one of the chairs for a bit of elbow room. And then, on the other side of the wall, there was an answering noise . . .'

He pauses for effect. But Grant doesn't know about Mrs Chalmers.

He takes a deep breath. 'That was our sign – Mrs Chalmers and me. They took her away, and I haven't seen her since, but that was how we communicated – a scrape of the chair from me, a little cough from Mrs Chalmers, and that's how we knew we could have a little chat over the wall!'

Grant laughs loudly. 'Ingenious! Like a code!'

'Exactly!'

'Never heard of messaging, Mr M?'

Ignoring that, John rushes on. 'Maybe by some miracle Mrs Chalmers has returned! I thought maybe she'd got sick of the gaol and ordered herself a taxi. My heart was racing. So, very carefully, I nudged the seat again. Silence.'

Grant's face falls. 'So that's it? No Mrs Chalmers?'

John shakes his head. 'I was thinking I'm starting to hear things as well as see things. I haven't told you about those things yet. That's a story for another time. But then . . . I swear I heard a laugh. A little titter.'

'A titter?'

'Well, I called to her, "Mrs Chalmers!", and I climbed up on those old slabs.' He points to the base of the wall. 'I thought I might smell her perfume – lovely and floral, it was – but no. Just garden compost and diesel.'

'Diesel? Did Mrs Chalmers have a car?'

'No.' John shakes his head again sadly. 'It wasn't her. I can't see over the wall, anyway. Maybe there were kids playing around in there. House has been vacant for months. The interesting thing is, I left one of those fly cemeteries on the table but when I went out a bit later it was gone. Very strange.'

'Seagulls, man.' Grant contemplates the sky again. 'They're mutating. It's all the hormones in the burgers they scoff.'

'Would they take a fly cemetery?'

'They'd take a baby, evil buggers.' Grant starts to sing a winsome little ditty. Something about three little birds singing sweet songs. 'Know that one, John?'

John shakes his head. It's hardly Glenn Miller, but there's a nice lilt to it. Grant chuckles and continues with his melody. He claps. 'You've a great voice, Tranter. Don't know that one.'

Grant makes a big show of pressing his hands to his chest as if wounded. 'You don't know the songs of the Irie Man? Bob Marley? He the tap i' the tap, man! I can see I'm gonna have to educate you!'

John has no idea of what's just been said, but he chuckles along anyway, and tips his face to the sky. It seems a brighter shade of blue, but maybe it's just his eyes playing tricks again.

Sarah

This journal is burning a hole in my brain. I just can't find the time to visit the museum. I'm longing for some space, but work has been exceptionally busy this weekend. As soon as the temperature hits a balmy eighteen degrees, the air fills with the smell of hickory and meat juices. It's a full-time job just keeping the barbecue section replenished, and we've had a run on Prosecco. The ice-cream freezer is down to a few Cornetto's languishing in a crushed-ice drift at the bottom.

I still haven't found time to speak to the new cleaner properly. She is the perfect cleaner, a tiny little ghost – unobtrusive, efficient, leaving nothing behind but the scent of the just washed. Even the cable of the vacuum is left neatly coiled, and the other day she washed the bristles of the sweeping brushes and left them propped against the back wall like a row of soldiers with new buzz cuts.

I come face-to-face with the girl in the janitor's cupboard a few days later. I'd turned up on the pretext of grabbing some of the blue paper we use for spillages, but I actually wanted to get a look at the black eye, if indeed she has one and it's not just a figment of Peggy's overactive imagination.

I remind myself that I'm responsible for her, that I have a duty of care, but actually there's a parallel here that hasn't escaped me. A young girl, presumably without her family, in Scotland. My girl, motherless, in India. Okay, Mai has a husband, or at least some kind of male figure in her life, and

Hannah is probably relishing being family-free, but the whole situation smacks of a rather bizarre cultural exchange.

Mai regards me with a question in her eyes. She's so petite and frail close up. Her hair is scraped back and she's wearing a pale foundation. Whether it's concealing a recent assault, I can't tell. I try so hard not to stare at her, I end up getting a bit flustered.

'There was a spillage in Wines and Spirits.'

'You want?' She gestures towards the mops, neatly wrung out in a line and leaning against the wall. Even if I did want, I'm blocking her exit.

'No, no. I'll just . . .' I grab a roll of paper and screw up my courage. Why is it so easy to talk behind backs, and not to faces? 'Mai, is everything okay at home?'

She looks bewildered. 'Home?'

I take a breath. 'Domestically. In your family? Is everything all right?'

'My mother, she sick.'

Is her mother here? Or is she in Vietnam? I try again. 'Your husband?' She looks blank. 'The man in the black van? Black Van Man?'

She stiffens. Her expression shifts from cautious to closed in a heartbeat, but I can't be certain she understands what I'm saying. Just when I'm thinking I've lost her, that this conversation is going nowhere, she nods towards my collar bone.

'Pretty.'

My fingers move to the familiar smoothness of the hagstone. 'Yes, it's a . . . a charm.' Would she understand that? 'For luck.'

Not strictly true, but it raises the trace of a smile. Her face softens, and she nods. 'Luck.'

'Yes, luck. It . . .' I pick over my words. There's a message I want to get across. 'It wards off bad luck. Bad luck. Bad *people*.'

She understands. I know she does. She looks so miserable I act without thinking and pull off the necklace. 'Here. Put it on. It will keep you safe.'

She's enchanted by it, and her enchantment transforms her into something alive and vibrant. Wriggling the thong over her head, a dozen thank you's tumble out, leaving me glowing inside. I really do hope it keeps her safe, that it keeps evil from her door. But all day long my fingers stray to my naked throat.

Wear it every day, Mum. It will connect us through time and space!

I hope I haven't given too much away.

*

Peggy had seen me entering Mai's domain and didn't waste any time in grilling me about what I'd seen. I can only shrug.

'If she did have a black eye, it seems to have faded now. And anyway, she could have banged into something, for all we know.'

'Banged into a door. The age-old excuse,' Peggy scoffs.

She's right, of course. Why do we always take the blame on ourselves?

'If that was *my* husband, I'd give him a bloody good hiding,' she pronounces. 'My father once slapped my mother and she took the poker from the hearth and gave him a good whack with it. He never bloody did it again.'

'I don't think that's going to work here,' I object. 'If there's a welfare concern, I think we should contact the appropriate agencies.'

'I think we should take it into our own hands.'

'Oh no, Peggy.'

'We'll intercept him at the entrance.' There's a slightly fanatical look in her eye that worries me. 'Just as he's dropping her off.'

'When you say *intercept* . . . ?'

'Why doesn't he drop her off at the door like any decent man? I think it's fishy.'

I try to stall her. 'We have to observe proper protocols. Strictly speaking, it isn't our concern. I could flag up a welfare issue with the cleaning contractor.'

'Or we could loiter by the gate and get a gander at his ugly puss. If he thinks we're onto him, he'll maybe back off. She's such a tiny wee thing. I hate to think of her being smacked around.'

'I'm sure she isn't being . . .' I stop myself. How do I know what she isn't? I'd just listened to myself spouting a load of corporate tosh. Mai is a person, for goodness' sake. Not just a cleaner, a nameless woman. Someone else's problem. Images of Alie Gowdie perched on the penitent's stool float into my mind. Am I going to be one of those people who looks the other way while an innocent woman is being abused?

John

John checks the calendar. It's a Wednesday. He thought it was, but once you give up work and going to clubs and so on it's easy to lose track of the days. He used to go to the Rotary on Wednesday morning. It was a reason to get dressed up, dust off the tie and iron a shirt. Now Wednesday is Grant Day: 10.30 to 12.30. The red-inked boxes on the calendar produce a smile.

He'd had Sarah buy some more of those chocolate tea cakes, because that's what Grant likes with his cuppa, although sometimes his mum sends little sponge cakes. They're as light as a feather. They always have a cuppa now after Grant does the chores. It's a chance for a catch-up. So far he's learned that Grant lives in a flat in the town centre with his mum, that he wants to train as a nurse, but he'd left school at sixteen and doesn't have the right exam results, or perhaps any exam results.

'It's never too late,' John told him. 'I never sat any exams – left school at fourteen. There was a war on, the last couple of years of it, at any rate. I still got to be manager of a building society, though. Hard work and night classes and determination. That's what you need, son.'

Grant had said he'd think about it, but in the meantime he had to help his mother pay the rent on their flat.

There was a bit of a mess on the dining table again. It all started because he'd been viewing an old black-and-white film and couldn't remember the name of the actor. It was Richard something. This getting-old lark was a curse. He had an idea that the film might be featured in the TV guide Sarah insisted on buying. Not that he could read it, even with the magnifier. There was a big black hole where the words should be. Somehow he'd ended up with the contents of the magazine rack all over the table. There were things in there he hadn't seen in years: puzzle books, coach tour brochures, a dictionary and half a dozen flyers from his local takeaway. He'd never had a curry in his life, thank you very much, and he didn't intend to start now.

He'd even come across a page torn from a newspaper and folded into a stout square. He recognised the bold headline – Hannah had brought it in one day, years ago, and it had resulted in a bit of a set-to between her and her mother. He'd tried not to intervene, and he couldn't remember the details now. It was all past history. He would ask Grant to chuck all this stuff in the bin.

Right on cue, the doorbell chimes. Sarah wouldn't let Grant have a key. 'Not until we get to the bottom of these visions you're seeing. We need to know who's coming and going.' Not that she had any intention of getting to the bottom of it. He'd stopped mentioning it now, because she didn't understand. He saw the Figures, plain as day, in the hall, in his bedroom. They came in and sat on the sofa, but he kept it to himself.

When he threw open the door, there was Grant on the step singing a wee tune.

'Buffalo Soldier . . .' he sang.

'. . . in the heart of America!' John sang back. It was a thing they did now, plus something that Grant called a fist bump. The young people did it instead of a handshake.

'How goes it, man?' The lad wipes his trainers on the doormat.

'Well, you might need to sort out the table today, Trant. I was trying to remember the name of an actor. Richard something.'

'Oh yes.' Grant surveys the jumble spread across the table. 'Burton? Harris?'

'No.' John sighs. Maybe it will come to him later when he isn't thinking about it. 'It was an old film. Long before your time.'

'What was the title of the film?'

'I can't remember.'

'Okay.' They fall into a companionable silence as Grant sorts through the pile. 'The Ganges? You get a top curry in there. Ever been? No? I'll take you there one day.'

John chuckles. 'Sarah took me to a place where they don't serve any meat. They're not for me, all those fancy places. I like a nice steak pie . . . Now, I can't remember why I kept that. Something about a bowl.'

Grant had picked up the newspaper. He begins to read aloud: '"Archaeologists have unearthed a 2,000-year-old drinking vessel from the base of a broch in the far North East of Scotland. The team, led by site director Dr Janine Lawrence, who has been completing a six-week dig in an undisclosed area on the Nigg peninsula, says: 'The vessel is made of alder, and gives us a valuable insight into life in the first to mid-second century AD. It has been dated from its location in the vicinity of an Iron Age broch, but further radiocarbon dating will now be carried out. It's an unprecedented find in this location, and a real credit to my team.'"'

'Ah yes.' John nods. 'That's Hannah's stepmother, Janine. Dr Janine.'

Grant studies him over the top of the newspaper. 'So Sarah is divorced then?'

'A long time ago. Hannah was quite young. I don't know what happened, to be exact – whether Ian left her for this Janine. The party line was that he met her after they'd parted company, but it was quite soon after. Indecently soon, if you ask me, but Ian never let the grass grow under his feet. Always a bit of a rover, while Sarah was more of a home bird.'

Grant makes a face, like he's considering something. 'So this woman, Janine, sounds like a bit of a history expert?'

'Oh yes. A leading light in her field. Hannah is very proud of her, but don't tell that to her mother. Sarah has a real chip on her shoulder about it all.'

'Mmmm, I bet. Still, Sarah has been doing a lot of research of her own.'

'All that witchy stuff?' John chuckles. 'Prancing around town in a black dress won't get you in the papers, or maybe for the wrong reasons! I keep telling her, she should stick to the day job.'

Grant goes a bit quiet after that. He sorts out the rubbish and takes the stuff out to the bin. He's gone a while and when he comes back he asks him about the Figures. John had confided in him the week before, and the lad had taken it in his stride, as if it were an everyday occurrence. That made it so much easier to discuss.

'Any more trouble with the Figures, John?'

It's so good to be able to talk about it. They have a cup of tea and a teacake each, and John tells him about the three shapes that were sitting on the sofa last night.

'Right where you are. Three of them. I can't make out their faces, but it's not pretty.' He worries the silver foil wrapping from the teacake between his fingers. 'They're like gargoyles, medieval, from a different age. I told them to leave but they just sat there, all silent. I ended up leaving myself. I got up and went into the kitchen and there, to top it all, was a girl in the kitchen! A young one, drinking out of the tap, if you please.'

Grant smiles, but there's a stillness about him, a watchfulness, a bit like the Figures themselves. 'There must be a rational explanation, John. But no harm in keeping your door locked. The back door was open, just now, when I went to the bin. Still, it must be scary.'

'It is scary, Trant, when I'm here on my tod.' John suddenly slaps the arm of his chair. 'Todd! Richard Todd. *The Hasty Heart*. 1949. First film I ever saw with my Marjorie.'

Sarah

It's another week before I can get to grips with the Reverend Wilkie. Charlotte brings him to the table, so to speak, and settles him in the foam rest. I flex my fingers and adopt a Bond villain voice: 'We meet again, Mr Wilkie!'

Charlotte raises a brow. 'You're enjoying this far too much. Have you found anything interesting?'

I check my notes. 'Not yet, but I've learned how to preserve quinces and make a lemon syllabub. He's actually included Mistress Telfer's "receipts"!'

Charlotte glances over my shoulder. 'That's not going to get the academics in a tizzy, is it? Still, we're planning a historic food and beverage exhibition this autumn, so that might be useful.'

'Surely the Reverend Wilkie is worth more to culture than Paul Hollywood?' I let out a sigh. 'I need more time.'

Charlotte checks her watch. 'You've got two hours and then I'm letting loose the mob.' She smiles at my expression. 'The pre-schoolers from Lumsdain House. They're having an old Scots music session in here.'

'Great.' My shoulders slump. Two hours is like five minutes in the company of Wilkie's convoluted handwriting.

'How's your dad's carer working out, by the way?'

'Oh, the carer.' I give a bleak laugh which makes her smile. 'Remember the guy I sacked? Well, I didn't exactly sack him, he sort of . . . resigned.'

'What? The lad with the dreadlocks, always hanging round the Black Bull? He's the new carer?'

'Yup.'

Charlotte gives me a shaky-head, rather-you-than-me look as she turns to leave. 'Good luck with that. Two hours. I'll give you a five-minute warning.'

*

I did have words today with Master Donald who tells me that the girl Alisoune does torment him yet. Is the penitent stool not harsh enough punishment for her? I thought her marriage to Robert the Weaver might fettle her tongue but if anything she exercises it more.

I visited the hospital today to check on the well-being of the poor children.

Robert Webster has agreed to give houseroom and work to one of the boys, a young heathen of a tinker familie. He will make a fair go of the weaving, I am sure. He has a delicate hand. His face too is most pleasing, a putto, with skin fairer than most of his ilk, and so soft. Some by-blow, no doubt, got upon his mother by a lordling, such is the sinful nature of such folk.

I have christened him Abel, after he who made the first Sacrifice to God and was so cruelly slain by his brother Cain. It is my Duty to separate him from the Sinful Companie of his brothers, lest he be tainted with their Wickedness. I have informed Master Webster that I cannot spare the lad at the present time and he must wait until Michaelmas.

I have taken to meeting the boy in privat that he might hear the Lord's Word in his ear more loudly. When I left the boy's presence, here is the Gowdie woman waiting on the stair. She did accost me for being closeted with the boy and I on the Lord's Work. What was she doing lurking on the stairway? She went into the room and pulled the boy out. He was weeping, overcome with the power of the Lord.

She is a very dangerous woman.

Dangerous woman? My skin is prickling. I google 'putto' on my phone. *A representation of a naked child, especially a cherub or a cupid in Renaissance art.* I re-read the entry, struggling this time not with the letters, but the space between the lines. Words jump out at me: *skin, so soft, in private.* All my maternal instincts are shrieking. I want to reach out to that vulnerable child. I imagine Alie creeping up the stairs, knowing herself to be powerless yet willing to put herself on the line for this child. She must have had her suspicions. But perhaps my twenty-first-century hypervigilance means I'm reading too much into the text.

When I hear real children in the corridor outside, it's both a shock and a relief. With a sigh, I push the book away and sit up. All my muscles are protesting. I hadn't realised I'd been holding myself so tensely. Time travelling is hard work, especially when you come across things you don't want to see. I tilt my head to the left and to the right, rotate my shoulders, stretch out my knuckles.

The door swings open. Two under-fives wander in, hand in hand, like babes in the wood. Everything about them is innocent, from their big open eyes and mouths to their shiny hair, shiny wonder. One of them is clutching a forlorn-looking teddy.

'Matthew! Regan!' A teacher bustles in, closely followed by Charlotte, who's itching to rugby tackle the journal into safekeeping. The children are lined up two by two beyond the threshold. The teacher puts a finger to her lips. When she turns towards me I can see that her face is smooth, with an amused expression, framed by a mass of unruly waves kept in check by a bandana. She's wearing the sort of harem pants I caress enviously in little ethnic shops and her sweater is riding low on her shoulder, as if she's somehow pulled it all together at the last minute because she's been busy with more interesting things.

'Thanks for the five-minute warning,' I hiss at Charlotte, who hugs the book to her chest and gives a wry smile.

'I kind of got caught up with the little people.'

The children are swarming through the room, chattering, poking at things, smearing the glass in the cabinets. It's time to go.

'We're just waiting for the musicologist,' says Charlotte. 'He's researching local children's songs and rhymes, and we thought it would be good to bring them all together!'

Not for the first time, I'm relieved that Hannah is off my hands and I no longer have to listen to 'The Wheels On The Bus' forty times a day and hide her recorder. The teacher smiles serenely. She has at least four little bodies hanging off her jumper. No wonder it's so shapeless.

'Feel free to stay and listen,' she says, as if offering me a rare treat.

In the background, Charlotte's smile widens. 'Yes. Old kiddies' rhymes are a great source material.'

'Mmmm. I'll leave it for the kiddies.'

I'm not sorry to leave. I've heard enough of the Reverend for one day and a nice hot cappuccino is calling me. Stepping out into the fresh air, I feel disorientated, a bit like when you leave the cinema in the afternoon, not sure whether to expect day or night. It's never really brightened, and as I start the walk home the rain comes on, big heavy drops pinging off my hood. There's a smell of damp burning wood on the breeze, the taint of witch fires and old books; one disposing of the evidence, the other obfuscating the truth.

For some parts of the journey we had to walk through the night, and the men beat us with sticks to make us walk faster. When I couldn't walk any faster, Ma dragged me along, tried to carry me until she got too weak. Then we were loaded onto the back of a truck for the trip across the water. We nearly froze to death. When we reached the other side, the leader of the men started banging on the side of the truck until the driver came out and opened the door. We ran to a forest, and more men came to pick us up. There were lots of trees around and then lots of houses. Everywhere was full of people. Ma said we were in Britain.

They put us in a big stone house. It smelled of stale water and cold and there were no cooking smells, no spices, no heat. The air was dead and the children were quiet, like they were dead inside. No one smiled, and there were lots of people, so that was a lot of not smiling.

There were no cupboards in this house, no little boxes like the ones at Grandma's that had buttons and ribbons and little pieces of cloth to play with. I tucked myself in a corner and played with the one toy I was allowed to keep.

My mother said this would lead to better things.

I think she lied.

Sarah

I catch myself thinking about Grant Tranter. Despite my misgivings I'm impressed with how well he's working out. I now tend to avoid my dad's on Wednesdays, but on Thursdays he's noticeably chipper and brimming over with Grant-isms. Odd phrases have been creeping into his vocabulary and he knows far more about Bob Marley than is appropriate for a man of his age. Grant's mother has even taken to sending cakes. She bakes everything from scratch, apparently, and her butterfly cakes are to die for. It makes me feel quite miffed.

*

I'm surprised to get a call from Grant one Thursday morning. I'm busily checking the stock in the hot cabinet. Thankfully, the chicken-leg saga has played itself out, with no more complaints, but there seems to be a discrepancy with our takeaway pasties. I can't figure it out. I hold the phone to my ear as I re-count the pasties and sausage rolls.

'Sarah?'

My heart does a little skip. Nothing to do with Grant's voice but everything to do with my tendency to expect bad news. 'Yes? Everything okay?'

'It's all good, Sarah.' I detect a slight smile. 'Sorry to bother you, but I'm wondering if I can have a word with you about your dad? Nothing urgent, just something that's come up. Probably best not to talk about it on the phone.'

'Yes, fine, Grant.' I do a quick round-up of the local cafés. Better to meet him on my own turf. 'I'll be home after four. Just come up to my house.'

I give him directions and stick the phone back in my pocket. I never wanted him taking the job in the first place, but now I find myself hoping he isn't planning to leave.

Sarah

'Your father's got duppy,' Grant pronounces as he saunters past me.

'Do come in, Grant.' I close the door pointedly. He's wandering through the sitting room, checking out the pictures on my walls. He seems to fill the space with an energy that wasn't there before. He's dressed casually in board shorts and flip flops, and a hoodie in the Jamaican colours. I presume he has the afternoon off. 'Take a seat.'

He remains standing, peering at a photograph of Hannah. 'This your girl? She looks like you. Same serious expression. She's travelling, isn't she?'

I nod. When he asks me if I've visited her I don't reply, but my sense of frustration must have made itself visible, because he gives me a look that's edged with sympathy.

'Maybe you can take some time off now the cavalry's here?'

I flinch away from his grin. 'I can't afford it. And anyway, flying is . . . I'm afraid of flying.' Why did I admit to that? I swerve away from Grant's interest. 'So, Grant, what do you want to talk to me about? And what the hell is a . . . a . . .'

'Duppy. Plural. Your dad's seeing ghosts, man.'

I give a little laugh which, even to me, sounds uncertain. 'He *is* seeing things but there's a logical reason. He's probably got a vision problem.'

'Says who?'

'Says the doctor. I'm taking him to the optician to get things checked out. I'm pretty certain it's not ghosts.'

'You're sure, are you?'

Grant is gazing at me so intently I can almost feel my certainty wilting. There are unknowable things in his expression which make me hesitate.

'Yes, I'm sure.'

'Okay.' He gives a little nod, as if he's convinced of no such thing, and whirls away to finger the treasures displayed on the ledges of my three back windows. A collection of Keiller's marmalade stoneware jars, an old poison bottle dug up in the herb plot, a smiling Buddha. He picks up the heavy figure and weighs it in his hands. 'My mum's a Buddhist. She chants a lot. *Nam myo ho renge kyo*. Are you a Buddhist?'

I move to wrest the figure back, but he's already picking up something else. He's like a toddler driven to explore. 'No, I'm not a Buddhist. I don't believe in anything. Please, put that down. It's really old.'

'Not even ghosts, apparently. What is it?' He aims the sharp point of a weaving shuttle at me, one eye narrowed like a sniper. I take that off him too.

'It was used in the weaving process. This upstairs room housed a couple of hand looms. They were huge, the size of two double beds.' I raise my eyes to the ceiling and so does he. 'Imagine them strung with coloured yarn – two sets of warp thread with a gap in between, like a tent, and that shuttle loaded with a different colour being passed between them. Sometimes, if the looms were very broad, a child was used to pass the shuttle from one side to the other, crawling under the clacking machinery, breathing in dust . . .'

I pause for breath. I'm storytelling again. I can't help myself. Slightly embarrassed, I rearrange the Buddha and the wooden shuttle on the window ledge. A vestige of grey thread clings to the innards of the shuttle, a remnant of a more industrious life.

Grant is scanning the room, trying to work it out. 'So why upstairs? Wouldn't it be easier to do it downstairs?'

I can't resist a smile. He has an enquiring mind and I'm drawn to it. 'Some weavers' houses were like that. It just depends on the light source. The occupants lived in the darkest part. Up here, not only do you have light' – I gesture towards the windows – 'you can just lug your bales of cloth to the top of the stairs and chuck them onto a cart! Labour-saving. You know this house was once owned by the Kilgour witch Alie Gowdie? Or rather her husband. I like to think it was specially built for their union. A state-of-the-art weaver's house, designed for a lifetime of industry, until—'

'Until they tied her to a stake and set her on fire. That's not in anyone's life plan, is it?'

'No, it's not.'

He wanders over to my desk, but I'm more relaxed now. I didn't think he'd know anything about the witches, or even care. Somehow we've found a groove. He feels less like an exotic species – a Venus flytrap perhaps, or something that only blooms at night – and more like me. The dodgy floor-board does not escape him. He tests it once, twice, head cocked, listening for the squeak.

'Mrs Sutherland! Look at that desk.' All my notes are spread haphazardly across the surface, and there are piles of books, empty mugs and crisp packets, scraps of paper bearing my scribbles. My inner world laid bare. 'And I thought you were a neat freak.'

I play along. 'Only at work, Mr Tranter. When the staff stress me out.'

He shakes his head. 'You need to get out of that place, Sarah. It's not good for you.'

I'm about to object, to launch into a spiel about responsibility and bills, but he's laughing again, holding up a book and wagging it at me. '*Scottish Witch Trials in the Seventeenth Century*? How can you believe in witches but not ghosts?'

I take the book from him. Our fingers touch in a way that discombobulates me, but I recover myself with what I hope is a stern frown. 'That book is *fact*, unfortunately.'

He picks up a second book and flicks through the pages, and the floorboard creaks a little more. I wish he'd stop. I know the vulnerable places in this house, the vulnerable places in me. I don't need anyone probing them.

'But what about the witchcraft?' he persists.

'Do I believe actual witches existed?' No one has ever asked me that before. My shoulders relax. 'No. I think they were ordinary women accused of extraordinary things. I don't believe they used magic or summoned up the Devil or saw him dancing in the market square. That's all figments of the male imagination, and the confessions were extracted under torture. You'd say anything, wouldn't you? The witch trials were just a way of controlling people, of turning them away from the old ways and back to the Kirk. This journal I'm reading, the Reverend Wilkie. He thinks he *is* God. He thinks . . .' I take a breath, dial it down. 'Sorry, I get too fired up about the past.'

Grant looks thoughtful. 'Ol' Higue is a witch who sheds her skin and flies around at night as an owl. If you find her skin you have to put salt on it so she can't put it back on.'

'Jamaican folklore?' Grant's words take me back to my father's strange visions and the reason he is here. 'I'm fairly sure my father doesn't have shapeshifting witches or the spirits of the dead living in his house.'

He makes a face. I can tell he isn't convinced. 'So . . . if your downstairs is upstairs, your upstairs must be downstairs?'

'Yes, that's right.'

'So where's the john?'

'Oh. So you go down the stairs over there' – I point past the stove to the spiral staircase in the far corner – 'and you just—'

'Follow the scent of potpourri . . . What?' He laughs at my expression. 'Come on. I bet you have potpourri in your bathroom and one of those dolls with the frilly knickers that hide the bog roll.'

I can't help laughing. And the fact that I'm laughing surprises me. Something deep within me rolls over and stirs. 'You think you know me, Grant Tranter, but you don't know me at all!'

It's strange watching someone disappear down that funny little staircase. I watch him grow smaller until only his head is visible. He winks at me. I think he says he wants to get to know me better, but it's just a murmur and I may have misheard. My world shrinks suddenly, until there is only the bounce of his dreadlocks and then he's gone. The room feels cold, and I'm standing there, alone, rubbing the tops of my arms. What have I done? I should never have invited him in.

I approach my desk again, slip on my reading specs, and look through the pages I'd been working on earlier. I don't particularly like people going through my stuff, or learning how I am when I'm off guard. Recalling his taunt about my untidy desk, I try to see myself as he must see me: a buttoned-up control freak in the office, and at home – what? Does he really want to get to know me better? More to the point, what will he find? I'm not sure I have it in me to throw up any surprises. What you see is what you get best describes me, but that's not strictly true. My best bits are kept away from the public.

That's the big question, isn't it? Do I want to surprise Grant Tranter? And how in the hell have I got to this place, given that a few weeks ago he was my arch enemy? It's the oldest cliché in the book, Sarah Sutherland. Your head has been turned by a handsome young man. You really should know better at your age.

As much as I try to talk myself out of this silly notion that I might be attracted to Grant – and that, incredibly, he might be interested in me – there's a splinter under my skin. A wicked little voice goads me. *Stranger things have happened . . . What if . . . ?*

By the time Grant reappears, I'm a jittery mess. I pretend to study the photocopies, but remember to slide off my glasses as he approaches. I don't want to look like a school marm. I notice he's dangling a chilled bottle of wine by the neck. He produces two long-stemmed glasses with a flourish, as if he's offering me red roses.

'I do apologise,' he says, totally unabashed. 'I don't usually go through people's stuff but I found the kitchen and then I found the fridge . . .'

'You've got such a cheek, Mr Tranter.' I pull a mock scowl. 'What do you think we're going to do with this?'

He sets the wine glasses down on my coffee table. 'Drinking alone is best avoided.'

'Who says I was going to be drinking that alone?' I counter. 'Or drinking at all, for that matter?'

Despite my objections, the fight is seeping out of me. I'm already anticipating the sharpness of the alcohol, the pleasure of having a conversation that doesn't involve some measure of anxiety. I perch on the edge of the couch and nervously flap the photocopies against my thigh.

'So what's with all the paperwork?'

I glance at the pages, selecting my words carefully. They're taking up such a huge place in my mind, it's hard to keep a sense of proportion, to find a starting place that might appeal to a layman. I suppose that's what happens when you spend too much time alone. Reconnecting is tricky.

'A couple of weeks ago someone handed in a box of old books to the museum. Among them were the journals of William Wilkie, the minister who was involved in the witch hunts.'

'Seriously?'

I nod. 'So, the last one, dated 1648, *should* give us a first-hand report of the witch trials. I'm trying to make sense of it, but his handwriting isn't the easiest. Like a hen scratching in the dust, as Dad would say. Charlotte at the museum is obviously very protective of the actual book, hence the photocopies.'

'You think it might provide some new info for your witchy walk?'

'Maybe.' I'm not sure how much of my inner workings I'm prepared to share with Grant Tranter, but I take a slug of wine and rush on. 'It's more than that to me. These are real people.' Warming to my theme, I lean towards him. 'There's a little boy, Abel. He was an inmate in the hospital – now Lumsdain House. Wilkie was supposedly a charitable benefactor, but . . . okay, maybe it's me, but how does this sound to you?'

I've managed to mess up the papers with my nervous fidgeting so I have to shuffle them. I drop one, and Grant picks it up and then I have to stick on my glasses, but eventually I give a little *ahem* and start to read.

'"Young Abel came to us some three summers ago. The day after the Martinmas Feeing Fair, a yellow-headed beggar woman was found sleeping in a ditch within the town boundary. The heathen was garbed like a man, in breeks and shirt. On inquiry, she had concealed beneath the shirt a boy-child, piteous small and starved."' I glance up to find Grant's eyes on me, curious. 'The Feeing Fair was when the farmers hired new servants. Maybe this girl couldn't get work, with the little one in tow. Maybe she dressed like that to ward off the men. It makes me feel sick, that this was happening here in Kilgour just a few hundred years ago.'

Grant makes a tell-me-about-it face. 'Still happening the world over.'

'There's more. Listen to this: "When the news was brought to me I reminded the Baillie and Session Clerk of their duty to God and the State. The art of begging is learnt as a babe-in-arms. By the law, no vagrant can be left with child underwing. I hear that it did take two men to prise the boy from his mother's grasp. She held him so fast she left red marks on his arm that stayed all week. He was taken to the hospital and will be brought to the Path of Righteousness."'

Grant swears and scratches his head, as if it might dislodge the image. 'Oh, man. He sounds like the worst kind of funda-mentalist nut. Basically, he abducts the kids of the poor and vulnerable and keeps them in Lumsdain House?'

I stare at the photocopies as if mitigating circumstances might present themselves. In the interests of historical accuracy, I feel compelled to smooth the waters I've whipped up. 'We've got to take an unbiased view, though, and consider the context. Scotland was in the grip of the Covenanters. They really believed they had God on their side and it was their mission to save people from sin. Wilkie was just doing his duty.'

'You're literally playing Devil's Advocate!' Grant sits back and views me with suspicion. 'The boy had marks on his arm because his mum was shit scared of losing him. It's inhuman.'

I drop my gaze miserably. 'This is my dilemma. I'm not an historian. I get tied up with the human stories, and I know we can't judge the actions of the past by what's acceptable today, but . . .'

'Ha! Tell that to all the abuse victims suing the Catholic Church!' Grant scoots to the edge of the couch and grabs the wine bottle, tops up our glasses with such force that wine splashes on the wooden surface. I hope it won't stain but I resist the urge to mop it up. 'Please don't tell me he keeps mentioning the wee lad in his diary?'

I look away, nibble on the leg of my glasses. This is my fear, that Wilkie uses too much ink in describing that little boy. Surely in the seventeenth century a tinker's brat, even a rescued one, would be expendable, invisible. And yet the child is cropping up more and more frequently in the text. The implication sits uneasily between us.

'Shit.' Grant struggles to remove his hoodie, as if the injustice of the past is making him hot and bothered. His T-shirt rides up as he drags the top over his head, revealing taut muscles and a smattering of hair. Primly, I look away. My thoughts return to the present with a bang. What the hell am I doing drinking wine with this guy? I'm not even sure what time it is, although beyond the high windows the sky looks ominously dark. The threat of rain, or thunder. I can almost feel energy humming from Grant.

I eye him up discreetly in my peripheral vision. He has strong capable hands and a whole shopful of beaded bracelets on one wrist. I'm starting to forget why I have a grudge against him, and remind myself that he has a serious attitude problem and a reputation as a troublemaker. According to Peggy, he was excluded from school for stealing the headmaster's car and abandoning it in the Cairngorms. He apparently got a train home and a huge search was mounted for the teacher, who was actually safely ensconced at a conference in Blackpool.

So Grant. A little giggle escapes me, and he narrows his eyes.

'What?'

'Nothing.'

I think of his upbringing, his background, so different from my own. His heritage is present in his face; in the dreadlocks framing high cheekbones, the wide good-humoured mouth. His skin is on the golden side of sallow. I suspect his roots may not be as romantic as he thinks, but he's young, idealistic. To avoid his amusement, I focus on his outstretched legs. The flip flops have seen better days. There's mud between his toes and his nails need clipping.

He pitches forward again. 'I have an idea. Let's go over there now!'

I blink at him. 'Where?'

'Lumsdain House! Bet it could tell some tales. You could add it to your witch walk, which, by the way, I'm coming along to next Friday.'

'You're what?' I sit to attention so quickly my drink slops over the rim of my glass. 'You can't. You live here! It's really for tourists.'

'So I'm barred? That's discrimination right there.'

'No, it isn't!' I chuckle at his injured expression. 'But you know all the stories, don't you? You'd be bored. Or you'd take the piss.'

His mouth drops open. 'Me? Take the piss? I'm hurt, Mrs Sutherland. And as for bored, your passion shines through.'

'Does it?' I level my gaze at him. I didn't think passion still existed in my emotional vocabulary, but stranger things and all that.

'Come on.' He takes the glass from me and seizes my hand. The sudden contact, the unaccustomed warmth of his skin, make me want to pull away, but he doesn't give me the option. He pulls me to my feet. 'Lumsdain House. Right now.'

Sarah

'We're just going to . . . what . . . break in? Grant, it's really dark.' I still have absolutely no idea what time it is.

He fishes a couple of keys from the front pocket of his shorts as I avert my eyes from his crotch. He dangles the homemade crocheted key fob. 'My mum runs the nursery. I have to hold on to her spare key because she's really scatty. Keeps locking herself out.'

I'm not sure that bodes well for the children. At least Grant has dropped my hand and I'm able to think straight, or as straight as two large glasses of wine on an empty stomach will allow. I scrabble around for further excuses. 'Isn't it alarmed?'

Grant laughs as if this is the funniest thing he's heard in a while. 'Have you seen the place? Seriously, who'd want to go in there after dark?'

'Us, apparently.' I rub the back of my neck. The top of my spine is tight with tension, but there's something else too. A tingle deep in my belly. Excitement. It's been missing for a hell of a long time. Welcome back, old friend.

*

I turn the lights off, leave the heating on and lock up. My iPhone is nestling in my back pocket. When I check the screen, I see a missed call from Hannah. 'Shit.'

'Who is it?' Grant appears beside my shoulder. He smells of hair products and incense.

'Hannah. She called a few hours ago, but my phone was on silent. I should phone her back.'

'Later. Come on.' He takes the phone from me and slips it back into my hip pocket. The intimacy stops me in my tracks. I can't do this. I need to call my daughter, but when I do the maths it's the wee small hours in India. Grant is already ahead of me on the road, humming a little reggae tune that's vaguely familiar. The street lamp turns his hair to grey. He is a ghost of the road. Something fleeting to be captured if possible. I jog to catch up with him. He grasps my hand as if we're mates of long standing, and tucks it into the crook of his arm. I hope no one sees us, and then I kind of hope someone does. I feel like I've rejoined the human race.

*

There are no lights blazing at Lumsdain House. Of all the places to run a nursery, I'm sure this isn't the best choice. In the darkness, the childish cut-outs and potato prints sellotaped to the windows look oddly flat and lifeless. Despite a rather grand stone portico, the main entrance door is a modern eight-panelled affair in deep gloss burgundy. It looks a bit flimsy compared to the solid stone architecture of the building. There's evidence of a more robust past: an iron boot scraper on the step, a disused Victorian bell-push. I'm surprised to see the brass nameplate from Dad's old building society still affixed to the wall on the left-hand side.

It takes Grant all of two seconds to unlock the door. I bet breaching its defences wasn't quite that simple back in Wilkie's day. It was probably even harder to get out.

Motherless, dependent on charity and the goodwill of the parish for your next crust of bread. I can almost hear an older, heavier, darker door clanging shut.

So many incarnations, so many lives played out within these walls.

We step into what appears to be a high-ceilinged vestibule. The chilly air smells institutional – soup and sour carpets. The soft whump of the door closing behind us sets up a far-reaching echo. I imagine crows fluttering from the battlements, if there are any battlements. There's a spectral green glow from the emergency exit signs but Grant fumbles for a switch and floods the place with light. I immediately go into a panic. Someone will see us and call the police, but he isn't listening.

The interior certainly offers clues to a grander past: high ceilings, stucco, a mahogany banister spiralling upwards. I try to remember Dad's old stories about the place. Did the bank occupy the ground floor with meeting rooms above? Before that, it had been home to a generation or two of textile barons, and before that, the Victorian pauper children from the city workhouses. Slave labour for the textile mills.

'My dad says his colleagues thought the place was haunted,' I whisper. Shivering there in the cold hall, it's easy to imagine that some of that pitiful energy might remain in the walls. We both stay silent for a beat, as if we're listening for something.

Three doors face us, their frosted glass windows strangely enigmatic. It occurs to me that I don't want to open them, to disturb whatever might lie behind them, but Grant is already moving, confident and curious. We peer into what must be one of the nursery rooms. Neat little tables and chairs in primary colours; trendy plastic trugs brimming with cuddly toys and building blocks. The miniature book cases remind me of Hannah. There'd been a rocking horse in her nursery class, one of those gorgeous handcrafted ones, dapple grey with a lush mane and a missing tail.

I slip a book from the nearest shelf. '*Haki the Shetland Pony*! Hannah loved this.' Flicking through the pages, it's like meeting up with an old friend. Grant smiles politely, but I suppose in your twenties you're not in the market for nostalgia. He isn't much older than Hannah. The thought is so disquieting I have to move away from it. I put the tattered volume back, suddenly feeling like an intruder.

'I'm really worried someone will see the light on,' I repeat. 'It's not going to look good, someone in my position, being here after hours, with—'

'Someone like me?'

'That's not what I meant.'

Grant's face has grown sharp and defensive. 'I didn't force you to come. Go back, if you want.'

Given the choice, I realise I don't want to. I don't want to turn the clock back. I don't say that. I remain silent, but I think Grant knows.

I sense him relaxing. 'Don't be such a wuss. No one cares. Come on. Let's go upstairs!'

*

The stairs creak. Would you expect anything else? Cold darkness, creaking stairs. All the elements for a gripping story, but I can't quite get a fix on this one. The telling of it has been whisked from my hands by the strange man ahead of me. He's all in shadow and I fix my eyes on the pale flash of his heels. The staircase turns and doubles back on itself beneath a huge stained glass window. During daylight hours it must be impressive. I pause for a second, try to make out the colours and the design, but it's grey and opaque, with a secret glimmer. There's a suggestion of faces, surrounded by darkness, like in one of those paintings of Hell. My stomach knots. I race up the last few steps, anxious to catch up with Grant on the next level.

When I try to speak, I sound winded, and my words come out a bit more panicky than I'd like. 'Do you think there's anything left? Of the original building, Wilkie's Hospital?'

'Upstairs. Up where we're going it hasn't been so mucked around. I reckon the timbers and stuff will be original, but you'd know more about that than me. I bunked off history lessons.'

He grins, and I do too. My unease slides away. Maybe I can pretend this is normal behaviour, breaking into a council building in the dead of night with a man young enough to be my son. The flare of the torch on his phone distracts me.

'Look at those bastards!'

The walls are festooned with mounted heads: stags, antelope. Something that looks like a bison. A forest of antlers and glinting glassy eyes. Add to that the portraits of long-dead councillors and aldermen and you have a lot of gazes following you.

'Oh God. This is too creepy. And cold. Look, I can see my breath. If I see breath coming out of one of those bloody things, I'm out of here.'

Grant sniggers and steps over to one of the dark mahogany doors that line the landing. There are a lot of them – I do a quick count and stop at six – but this one is set into a little alcove.

'I think these used to be the council chambers,' he says.

'Until the cutbacks. But here' – he whips the key fob from his pocket – 'is the portal to another world . . .'

He indicates a second, narrower archway in the alcove, off to the side – you'd only notice it close up – but this one has an iron grille, like one of the cells in a Wild West gaol. Grant makes short work of the padlock and we're in. A narrow stone staircase leads upwards, and a stone-cold breath of air rushes down to meet us. *I don't like this*. I don't say it; I'm trying to be brave, but I stick as close to Grant as I can get without actually touching him.

Maybe there are battlements after all. The only way is up.

'See what I mean? I reckon this leads to a much older part of the building. I've been up here once or twice with my mum, and it's seriously creepy!' His voice has turned into an echo somewhere above me. The slap of his flip flops echoes the clump of my boots as we spiral up, up. We pass an arched window, like something out of a storybook, before we find ourselves on another landing. The air is cool, damp, and the floor creaks as if we're suspended. I feel very high up. All the doors on this corridor are closed too. I think we should leave them that way; Grant has other ideas. He opens one. It creaks, naturally, and we peer into darkness until he locates a light switch. The room is big, square and unremarkable – empty apart from some boxes, a few cobwebby chairs, ladders and empty paint pots. I feel strangely relieved.

'They use this for storage, but Mum reckons these may have been the dormitories for the workhouse kids. Boys and girls, separate.'

I make a face, wander around, scanning the walls. I remember Dad's comments about the kids drawing on the walls, but there's nothing to see here. Had he got that wrong, or is there something in one of the other rooms? Perhaps he's misremembering. It was all a long time ago. I poke around in a cardboard box – I can't help myself – but there's nothing more interesting than some folded dust sheets scattered with mouse droppings. I withdraw my hand as if I've been stung.

'There's more. Better than this.'

We close the door softly and I hurry after Grant as he strides along the gloomy corridor. I'm not convinced that 'better' is the right word. It's interesting, *intriguing*. We're peeling back the layers, stripping the place to its bare bones, but I'm no longer sure I want to gaze upon the bare bones of Wilkie's world. The journal is one thing, but this feels a bit . . . ghoulish. A chill creeps over my shoulders. There's another door at the far end of the corridor. Grant opens it and I nearly collide with him in my haste not to be left alone.

Laughing, he steadies me and feels around for another switch. He's holding my hand. I don't object.

'This feels older, doesn't it?'

A single low-watt bulb casts yellow light on unrendered stone walls, dusty floorboards and a small fireplace. The bulb is suspended on a length of old cable, and as we glance around, it begins to sway with a circular motion.

Grant is watching my face. 'If you don't believe in ghosts, now would be a good time to start.'

'Stop it.' I snatch my hand away. 'It's just the draught.'

We look up, past the light fitting. There is no plaster ceiling, just bare rafters. The black yawn of the roof space is scary. I try to picture the place from a child's perspective, see it as Abel might have done, or any of the other beggar children: all those pockets of dark that you might fall into; nowhere to run, nowhere to hide; footsteps on the stairs, the key in the lock. Little ones crying in the night, and no one to hear. Did they even leave them a candle?

'It feels ... I don't know ... like it's waiting for something.'

I'm not sure I intended to say that out loud. Sitting on the sofa with a wine feels like a long time ago. We've most definitely sobered up.

'I know what you mean,' Grant says quietly. 'Look. This is why I brought you up here.' He guides me over to one of the solid oak uprights that support the roof beams, focuses his phone torch on the surface so I can see better. The wood glows, rough-hewn and suddenly alive in the artificial light.

'The kids, they scratched shapes and things on the timber. Mum once told me it's because there's no window in here. They drew the things they couldn't see.'

'That's what Dad said! He seemed to think it was the workhouse children, but this is earlier. Definitely earlier.'

He points out the marks, each little pictogram carefully carved – no *dug* – into the blackened grain with a crude nail or knife. They form a haphazard row, a daisy chain, about three feet up from the floor. Child height.

'See?' Grant plies the light beam across the surface. 'That's like a sun, and this – a crescent moon? Stars. Lots of stars. All the things they must have imagined were outside.'

I peer closer. Slipping the phone from Grant's fingers, I move the light across the pitted surface until I can see the slant and slice of the marks. Grim, determined. Urgent. Hard-edged, like runes. What are they saying? What is it I'm not seeing?

And then it clicks. A memory unreels. A random internet search, an old reference book in the library – I've seen these shapes before. My breathing slows down and my heart starts to gallop. Excitement is tinged with a prickling sense of dread.

'They're not stars.'

'What? What are they then?'

I straighten up and return the phone, as if I've seen enough. The creeping feeling has taken over my gut. 'I've seen these before. They're apotropaic marks.'

'Apo-what?'

'It means to ward off. They're symbols – patterns scratched into the fabric of a building with the intention of keeping witches out. They're like talismans, I suppose. To ward off evil. You know, like an amulet you'd wear around your neck.'

I think of my little hagstone, the amulet I gave away. Grant traces a finger over a star which isn't a star, and I place my finger next to his.

'Look. That's a series of double Vs. They invoke the Virgin Mary for protection, and these circular designs – not suns and moons, but overlapping circles – hexofoils. The idea is that a malevolent spirit would be confused by the never-ending lines and become trapped in the design.'

'Like flypaper?'

'Kind of like flypaper.'

The smile we share lifts the chill, just a fraction. 'It was a common practice. Not many studies have been done on domestic settings, but from what I know, they can often be found in the places where witches could enter, like window-sills' – our eyes stray to the blank wall where there should have been a window – 'or the fireplace. Witches were thought to come down the chimney.'

We cross to the grate, which is filled with a tangle of fallen nesting material and ancient soot. Grant plays the light across the lintel and the modest hearthstone. Nothing to see here but the chips and gouges of long-term use.

I glance at the exit. 'Or the door. Witches can come in through an unprotected door.'

Immediately Grant crosses to where we came in. I deliberately lag behind, afraid of what we might see, dreading the implication. His words don't surprise me.

'They're here too. The same symbols on the door frame, about' – he measures with the flat of his hand – 'waist height.'

I come up behind him. 'Child height.'

'They were trying to stop the witch coming in from this direction. Imagine, little kids being so terrified.'

There's a bleakness in his expression as he turns to look at me. A ghastly realisation settles all around us, and we don't speak for several minutes until I step forward to inspect this new batch of marks.

'But who was the witch? Who were they most afraid of? Who were they expecting to come through this door?'

The double Vs march before my eyes. Frontline protection – Virgin of Virgins. VV VV VV.

Or were they Ws?

I'm good at hiding, at making myself small. It's easier to hide when you're all curled up. You can fit under things, behind things. Stay invisible. The world is less scary when you look at it through the gaps.

That first day, I didn't know where they'd taken my ma. I hid under a table with a cloth that trailed to the floor. The cloth stopped me seeing most of what was going on, so I can only remember a triangle of that day. I can remember the hard ground and the way it made my bones ache. I remember being hungry.

I could see bits of people – legs and feet – and I tried to guess what they looked like. The ladies' legs were brown and bare. The men wore boots. It must have been wet outside, because the men left footprints on the floor so huge I could fit both my hands inside the shape. They spoke words I didn't know.

All that day I tried so hard to hear my ma's voice my ears hurt. I was hungry and thirsty, but I didn't dare come out into the light. I stayed under the table. I thought it was safer under there.

Sarah

The unexpected high of finding the hidden treasure of Lumsdain House is followed by a week of lows. Dad succumbs to a cold and keeps me busy making hot drinks and fussing over him in the evenings, while at work we have a freezer malfunction. The wastage figures are through the roof and I have to suffer a visit from the area manager, an ex-soldier who thinks he's still in the military. I tell Dad about it and do an impression of Captain Mainwaring, which makes him cough with laughter.

I barely have time to think about Alie Gowdie, or Grant Tranter, for that matter, although maybe I ought to spare him a thought. Discovering those crude symbols of protection had filled me with conflicting emotions. True, it was an exciting historical find (in your face, Dr Janine, with your Iron Age pot) but still, it made me sad. Too real, too raw. Grant was more logical. There's no way of knowing for definite that this was the work of seventeenth-century children, he'd pointed out after we'd left, or whether kids had ever been housed there. It was all supposition.

'And gut feelings. Don't dismiss intuition, Grant,' I'd said airily.

'Whatever. It was all a long time ago.'

He'd yawned, and that had pissed me off. It was like he'd been up for a jolly jape and now he was dismissing it all.

'That's not the point,' I'd argued. 'It's like the Suffragettes, or the soldiers who died in the war. Lest we forget, and all that. We owe it to them to remember what happened.'

Grant shook his head a little, as if he wasn't convinced. 'This is different, though. What good does it do to dwell on those little kids, locked up and abused, when we can't do anything to help? There's enough stuff going on in this century without a guilt trip over what happened three hundred years ago.'

'It's not a matter of guilt, it's a question of justice. We can get to the truth!'

'And the truth is?'

'The truth is that the witch wasn't Alie Gowdie! The witch was the Reverend Wilkie. *That's* who they were trying to stop. *That's* who they were so afraid of. Pure evil.'

'You think the mad minister went around burning innocent women to take the heat off him?'

It's a big departure from the story we'd come to know in Kilgour. I know it is, and I don't know how I can prove it, but I know I have to try.

*

My amateur status in the history stakes takes a bit of a kicking from Charlotte of all people. Maybe she was having a bad day. With a Thursday morning off and nothing planned, I head to the museum intent on studying Wilkie's journal in peace and quiet. Instead, Charlotte thrusts a pile of photo-copies at me and offers a hasty apology.

'We've got the musicologist in again. He's doing some great work with the nursery classes. He's planning on releasing a podcast of them singing.'

'So I can't get a slot in the research room?'

Charlotte frowns. 'Sorry, Sarah. Not today. That's why I copied a few more pages for you. And I meant to tell you, I've got to hand the journals over to the archivist next week.'

'Oh.' The imminent loss pricks me sharply.

'I did give you the first look at it,' she reminds me. 'You must have enough information by now to ramp up the tour.'

Her throwaway comment leaves me feeling a bit dismissed. Discounted, as if my interest is not to be taken too seriously. An idle fancy, not serious study. I'm not an academic, an historian, a researcher. My finds will never set a conference alight or alter the course of history.

I leave, clutching my photocopies, feeling sidelined and irritated. Bloody musicology. How much social history can they teach three-year-olds?

I'm not sure how it happens, but at some point after the age of forty, cake becomes a panacea for every ill. I emerge from the library into strong sunlight. I should go for a walk, clear my head and shake off the blues, but I know I'd just end up mulling over everything I think I've figured out: a minister with an unhealthy interest in small boys, and a girl who's fallen foul of some conniving men. All that stuff about her seeing the Little People and dancing with the Devil. Not so entertaining when you really get to the nitty-gritty. I have an irrational urge to take a pair of scissors to my lacy black dress and burn it beneath the mercat cross as a sort of protest. Maybe Charlotte's right. Maybe this is best left to the professionals, with their proven methodologies. I can see it now – the burgh archaeologist commissioning a study into the witch marks, and someone like Dr Janine Lawrence doing a piece to camera on the evening news.

I find myself staring in the window of the Pantry. It's as good a place as any to go and lick my wounds. The café is warm and comforting, everything nicely muted: a babble of conversation, the soft hiss of the coffee machine. One of the girls behind the counter gives me a smile cheery enough to guarantee a good sale and a decent tip. Yes, I'll have today's special coffee beans and an almond croissant on the side, thank you.

Selecting a table for two in the window, I flatten out Charlotte's pages, feel around in my bag for my notebook. But Alie and her world seem very far away today. I have to face it. In the great ocean of Things That Matter, she's hardly a ripple. I gaze out of the window, nibbling the end of my pencil.

From here I can see across the square towards the museum and Butter Wynd. Someone is crossing the square, negotiating the road in front of the café. I'd know that jaunty gait anywhere. My stomach does a little flip, in a way it hasn't for a very long time. Bobbing dreads, the purple lanyard and the black top with its slogan, 'Resist the System'. No jacket. It's not that warm, he'll catch his death.

I'd given Grant my mobile number, for Dad-related business. Apart from his concern over the hallucinations, he hasn't contacted me, but that hasn't stopped me toying with the idea of sending him a message after our Lumsdain House escapade. My rational brain warns me that would be a bad move. Our boundaries are already inexplicably starting to blur without that sort of help.

The trouble is, I can't stop thinking about the breathy excitement of that night, the spontaneity and the touch of his hand. Maybe I'm just lonely. What do the psychologists call it? Skin hunger. Maybe it's not Grant I want to be intimate with but simply another human being, one I'm not responsible for. Someone young and carefree who can see the young and carefree someone I used to be. Is that too much to ask?

Oh God. He's looking over. Be cool. Let him go past. Don't stir things up . . . I press close to the window and wave like a maniac until I attract his attention. He's wearing earphones which he slides from his ears. Flashing me a broad grin, he strides into the café and slides into the seat opposite. Oh no.

'I was just thinking about you,' he says.

'Ditto, but probably not in a good way.'

'That's nice.' He pretends to look offended, making me smile. 'I've just popped in to see your dad, actually.'

'What? It's not a Grant day. How's he doing?'

'Still seeing duppy, but otherwise A1, in his own words. You know it really bugs him, seeing these things. Are you going to take him to the optician?'

'I am! I'll make an appointment.' I'd meant to do it last week, and my guilt and irritation must have shown in my face.

Grant surveys me curiously. 'I'll grab a drink. Do you want another?' He nods towards my mug, and I shake my head. He saunters over to the counter, indulges in some banter with the smiley girl. They must be around the same age. Her flirtatiousness makes my heart sink. When Grant returns to the table with something fizzy in a can, I am unreasonably cranky.

'Don't you drink tea, or coffee? That can has got about ten teaspoons of sugar in it.'

He laughs. 'What are you, my mother?'

Something passes between us. I say no with such vehemence he looks at me for a second longer than he should. And then the moment passes and he's talking about going for a beer.

'Aren't you working?'

'Half day on a Thursday,' he says. 'What about you? Want to come for a drink?'

'I'm working late. Keeping an eye on the twilight team, although I suspect they're finding it all very boring since you left.'

'Ah, the glory days of forklift scooter.' Grant shakes his head in mock sadness, toying with the unopened can.

'Maybe another time, though . . . for a drink,' I hear myself saying.

He looks up sharply, eyes dark, glittery and alert. There's no hiding place. I'm lost in the full beam of his interest. Slowly he lifts the can in a toast. 'I'll hold you to that, Mrs Sutherland.'

Suddenly he's on his feet, sweeping his energy away like a tablecloth. 'I'm off to the Black Bull then. Hate cafés. But until we meet again . . .'

He leans towards me. I don't see it coming. I'm out of practice. He kisses me on the lips, slowly, deliberately. And then he's gone.

*

I can barely eat my croissant. I'd like to say my heart is turning somersaults, but my reaction is even more visceral. The truth hits me in the solar plexus, and I feel sick. Has this attraction been fizzing away since we first met, like an electrical fire in a cavity wall? Just waiting to consume me. I can't do this. How can I? The age difference is preposterous. I do a quick calculation and cringe. No, he needs to be with someone like the smiley girl behind the counter. What would he think of me, with my greying roots and extra pounds, creaky joints and dry skin?

Oh for God's sake! I've suddenly jumped from fancying him to imagining myself in bed with him. Don't go there.

Don't even consider it. Like a sleepwalker, I take a sip of my cooling coffee and tidy the papers in front of me, trying to lose myself in the Reverend Wilkie's spiteful meanderings. It worked before, but now I can't get Grant Tranter out of my head. I can still feel the imprint of his lips on mine, slow with promise. *Shit.* I end up reading the same passage half a dozen times before realising that I *have* actually read it before. Charlotte has photocopied a section I've already seen.

With a sigh, I glance across the square to the old tolbooth. I'm still smarting from her dismissive attitude earlier, and I don't really want to go back in with a complaint. I fish around in my bag for my phone to check the time. There's a message from an unidentified number. A picture of a pint and a simple: *See what you're missing* 🍺

I can't prevent the grin that spreads across my face.

*

Over breakfast the next day, I give myself a stern talking to about responsibility and doing the right thing. My heart refuses to listen. It's tired, it needs a break. Like the pigeon in the tree outside when she thinks she's caught the eye of some young squab, my soul is all puffed up and hopeful. I'm not sure how to deal with that.

I take my toast over to the desk and chew reflectively. Sunlight streams in through the high window and bounces off Charlotte's new photocopies. The ink seems sharp and vivid today.

After The Kiss (in my head, it's now capitalised) I'd bitten the bullet and gone back to the museum to point out Charlotte's mistake.

'Twice in one day,' she'd greeted me, nodding at the pages in my hand. 'You're keen!'

I held up the photocopies and made an apologetic face, even though it wasn't my mistake. 'I'm not *that* keen. It's just that you photocopied the wrong pages. I've seen these already.'

Charlotte laughed. 'Oh no! Sorry, I've been so busy. Why don't you come in, and I can sort it out?'

Our little tiff of that morning had been firmly over-shadowed by a new and pressing anxiety, which was sitting undigested in my belly alongside the croissant. I managed to tamp it down until we reached the research room and then it all tumbled out.

'He kissed me. Or maybe I kissed him. There was kissing. It just happened.'

Charlotte attempted to find the right words. 'Uh, who exactly?'

I rewound. 'The carer. I mean Grant. Grant Tranter. Just now in the café. He came around to my house the other evening and we had some wine and then we decided to go to Lumsdain House. He has a key so it wasn't breaking in.'

'Woah! So this is Grant, your dad's carer? The guy with the dreadlocks and the attitude? Sarah, he's in his *twenties*!'

'Yes. I know. Late twenties, actually, but thanks for pointing that out.' Irritation flared. 'You can talk. Sophie is ten years older than you!'

'It's different for us.'

'How come?'

'Because we're used to it. I've been the subject of wagging tongues since school. You know, the only gay in the village. Small town, small minds. But you're so . . . mainstream.'

'Mainstream?' Translates as safe. Boring. Staid.

'You know what I mean. Pillar of the community, never

kicks above the traces. The gossips will have a field day if you start walking out with Grant Tranter.'

'Walking out?' Laughter spluttered from me. 'You're funny. I'm a big girl, I think I can handle the fallout. And anyway, it was just a kiss. I'm sorry I even mentioned it now.'

'Just a kiss today. He'll be moving in before you know it and you'll be washing his socks. You just got rid of one adolescent.'

My face closed into a scowl. 'He doesn't wear bloody socks.'

I no longer wanted to be the Sarah they all expected me to be – the 'mainstream', staid, boring, predictable Sarah with the ageing father and the empty nest. I didn't *have* to be that person. Life is full of possibilities. I sensed a sea change coming.

*

I take another bite of my toast, the marmalade tart on my tongue. It's all a matter of perspective. People aren't always as they seem. Take religious fanatics, for example. On a whim, I gather up the new photocopies and whisk them into my briefcase.

The supermarket is mercifully quiet. The summer holidays are a weird time in the shop. It's either swarming with kids or deathly quiet as the residents of Kilgour explore the delights of Disneyland and Center Parcs. It gives me the perfect opportunity to close my office door and devour the latest offerings from the mad minister. But somehow it's impossible to concentrate; my thoughts keep reeling back to what happened after yesterday's museum visit. The implications are so profound I'm still processing it. This is why I can't connect with the Reverend's words. They're just words. He's not telling us the truth. Oh no. Just his version of events.

As I was leaving the museum, I managed to get mixed up

with the children from the nursery. They were all on a high after their music session, shrill and jostling, taking up the whole foyer. I tried my best to dodge past them but Charlotte called me back to look at the visitor book.

'Look!' she cooed. 'One of them has signed my book! Aren't they adorable?'

'Gorgeous,' I agreed without conviction. I pretended to admire the scribble: a smiley face, with two dots for eyes and a half-moon mouth.

Somehow I ended up tailing the children back to Lumsdain House. Was it the silly little emoji or a snatch of a song overheard? I'm not sure. But as they made their way down Butter Wynd I was hot on their heels. The Reverend Wilkie calls my attention back to the photocopies on my desk. One of the entries leaps out at me.

> When I visited the poor children this week, it occurred to me that one was missing. Abel, the little martyr. The Nurse informit me that Mistress Gowdie had called and taken the child to help with her tasks. They were seen carrying a pail to the well, she said. I did return home in a strange temper. I wit that the strumpet did take the childe away for her own wicked purpose. She cannot suffer him to be the instrument of Good.

I gasp and peer more closely at the paper. She couldn't suffer him to be left in your clutches, William Wilkie! Mention of the well makes my heart beat a little faster. Does this mean that Alie took Abel to the well, and not one of her siblings, as the story goes? I read on, my eyes wrestling with Wilkie's script. It's like unpicking the stitches of political spin to get at the truth.

Not an hour later, the Butcher Donald did make haste to me and did declare that he had smelled Brymstone on the head of the child. I lay this abomination at the door of Alisoune Gowdie. She is a persone who dost consult with Devills and Familiar Spirits and we cannot suffer it more.

I sit back so heavily in my swivel chair it spins me round. How things can change in a moment! These are facts that could change the story of the Witch of Kilgour, shake up the narrative. Alie Gowdie, you've been stitched up. This is your death warrant in black and white. Archibald Donald couldn't have you and William Wilkie couldn't have the boy.

Someone had to pay. And it was you.

Sarah

After work, I have my usual shower and cook some pasta for my tea. I only eat half of it. I can't settle. I end up wandering around the house, trying to banish a great many people from my thoughts – Alie, Abel, William Wilkie, Grant – and ducking and weaving amongst them. I have two hours before Mrs Sutherland's Witch Walk. I need to calm myself. Concentrate. As a distraction, I play my favourite game: how would things have looked in 1648? Softening my focus, it's time to blot out my widescreen TV and conjure up instead a world of weaving looms and rush lights. I've painted Abel vividly in my mind: undersized, frightened, his fair hair and fine features setting him apart from a dozen other poor boys. I can imagine the little lad in my sitting room, dwarfed and deafened by the clatter and throb of the weaving frames. I can see Robert working the threads, a pattern growing steadily beneath his hands, and the child crouching beneath the loom, waiting to pass the loaded shuttle from one side to the other, in his own little cave of dust and scraps. Did he feel safe here with Robert and Alie, or did the charm of protection evaporate as soon as Alie was bundled away to the tolbooth? I clutch at my throat where the little hagstone used to live. Did luck run out for all of them? I imagine Robert spending all his hours negotiating with indifferent officials, and Abel cowering here, listening for the click of the door, the flickering of the candle flame, the squeak of the floorboard as Wilkie lets himself in. Did he frantically scrawl witch marks in the dust beneath the loom?

*

According to my inbox, I have five guests lined up for tonight's Witch Walk. I try to second-guess them; it's another game I like to play. Mr and Mrs Smith (illicit lovers), Joanna Haliburton-Forbes (slumming it), Michael Seegers (American exchange student), Helen MacDougall (librarian). Sometimes I'm right, sometimes I'm spectacularly wrong. I email receipts and make a note on my income and expenditure spreadsheet. I always pay my taxes.

I shake away my demons and slap on some vampy make-up, iron the creases from my black lacy dress.

I have a feeling tonight will be different. Things are changing. Things *have* changed; I feel it in my bones. Alie Gowdie is reaching out to me, demanding I put things right, and my own life, which has become buried beneath the weight of everyone else's expectations, has rolled over and is sitting upright, rubbing the sleep from its eyes. I feel alive. On fire. The touch of Grant's lips has set something aflame, but not in a purely physical away. He's lit a fuse. It's burning, and I don't know where it will lead.

I finish off with a slick of red lipstick – there's red lipstick in all the best stories – and get up from my chair.

It's that time again.

*

I walk into the snug of the Black Bull to find Grant Tranter occupying a long table with the other would-be Witch

Walkers. He's halfway through a pint and chatting to a girl with pink hair. I can't say I'm surprised to see him – he had mentioned coming, after all – but he's out of context, out of time, and the kiss is very much at the forefront of my mind. I need to get a grip. I'm not used to this weakness, this slow dissolving. There's other stuff too. I'm desperate to tell him what I've found out today, another piece of the puzzle. Grant will understand. He'll share my excitement at this new development, but right now I have my witch's hat on. Time to be professional.

'Grant, you haven't booked!'

'Was I supposed to?' He looks all innocent.

'We paid online,' says a heavy-built balding man who may be Mr Smith. Mrs Smith – if it is she – is tucked into his elbow and nervously sipping a ginger beer.

'Can I still come?' Grant tilts his head, eyes gleaming like an eager spaniel.

'I suppose so.' I shoot him a look that says behave yourself or you're out. 'You can pay me later.'

The pink girl smiles at him. She's seriously pink. Not just the hair, but the frames of her specs and the fingerless gloves wrapped around her pint glass. They're studded with tiny silver skulls. Joanna or Helen? Textile student, definitely.

After my introduction and safety talk – the cobbles and steps are a trip hazard – we emerge from the pub and congregate at the mercat cross, where I do my usual spiel. How do you spot a witch? Trust Grant to say 'red lipstick'.

We move on to the tolbooth, the scene of many an extracted confession.

'So how did they torture them, the witches?' Pink Girl wants to know. She's wearing a pink net tutu over ripped black leggings and sparkly DMs. Does she *really* want to know?

'I spend a lot of time in here.' I glance up at the inscrutable mullion above us, but I can feel their eyes on me. 'Research. I can tell you what happened to the town's most famous witch, Alie Gowdie. I can tell you what happened to her.'

I look around the circle. The eyes are keen, eager. I smile.

It's time to begin.

'In modern parlance, you might say Alie Gowdie was "known to the authorities". There had been several allegations against her, which I'll tell you about as we walk.' I'm thinking of the cow charm debacle, the unexplained Little People and the Brimstone Boy, who now has a name, thanks to Wilkie's sordid meanderings.

But these people are here for a night out, I remind myself. They've come to hear a story. I should stick to the facts as I know them, and not this new unfolding version. Another phrase springs to mind – *for entertainment purposes only* – that Get Out of Jail Free card for those paranormal TV programmes that make spurious claims, the modern equivalent of the Victorian séance. Maybe that's me, not so much an historian as a charlatan, a fake medium channelling what might have been. I decide to get straight to the crux of the matter.

'One cold day in September 1648, Alisoune Gowdie was bundled from her home and marched here to the tolbooth. It's reported in her trial transcript that her husband Robert pleaded on her behalf and accompanied her on the short trip to gaol, but he was not allowed through the door.' I wave in the direction of the museum. 'She was taken to the room above' – we all look up – 'and stripped naked . . . I'll ask you again: how can you identify a witch?'

There's a shuffling as the spotlight falls back on the group. It's an exam, a test, and no one wants to speak up, apart from

Grant, who opens his mouth and shuts it immediately in answer to my hard stare.

'Marks,' Pink Girl suggests. 'Moles and stuff.'

I nod my approval. 'Moles and stuff. The mole or birth-mark is prodded – or brodded, in the Scots tongue – with a needle. If the accused feels no pain, it means it's the mark of the Devil, the site where he nipped, bit or kissed his disciple.'

'I've got a little mole on my hip!' There's always one in every group who fancies themselves to be a witch. I smile at Pink Girl and wonder how long she would have lasted in 1648.

'A professional witch pricker was brought in from Tranent, one George Cathie, who appears to have made a lucrative living travelling from parish to parish identifying witches. Devil's marks were believed to be located in secret places: under the hair, the eyelids, body cavities . . .'

I let that sink in. There's a bit more uncomfortable shuffling, but I won't dwell on the reality. *For entertainment purposes only*. I won't linger on the facts, that these women were strip-searched and shaved and humiliated in front of strange leering men. The transcripts show that William Wilkie was present at Alie's 'brodding'. I bet he loved the chance to see her brought down.

'No marks were found on Alie, but that wasn't enough to save her. They tried to get her to make a confession, to implicate some of her neighbours who had been apprehended at the same time. According to the Kirk, witchcraft was like a disease. It was contagious, and even to be seen having a laugh with someone who was accused in this way was highly dangerous. The last years of the 1640s, just before Cromwell's invasion of Scotland, saw a particularly zealous witch hunt. The minister of Kilgour seemed eager to do his bit to rid the town of what he described as a scourge of witches, and he had a particular axe to grind with Mistress Gowdie.'

I've broken my own rule and, sensing a ripple of renewed interest, I change tack. 'Torture. That was the next step. Sleep deprivation, lack of food. Some of the confessions we have on record are so ludicrous and embellished it's almost as if the suspects *want* to be executed, but the reality is that hallucinations can occur when the body is exhausted and stressed. The women quite literally were losing their grip on reality, and the confessions were extracted under extreme duress.

'If all that didn't work, you also had the bootikin, which was a kind of wooden boot that encased the leg. They drove wedges into it until it shattered the limb, rendering it "unserviceable". Or there was the witch's bridle, a nice little iron number that fitted over the face. It was usually accessorised with a spiked device that went into the mouth. You couldn't move your tongue, swallow or cry out. They literally robbed you of your voice. And then we have—'

I stoop to take a prop from my Gladstone bag. 'Pilniewinks!' With a flourish, I produce a compact metal thumbscrew, which is passed from hand to nervous hand, with the expected groans and pained face-pulling. Grant, of course, tries the device for size and gets his thumb stuck. There's a brief interruption as Mr Smith struggles to release him.

I press on. 'Alie Gowdie was a strong, strong woman. She refused to implicate any of the neighbours incarcerated with her and denied all of the charges levelled against her. However, she was overheard telling the witch pricker to search the Reverend Wilkie.'

I inhale deeply. I've read the transcript of Alie's trial online, but that was several years ago, when I was researching this walk. Only now are the pieces of the puzzle starting to drop into place. A new chapter is writing itself, I can feel it, like a second heartbeat alongside my own. 'She was heard to say that the minister had a black mark shaped like a heart at the top of his left thigh.'

'How did she know?' More than one voice pipes up, the tone slightly accusing. Like the voice of a mob.

'They could either accuse her of having carnal knowledge of the minister, which would implicate the man of God, or they could accuse her of having the magical powers of second sight bestowed by the Devil.'

'It comes down to the minister's word against hers, doesn't it?' Mr Smith decides, staring down at the cobbles. 'No contest.'

'None.' I catch Grant's eye. I know what he's thinking. We know where Alie got that information from. From Abel. We are closer to the truth than anyone can imagine, but how can we prove it?

As we turn down Butter Wynd, my thoughts drift back to yesterday.

*

After tumbling out of the museum, the kids were arranged into pairs for the walk back to Lumsdain House. They were still singing snatches of the old songs they'd learned in their music session, and on a whim I followed them, observing their Day-Glo backpacks and expensive trainers. I couldn't help sparing a thought for those long-ago kids, the babies of vagrants and beggars and prostitutes. Were they marched to their fate, ragged and barefoot, down the same route? At the mercy of the parish and men like William Wilkie.

Childish voices floated back to me on a nursery rhyme. I struggled to place it. Funny how you forget all those things once the toddler years are past. My last musical memories of Hannah are heavy rock, but I definitely knew this one.

Crying through the windae ...
Yelling through the lock ...

Of course! I gave my head a virtual fist bump. 'Wee Willie Winkie'. The old bedtime rhyme was never a favourite in our house. Many Christmases ago, my parents bought Hannah a storybook with reproductions of vintage illustrations: a procession of fat piggies, rosy-cheeked farmers' wives and hapless gingerbread men. The old Sandman himself was a grotesque caricature with a shock of white hair, a parsimonious twist to his mouth and pince-nez perched on a warty nose. With his sputtering candle and striped nightgown, he really was the stuff of nightmares. The very sight of him used to terrify Hannah. She'd insist on her bedroom curtains being pulled across so tightly that not a chink of night could be seen. You definitely wouldn't want Wee Willie Winkie peering through your curtains.

Are all the bairnies in their bed?
It's past ten o' clock.

The children were drawing away from me, lining up beneath the portico of Lumsdain House. One child at the edge of the group, a little blond boy, was still singing his heart out.

Wee Willie Wilkie,
Dinnae let him in ...

A shiver of fear edged up my spine. Rooted to the spot, I stood there, gaping like a fool until one of the teachers picked her way towards me. She looked hesitant, apologetic, and I instantly recognised her from the research-room invasion. Her hair was shaved behind her ear on one side, but long and curly on the other. She had various piercings and colourful rag-doll dungarees with huge pockets. I stammered an apology.

'I just wondered if I could help you with something?' She was mild-mannered, unthreatening, but I could tell her child protection sense had gone into overdrive. She looked me up and down, before recognition dawned. 'Aren't you Charlotte's friend, from the museum?'

'Yes, I'm Sarah.'

'Mirren.'

We shook hands. It was incongruous and a bit odd. It dawned on me that this might be Grant's mother. I went hot with embarrassment and withdrew my sweaty palm quickly in case she noticed.

'I've been doing some research into the witch trials.'

'Oh yes! Fascinating. We've been working on some old rhymes.'

'That's what I was listening to. But the words . . . they seemed a bit strange, different maybe?'

'Ah, they're a local variation. You should speak with the musicologist. He's a real expert on all these old rhymes. He'd be able to tell you the history. You might catch him before he goes.'

As she spoke I tried to calculate her age. Smooth skin, zero lines around her mouth. Like me, she fell pregnant at a young age, if the gossips are to be believed, so now she'd be about . . . Oh my word. Am I'm thinking of sleeping with a guy whose mother might be the same age as me? Am I? Is that what I'm thinking of?

*

I pull myself sharply back to the present, to find that Grant has fallen into step beside me as my Witch Walk proceeds down Butter Wynd. I'm hyperaware of every little detail of him, the slap of his flip flops on the cobbles, the taut line of his jaw. What can he possibly want from me? I let my gaze drift up to his. There's an honesty in his eyes that I could well do without.

The sunset is beautiful tonight. Down at the bottom of the wynd, the colours are framed by crumbling walls: stripes of peach and indigo. I think of my dad, his house turned to orange by the last burst of the day. It's just coming up to nine; he'll be making his final cup of tea, drawing the blinds in the kitchen. He usually watches the ten o'clock news before heading off to bed.

I haven't had time to speak to him today. Guilt oozes up. My life has been so crammed with the unexpected, he's been toppled from my thoughts. I hope he's all right, but resist the urge to check my mobile for missed calls.

I take a left turn into the courtyard of Lumsdain House. It's sleeping. The last low rays of sun have turned its windows into mirrors, and my little gang crowd around and peer in. Grant stands a little apart. I pray he won't produce the key and offer everyone the grand tour.

'So this is Lumsdain House,' I start off. 'The facade is plainly Georgian, but it's undergone a number of changes over the years – a building society, council chambers. In the nineteenth century it was used to house orphans. After industrialisation it was common practice to take kids out of the workhouse and use them in the factories.'

There was the customary murmur of regret, a mention of 'slave labour' from Mr Smith and a quiet pause for the lost little souls who'll be conveniently forgotten the minute they hit the pub afterwards. But they didn't come for a history lecture. They've paid to be entertained.

'But . . .' I pause for effect, give an affected twirl of my lacy sleeves. 'We have discovered that in the seventeenth century this building was actually a paupers' hospital, run by the Reverend Wilkie I mentioned earlier. He features a lot in this story, has a starring role, you might say. He was even immortalised in song.'

Grant gives me a sharp look. He hasn't heard this part. This is the best part, the part I discovered yesterday.

*

After parting with Mirren – can she *really* be Grant's mum? I make a mental note to find out – I scurried back the way I'd come, skidding over the cobbles in my haste to catch up with the music man. I was panting by the time I reached the museum entrance and asking myself how the hell I'd be able to keep up with a younger man. Staggering up the steps, I bumped into Charlotte in the foyer. As luck would have it, she was deep in conversation with a thin man in a brown suit that was too big for him.

'Are you the musicologist?'

They'd both looked a bit shocked at my abruptness, but the man nodded slowly. Charlotte looked hacked off. She folded her arms and was about to give me her prim 'What are you doing, Sarah?'

I ignored her and blurted out my burning question: 'What do you know about Wee Willie Winkie?'

The guy visibly relaxed. I was not an irate mother or a stalker. 'You heard the children? They love that one.' He swelled with pride. 'I have a series of recordings made in the fifties –

playground rhymes and songs. There was a study done in 1958 that documented the slight regional variations between—'

'But Wee Willie Winkie?'

'That's an interesting one. What we assume to be the original poem version was published in 1841 by William Miller.'

'Can I hear the recording?'

'Sarah, Eric is on his way to the high school.'

I gazed at Charlotte imploringly, my hands locked in a surreptitious prayer position.

Eric jumped to the rescue, all fired up by my interest. A glance at his watch. 'I have half an hour. I'm sure you'll find it fascinating.'

Like most people with a passion, Eric came to life when discussing his work. I'd dismissed him as a bit of a nerd. Beanpole thin and very pale, his mud-brown jacket was so broad on the shoulders it looked like he'd forgotten to remove the hanger. I wasn't terribly sure what a musicologist did, but it was easy to imagine him in a basement surrounded by amplifiers and keyboards, deprived of daylight and forgetting to eat.

We regrouped in the research room, which had retained the powerful popcorn whiff of sweaty kids. Charlotte banged around, opening a window and generally putting things to rights with the air of an offended cleaner. I suspect she didn't want me bothering 'the expert' with my amateur theories. Eric cracked his knuckles and opened up his laptop, a maestro lifting a piano lid.

His recordings were stored in a bank of password-protected sound files. I was struggling to breathe at this stage: my hunch was alive and well and nibbling at my stomach lining. I knew I was right. I *knew* what I'd heard. I was either set to listen to the most boring lecture in history, or I was about to learn something that would twist the narrative even further.

Click. Crackle. The recording bursts into life.

Children's voices from across the decades, tinny and insubstantial. Discordant ghost voices on another frequency.

Wee Willie Wilkie rins through the toun
Upstairs and dounstairs in his nicht-goon

Keekin' through the windae for a laddie on his lane.
Hide away the bairnies, syne there be nane.

Eric pressed pause. 'You understand the language? "Keeking" is an old word for peering, of course, and "on his lane" means alone. Quite sinister, isn't it?'

'Yes, it is.' My voice was faint. 'Hide away the children, soon there'll be none.'

Eric rubbed his chin. 'We think the name Wilkie, as opposed to Winkie, might be a nod to a local character. We see this frequently in the variations. It may be that Miller's poem was created from the remnants of older, darker verses. Certainly, the titular character is believed to be an earlier Jacobite nickname for William of Orange, but in this case . . .'

Charlotte stopped wiping down books and glanced at me.

I took a deep breath. Unbidden, the witch marks of Lumsdain House scratched their way into my brain.

VV VV VV

W W W

Wee Willie Wilkie?

'Eric, what do you know about the Reverend William Wilkie?'

Sarah

'That was amazing!'

Grant kicks off his flip flops and collapses on my couch. I know he's referring to the walk, but my thoughts are on my recent findings. I can still see the faces of Charlotte and the musicologist as I told them what I'd uncovered, from the diary and from the strange marks in the old building. The satisfaction when the penny dropped. I *was* onto something! There's not much space left for me on the couch – Grant's doing his manspreading thing – so I go and get some beer. Yes, I'd bought a few bottles on the off-chance. I think I'm probably still smiling when I return. I feel buoyed up, vindicated.

'So, come on then! What did he say, the music guy?'

Grant flips the top from his bottle with an opener he has on his key ring. I hand over my own beer for the same treatment.

'You should have seen his face! He didn't know anything about the minister, so when he saw how the profile fitted with the songs . . . Wow. He's going to dig a bit deeper.'

Grant hands back my opened beer. The smell of hops and the freeze of the bottle against my palm make me feel alive. We clink bottles and take a simultaneous slug.

'So, this guy, Eric, he confirmed that this song is peculiar to this parish?'

'This parish only. He can't date it – it's obviously been handed down as these things are – but doesn't that say it all?'

'They were scared of him. They didn't want to let him in.'

I think of Hannah's bedtime bête noire, the peculiar Sandman figure with his shock of white hair scrabbling at the window. I can still see the windows of Lumsdain House lit up like fire in the sunset, opaque, hiding secrets that are only now beginning to come to light.

'Okay, let's do a recap. Alie was propositioned by Archibald Donald the butcher, but was presumably in love with Robert the weaver?'

'A better match, perhaps. A secure future. Wives had to be a helpmeet. I'd much rather fold cloth and keep the books than dice mutton and make pies.'

'So Archie was determined to get his own back for the cow prank – that was hilarious, by the way – but meanwhile she's become aware that Abel, the little lad they'd promised to employ, was being abused by the mad minister.'

'Not mad. Just perverted and all-powerful.'

'Where have we heard that before? Nothing ever changes. Why don't you sit down, Sarah?'

He looks right at home in the corner of my couch, sipping a beer, one long leg resting along the length of the cushions, the other foot scuffing the floor. The only space is effectively between his thighs and he doesn't look like he has any intention of moving. It's a trap. Seriously, what was I expecting when I invited him back to mine? I mean, it's not a power struggle; I've just forgotten how to play the game, that's all. I park my bottom warily, tucking my trailing black skirts beneath me.

'You look bewitching,' he quips.

'That's such a line!'

In answer, he snakes his arm about my shoulders and pulls me close, so my back is snuggled against his chest. If it's a trap, it's a very warm, comfortable one. I suppose, back in the day, I sat like this with Ian, but it seems like such a long time ago. I've forgotten how to do this, so I take refuge in small talk.

'I think I met your mother today.'

'At the nursery? Yeah, you would.'

'Mirren?'

'That's her. She's bonkers. Crazy woman, man.' It's not said with any rancour, just a statement of fact.

I sip my beer, wait for words to form. Don't ask her age. *Don't.* 'So there's just you?'

'Yeah, I was an accident. An unexpected consequence.'

'Of what?' I can feel his heart bumping against my ribs. I move slightly, the better to watch his face. There's a tightness to his jaw. I'm so used to the rakish grin, the laughing eyes, this new subdued Grant worries me. For the first time I glimpse what lies beneath the brashness.

'A fling.'

'Didn't you ever know your dad?'

'Nope. My dad's just an idea to me. I don't know what he looks like. What he thinks. What he would think of me. I've grown up with my mother's story of who he is, but I know it's just a version of the truth.' He looks sad, apologetic almost. 'She's embroidered it over time. Maybe it makes her feel better. It's not easy raising a child alone.'

I think of Hannah. 'No, it's not. I mean, I was alone, but not a lone parent. Ian was always around, even when I didn't want him to be!' We both laugh softly. 'Do you know where he is, your dad?'

A little of the old bravado returns. 'He on the islan', man! One day I'll go and find him there. Until then . . .'

'Until then?'

'I'll be like those nameless wee souls in Lumsdain House. I'll always be a lost child.'

*

I suppose we never grow up, not really. Maybe we stop at a certain age inside. Inside, Grant and I are the same, searching for something. At least he has a vague shape to what he's looking for. Me? I suppose I'm looking for the woman I could become. I don't know if my timing works, but I turn my head and kiss him. It seems like a good thing to do. He's lost, a little sad. I know how to deal with such things, make them better. His lips are soft and unresisting at first, as if he's listening for a change in me, a note of caution, but my spirit of compassion quickly flows into something else.

I'm acutely aware of his heat, the way we fit together, the sudden urgency of his body. The spell stretches and snaps. I'm suddenly outside myself, a wary observer. Is this really me? What am I doing? I pull away, even though Grant tries to hold me fast.

'I can't do this. We can't . . . it's . . . it's ridiculous.'

I sit up, try to put some cold air between us.

Uncertain now, he lets me go. 'Why is it?'

I flap my hand between us, agitated. 'Isn't it obvious? I have a child born in the same decade as you. I'm *flattered*, of course I am, but this could never work.'

I'm staring at the coffee table, the abandoned beer and my black pointy shoes kicked off beneath it. I can't look at Grant, but there's a definite pulling away.

'Work? It only has to work for tonight,' he says. 'Don't overthink things.'

Oh God. We're on completely different wavelengths. Heat surges through me. I feel sick with embarrassment.

I've totally misread the situation. What was I expecting – a love story?

'Even for one night, it's . . . inappropriate.' Now I sound like a schoolteacher.

Grant chuckles, but the sound is dry, devoid of his usual good humour. 'You sound just like that other Sarah, Wisebuy Sarah. I guess this is against your health and safety policy.' He shuffles into a proper sitting position, so we're side by side, not touching.

'Grant—'

'No sex until you've done a proper risk assessment.'

'That's not fair.'

'And you're certain that there's absolutely no danger of you getting hurt.' He takes an angry swallow of beer.

'I'm pretty sure this would end in tears.'

Grant looks at me steadily. 'I guess we'll never know.'

There's that vulnerability again, a naked awareness. I shy away from it. Stare at the floor. Even when he gets up to go, I can think of nothing to say. Everything sounds like an excuse, because of course it is. Afterwards the house is too quiet, too empty. I think I've hurt him. He sees my caution as a rejection. And I've definitely hurt myself. I should have just gone for what he was offering. Damn the consequences. Now it's too late.

*

I sleep very badly and wake up feeling miserable. I have three missed calls on my mobile, but none of them are from Grant. The first call was from Dad at nine last night. He's left a message, his tone passive-aggressive. 'Nothing to worry about, Sarah. Just checking you're all right.' Another one from

Hannah. Bugger! I forgot to return her call. The third one is from the shop. I decide to deal with that one first.

'Is that you, Rosie? Any problems?'

'Oh, Sarah, hi. Are you coming in today?' I glance at my clock radio. It's not even eight.

'I am, but I'm on a late. What's happened?'

'Nothing to worry about.'

'When people say that, I worry. What is it?'

'Remember the missing chicken legs? Well, Peggy's cracked the case. I can't really tell you over the phone.'

She's in the warehouse. I can hear cages being rolled around and someone swearing.

I grimace and let out an impatient breath. 'Okay. Give me thirty minutes and I'll be there.'

*

The remains of a witch are scattered across my bedroom carpet, as if she's been spirited magically away – black lace dress, the sexy black underwear that no one ever gets to see. I feel like a failure. I wonder if Grant will laugh about this with his mates in the Black Bull. His disappointment was obvious, but for a second I could let myself believe that there was more to it, that he was hurt. He was hoping for something I couldn't deliver, and it wasn't just sex. I talk myself out of that notion as I step into the shower. The message was clear: *don't overthink things.* No, he's a player, as I always suspected. A young guy on the pull. Older women are a good option, aren't they? More independent, not as needy as these young girls with meaningful relationships in mind. I was fair game for a one night stand.

The water is hot. The shower gel smells of roses. I imagine

showering with Grant, and for a second my body flames beneath my hands. A vicious pang of loss radiates through my belly. I'd done the right thing, though. There's no way I want to be a notch on Grant Tranter's bedpost. I've had a narrow escape.

Sarah

In the great scheme of things, stealing food is hardly up there with manslaughter, but we've become so overregulated in the retail industry. Wisebuy operates a strict anti-theft policy. Bags are searched and everything has to be accounted for. Staff scoffing chicken isn't something I have to deal with on a regular basis.

By the time I arrive, Peggy and Rosie have Mai corralled in the canteen. They're playing good cop, bad cop. Peggy's standing over the cleaner, who is weeping into her hands; Rosie's people-pleasing expression is marred by an uncertain frown. To balance out the menace, I sit down at the table opposite the crying girl and try to keep my voice low and non-confrontational. She's scared, and when people are scared, they lie.

'What's all this, Mai? Peggy found you eating some chicken in the cleaning cupboard?'

'I went down for a wet floor sign and there she was,' Peggy elaborates. 'Eating the crispy skin, if you don't mind, thinking no one would notice!'

'She was taking bits home too.' Rosie produces a small parcel: one chicken leg and two barbecue sausages. 'Oh, Mai. You should have said you were hungry.'

'Is that it, Mai? Are you hungry?'

The girl lowers her hand. Her face is tear-stained and blotchy. She rubs her tummy, the global indicator of hunger.

'But this is a canteen. You can eat here.'

'Not strictly true,' says Peggy. She puffs herself up in her white coat like an angry swan. 'She's a contractor, really. Canteen is staff only, but still . . . I would've given you a sandwich, Mai.'

I'm at a loss. 'Are you short of food at home, Mai? Are you being paid?' If she understands, she doesn't give any sign of it. She bows her head and her hair falls forward like a curtain. I sit back with a sigh. 'Hmmm. We need to find out if she's getting her wages. I'll call the cleaning contractor. Meanwhile . . . Look, ladies, I really don't want to take this any further.'

They stare at me. They both know that appropriation of the firm's goods means gross misconduct and instant dismissal, but, as Peggy pointed out, Mai isn't staff. I would need to report it to the cleaning contractor, and if she's stealing because she's hungry, how is firing her going to help?

I can see a war going on behind Peggy's eyes, but the mother in her wins. 'You're right. No one else knows. Let's keep it between us.'

Rosie nods, happy to go along with the majority. 'But NO MORE CHICKEN, Mai!' She's raised her voice, the way people do with non-English speakers. 'The customers DON'T LIKE IT. NO EAT CHICKEN!'

'All right, Rosie, you've made your point. Go home, Mai. Rosie, give her the bloody chicken.'

*

Back in my office, I find a mobile number for the cleaning firm's area manager, but there's no reply. I try calling our head office, but they can only give me the details of the cleaning firm's main switchboard and I end up being passed through multiple divisions only to end up back where I started – an area manager who doesn't answer his phone. Maybe he doesn't work Saturdays, lucky beggar.

By now, I'm thoroughly hacked off and it's not even lunchtime. I haven't called my dad, either, and Hannah will just have to wait until tonight. I twiddle my pen and wonder what Grant is doing now. Is he thinking of me, or is that it, over before it starts? Relationships are so disposable these days. The kids seem to do things in reverse, going to bed with someone and then agreeing to date if they actually like the person. Maybe that's what we were doing, trying to figure out the spark. Can we go back to the 'friend zone'? Grant the carer and me, the client's daughter?

Don't overthink things. Older people spend a lot of time thinking, wondering, analysing. I can't expect someone of Grant's age to understand that, and what did I expect, seriously? Nothing could ever come of this. The age thing is too great. The attraction is intense, a bit taboo. We got carried away. End of story. Chalk it down to experience.

But already I have my phone out and I'm contemplating texting him. I compose something in my head which I won't send. *I'm so sorry. I'm really attracted to you but I'm scared. Scared of you. Scared of my feelings.* God, no. That will never do. Just put the phone down and forget about him.

Hey. Last night was awesome. I'm sorry I messed it up. ☹

Peggy barges into the office as I press send. I whisk the phone out of sight. 'Can I help you?'

Peggy looks indignant. 'You need to come,' she says. 'Mai hasn't gone home. She's sitting on the wall out front like she's waiting for something. She'll be waiting for that bastard.'

Sighing, I rub my eyes. The combination of last night's Witch Walk, the whole Grant thing, the beer and lack of sleep is beginning to take its toll. I think of all the things I have to put right: Dad's ghosts, Mai's nightmare husband; Hannah. Okay, Hannah is probably just fine, but I haven't spoken to her since . . . When did I last speak to her? And now I've added Grant into the mix. What the hell am I doing?

I've no choice but to stick the mobile in my bag and give her my full attention. 'It's not a crime. Maybe she lives far away and needs a lift?'

'She doesn't. She lives over the bridge – at least that's what she told me.'

'Maybe she's embarrassed.' I'm already following Peggy reluctantly from the office, back along the corridor and into the canteen. The red line infuriates me as soon as I step across the threshold, and there's Rosie, leaning on the windowsill, breathing on the glass.

'Rosie, time to get back to work. We've spent far too long already on—'

'The chicken' – she nods towards the car park below – 'she's just chucked it in the bin. I bet she's scared of him.'

'Terrified.' Peggy jumps in. 'Scared of another belting.'

Rosie agrees. Presumably the entire workplace knows about the cleaner's domestic strife. The window ledge is wide enough for us all to squash together, elbow to elbow. It affords a bird's-eye view of the situation below. There's the slight figure of Mai, sitting on the low wall at the entrance to the car park. She's facing out the way, towards the road with her back to the shop. An elderly couple pass by, glance at her curiously, but she keeps her head averted. There's something about her that makes me think of Hannah: the youth, the fragility. A sudden primal longing for my daughter engulfs me like a flash flood. I think back to the time I gave Mai the little hagstone. Is she wearing it? Does she believe it will protect her?

'Let's go down,' I hear myself saying. 'She looks so alone.' Rosie scrambles away from the window. 'Not you, Rosie. Aren't you on Wines and Spirits?' A sullen nod. 'Then off with you. Scoot.'

Peggy and I steal down the stairs and exit through the staff door like cat burglars. I haven't thought this through. I stop short on the outside and Peggy collides with me.

'What exactly are we going to do, Peggy?'

'We'll take the registration number and tell the police.'

'But we haven't any proof of anything, other than the black eye. As for the food, if it comes out that I've let her off with it . . .' I let the sentence go unfinished. If head office find out, I'm going to be in deep shit. I should really have barred Mai from the premises.

'Social services, then.'

We stare at Mai's back. She's a problem. And now, it seems, she's our problem.

Right on cue, the black Mercedes van glides into view.

Peggy jumps to attention. 'Right. You distract Mai. See if you can get a gander at his ugly puss, get a description, and I'll take down the number!'

'Did you bring a pen? Paper?'

From the pocket of her white coat she pulls out a fist of paper towels and an eyebrow pencil.

I'm impressed. I give her the nod. 'Okay. Let's go.'

We slot into position. I straighten my jacket and call out to Mai, trying to strike a friendly, chatty tone. She looks confused, because all her attention is on the van. I glance uncertainly at Peggy. She's skulking behind me like a pensioned-off Charlie's Angel.

The sound of the engine is loud. The vehicle draws level with the kerb and Mai gets to her feet. Low light is glancing off the windows, rendering the driver anonymous. There's something menacing about the vehicle. If this were Hannah, there's no way I'd want her stepping inside.

'Mai,' I try again, 'you don't have to get in. Can we talk? Please?'

I'm trying to stall her and she knows it. She looks back once, like the girl in that movie about the Mohicans, the one who leaps to certain death from the cliff face with an unnervingly serene expression. Mai is like that. Her resignation is deep and complete. She slides open the door. In that instant I see the face of the man who presumably 'gave her a hiding', as Peggy would say. He's unremarkable, darkly stubbled, with a grubby baseball cap pulled low over his eyes. I don't get much visual information in that brief moment but I can tell he's not Vietnamese. Is he even her husband?

His expression is fierce. Mai hops in and pulls the door closed. She's back behind glass, enclosed in her own unknown world. Peggy and I are standing there, blinking like owls, when the van starts to reverse into the entrance. I get a faceful of exhaust fumes and a twist of something else. The smell of it reminds me of a building site, a strange whiff of mortar and diesel.

Peggy is at my elbow, eye pencil at the ready for the moment the van moves forward, heading back down the road, but it stays put, engine idling. I imagine a moment of reckoning inside the cab. Is he questioning her? Have we made things worse by being out here? He'll want to know what we're doing. She'll try to placate him, make up some lie. I've seen it all on the soaps. I'm just about to say to Peggy that this was a mistake, when in the next breath the van begins to rev. It reverses another metre, tyres spitting gravel.

Peggy races around to the back of the van, faster than I've ever seen her move. She is a paparazzo, brandishing her pencil and her pad. I follow her, until I'm face-to-face with the dusty rear door. There is the heart shape, and a fingered outline – a circle with two dots for eyes and a mouth that's a frown, a downturned curve of misery. Without thinking, I sketch a second circle, with two eyes and no mouth.

'What the hell are you doing?' Peggy is scribbling down the number, but she only gets the first three letters when her pencil breaks. 'Bugger!'

I begin to dictate the final numbers, but the engine noise drowns out my words. My warning shout is lost, too, as the wheels spin and the vehicle suddenly takes an unexpected lurch, not forwards, as expected, but backwards, back towards us, with a crunch of gears and gravel.

Peggy has to leap out of its path. She stumbles and falls. The paper towels scatter to the winds, and a *hey!* leaves my mouth.

Suddenly I'm on my knees beside her. 'Are you okay, Peggy? Are you hurt?'

She recovers enough to swear like a trooper. 'I'm fine but what the fuck do you think of that!' She shakes her fist at the disappearing van like a cartoon character. 'The bastard. Did you see him? Did you get a description?'

I shrug. 'Yes and no.' Part of me is thinking, who's going to care? It's our word against his, and is Mai really going to take a stand?

'What does that mean?'

Peggy is winded. I help her to her feet.

'He looked kind of, well, Eastern European, maybe? I don't think . . . I just have the feeling that that *isn't* Mai's husband.'

'So what is he?'

We both stare at the now empty road. 'A bigger complication than we thought.'

John

'Is that your best jacket?' Sarah gives him the once-over and sniffs.

John bristles at the expression on her face. 'Of course it's my best jacket. You think I'd go to the optician in my gardening jacket?'

She tweaks the soft blue gaberdine. 'Spots of paint – look! I'm sure you ordered a new one last autumn. Go and put that on.'

He lets out a sigh loud enough to make her eyes roll and huffs off down the hallway. Marjorie always loved the idea of having a 'cloakroom'. It's actually a walk-in closet, with hooks on the back of the door. You can't really walk in, because the vacuum cleaner occupies the middle ground and the stuff hanging from the walls seems to be sprouting: plastic bags stuffed with plastic bags, random umbrellas, a plastic laundry basket as big as a turtle shell, a mop and bucket, a garden rake which should be in the shed if only he could summon the motivation to go out into the garden. He has a gardener come once a fortnight, so he feels a bit redundant now.

Sarah's right. Why is she *always* right? The newer jacket is hanging up underneath his rain mac. He gets a wee catalogue every month, *Leading Man*, and he feels it's only polite to order something: a bumper pair of socks, a sweater or some nice slacks. He made a mistake in February with the sage green car coat. It was at least four sizes too big and made for a lumberjack. Sarah had to faff around sending it back, which went down like a lead balloon, but the lady on the order line is lovely. She's always happy to have a wee chat and tells him what the weather's like in Newcastle, where she's based. He read somewhere that the Newcastle accent is very popular with those who contact call centres.

The new jacket smells box fresh, like brown paper and Sellotape. He holds it up to his face and backs out of the closet. Something catches his eye through the open door of the bedroom. A Figure sitting on his bed. He goes to shout but it sticks in his throat when Sarah comes to help him shrug into the coat. He checks her face but she's wearing that closed competent expression, not the expression of someone who's just clocked a ghost in the bedroom. So he says nothing.

'That's better. Now, have you got your glasses? He might want to check the lenses or something. Wallet? You can buy me a coffee after.'

'Oh, can I indeed? You should wait to be asked.'

She laughs and squeezes his shoulder. She looks lovely when she laughs, years younger. He smiles too, feels his whole body relax. She opens the front door and helps him out to the car.

Sarah

We're running late. I'd had to nip into work to fill out an accident form for Peggy. She'd suffered a scrape to the elbow from Saturday's fracas, and I'd been deliberating about it all Sunday. The Circumstances of Accident box was causing me a headache. I'd drawn a blank. Could I make something up? Waiting for a delivery. No, that wouldn't do. There'd be questions about hi-vis workwear.

'I'll just put that we were entering the car park to start our shift, Peggy. Minding our own business. I won't mention Mai.'

'Write what you have to write, lass,' she'd replied. 'I don't suppose they have a box for attempting to uncover a case of domestic abuse, do they?'

No, they don't have a box for that. I mull it all over as I look for a parking space in the centre of town. Sometimes the words on the page don't tell the whole truth: the Vietnamese cleaner, the Kilgour Witch, their circumstances reduced to a few lines of text. We don't want the extra paperwork, the extra responsibility. Or maybe, in the case of Wilkie's journal, he can write what the hell he wants and convince himself of anything. There was no one looking over his shoulder. Nothing between him and his God. He *is* the Truth.

Dad's voice breaks into my thoughts. 'Have you heard from Hannah?'

My stomach lurches with guilt. Checking my rear-view

mirror, I signal left and nose into the car park. 'Not lately. I've been so . . .'

What? Too immersed in your own life to return your daughter's call? As I reverse into a space I detect a faint air of disapproval around my dad, shimmering just out of sight. Tonight – I'll call her tonight. If I leave it until about midnight, perhaps I'll catch her as she's getting up. With a flash of horror I remember about the job she was applying for. Maybe she got the job and wanted to tell me. Or she didn't get the job and needed consoling. And I wasn't there for her. Even across the miles, how could I not be there? If I call her when we come out of the optician's, I might just catch her before she goes to bed.

'She seems fine,' I add lamely. 'She's with an Irish girl, Aisling. Sounds like they're buddying up to see India.'

'Hmmm. Not someone we know.' Dad doesn't expand, leaving me to wonder whether what he's thinking is good or bad.

The cutting edge of spectacle technology is on display in the window. Cool titanium frames rest on driftwood, up-lit by hidden spots. The windows themselves are smear-free, as if someone's gone over them with one of those black lens cloths you get with your glasses. Inside, the woman behind the desk looks like she's wearing a tunic of the same material. She's a living, breathing commercial, tapping away at her keyboard in the latest top-of-the-range eyewear. She glances up as we enter and smiles. Her eyes are owlish behind her lenses, mascara magnified into alarming spikes, which take away somewhat from the warmth of her smile.

'Mr Milton?' She taps something into the computer and we're in, on the system. Box ticked. 'Please take a seat. We'll be ready for you in a moment.'

She goes back to whatever she was doing, tap-tap-tap, and we sink onto neighbouring armchairs. Dad runs his hand over the soft butter-coloured arm. I can tell he's weighing up the cost of them against the possible price of a new pair of specs.

'I'm not sure they're going to help, new glasses,' he says sadly. It's the first time I've ever heard him open up about his sight. I've suspected for a long time it wasn't good; the way the sugar ends up on the floor rather than in his cup, and all the worrying stuff like seeing ink on the table where there was none, and those ghostly figures, not to mention the flames. I hold my tongue, wait for him to say more, but he just shakes his head and stares down at his knees. My hand covers his on the arm of the chair. His skin is cold and dry and ridged with veins, the knuckles swollen with arthritis. He still wears his wedding ring. I wobble it between two fingers.

'Mum used to like to come here, remember?'

Dad looks up and smiles. 'She loved that old Mr McTear. He was a bit of a one for the ladies back in the day. He was a Rotarian too. We used to call him Teary McTear. I mean, what a name for an optician!'

I chuckle. 'Do you think he chose the profession deliberately?'

'Who knows? They've certainly kept it in the family. Tim is the son. He's a handsome lad too. Don't you be going all misty-eyed when he comes in!'

Tim McTear takes off his specs and rubs his eyes. He's quite a robust sort, resembling a farmer rather than an optician, with ruddy cheeks and tousled hair. He wouldn't look out of place on a grouse moor with a shotgun crooked over his forearm, and as if to prove it, a rather natty tweed jacket is hanging on the back of the door. His freshness is marred by the puffy bags under his eyes. He's either an insomniac or the pollen count on the grouse moor has done for him. He catches me looking, wipes his eyes with a tissue and smiles ruefully. This is not a good look for an eye doctor.

'Hay fever. All those hanging baskets might look pretty, but it's two months of hell for some of us. Anyway, we're here to talk about your eyes, Mr Milton, not mine.'

Dad remains impassive throughout a taxing battery of tests: red lights, white lights, no lights, freezing puffs of air and digital numbers on the wall so tiny even I can't read them. Now he slumps in his chair, flexes his neck inside his shirt collar and fiddles with the trilby hat in his lap. My eyes on him are sharp as lasers, but he's avoiding them at all costs.

The optician considers my father in silence . What is it about being stuck in a stuffy windowless room with a professional that sets your nerves jangling? Doubt comes crawling back, stale and sickly. I realise I'm holding my breath. My thighs are sweating in the plastic chair and I've been pulling at a loose thread in my cardigan.

'You have very limited vision in your right eye, Mr Milton.' Tim pronounces the words slowly and loudly, as if Dad is deaf too. 'In fact, there's a marked deterioration since your last visit. I think at that stage I mentioned to you about AMD, didn't I? Age-related macular degeneration.'

'Macular what? I haven't heard about this.' My voice has a sharp *why wasn't I informed?* edge.

Dad is now staring stubbornly at the floor. He'd attended his last appointment alone and informed me afterwards that he was 'A1'. We'd left it at that, but now I experience a fluttering of panic. Dad has always been an open book, a stalwart ledger with all the information neatly printed. His subterfuge hurts.

Tim removes his glasses again. He seems irritated by

them, fiddling with the metal legs. 'Age-related macular degeneration can be either wet or dry. Your father has the dry condition, which means his vision will deteriorate slowly over time. It affects the middle part of the vision, so things can look distorted or blurred – objects, faces. It's a condition of old age and there is no treatment for dry AMD, I'm afraid. It's very common. I did discuss this at the last appointment.'

He's looking at me now, his expression slightly wary. Maybe he fears a bit of a family bust-up, but that can wait till we get home.

He turns to Dad again. 'Living with low vision can affect your daily life, Mr Milton. How are you coping around the house?'

'Absolutely fine. A1.'

'You're sure? We can refer you to a low vision clinic and I can give your daughter the contact details of some organisations that—'

Dad grunts, as he does when he wants to sweep things under the carpet. 'We've already gone down that path. Social services and what not.' It's his turn to glare at me. 'I'm not needing any more help, thank you very much.'

Tim replaces his glasses with a sigh. 'Is there anything else worrying you?'

'The current political situation. Our national debt . . .'

'Dad! Tim – Mr McTear – is talking about your health. Your vision. What about the fire and those figures and—'

'I'm perfectly fine, thank you. I can look after myself.'

'What about the *hallucinations*, Dad? You're seeing things that aren't there!'

'If we're finished, I'll bid you good day, sir.' Dad gets to his feet, replacing his trilby with a dignified defiance.

'Wait!' I get up too, intending to block his exit. I bet Tim doesn't get a family spat in here every day. 'Dad, will you please just sit down? There's a reason we came here. We need to get to the bottom of this.'

'There is no bottom,' Dad snaps. 'And if there is a bottom, it's mine, and I'll deal with it myself. Good day.'

He doffs his hat and goes to leave. We watch as he struggles to find the door handle. By this time, Tim is on his feet. He rests a hand gently on my father's shoulder. If that were me, he'd shrug me off. Instead, he looks around and appears to make eye contact with the eye man. I can't see his expression from where I'm standing, but something must have passed between them because Dad returns reluctantly to his seat.

'Sometimes,' Tim resumes the conversation as if nothing has happened, 'people experience some unexpected visual disturbances as a result of macular degeneration.'

'You mean like fires that aren't there and people that appear and disappear?' I blurt out, causing Dad to huff and shake his head, as if I've just taken the family skeleton for a walk.

Tim beams. 'Ah! Now *that*'s where it gets interesting.'

John

So that was it. They have an ANSWER at last. How people love to put a label on things. He breaks up a few slices of Sarah's wholemeal bread for the birds. It's as crusty as a fisherman's jersey. There's only one good place for that. He tears the loaf into little pieces and piles it into a plastic bowl.

Even now, Sarah will be tapping away on that computer of hers, *looking into it*. That's what she said when she'd dropped him off after the eye appointment. *I'll look into it.* Whatever that means. It's obvious, isn't it? He's as blind as a bat and his head is making things up. At least it proves he isn't going doolally. Sarah had made him a salmon sandwich with that gritty bread and gone around plumping up cushions, her eyes all watery. She loves a mystery, and now she has a name for what's wrong with him. Charles . . . Charles . . . something.

Sighing, he searches for the back door key. He can't recall the name of the condition, other than it had a chap's name. Young Timothy had said it about three times. It's a syndrome caused by his lack of sight in the right eye. 'Think about it this way,' he had explained. 'The brain is making up for your loss of vision. It's overcompensating by inventing things that aren't there. People see all sorts of things, Figures, faces – and yes, even flames or liquid.'

'How fascinating!' Sarah had said. 'I must look into it.'

Fascinating? Not so much from this end. He can't find

the key. Maybe young Trant put it somewhere else. He'll just leave it open. The side gate is locked, so no one can get into the garden. Sarah has been – what is it they call it? – goggling his symptoms on the computer, and she's printed off a lot of advice that he can't even see to read.

With the birds fed, he goes back inside and settles himself in his chair. His old magnifying glass is always to hand in case he needs to see the TV guide, and now he slides it from its felt pouch and cleans it on the hem of his cardigan. He used to collect stamps back in the day. Marjorie thought it was all a bit of a laugh. *Philatery will get you nowhere*. It was a standing joke between them. He misses that more than anything, having a laugh with someone. Not belly laughs or full-scale stand-up routines night and day, just the companionable chuckle of a shared sense of humour.

With the magnifying glass polished, he shuffles through the papers, but his mind has skipped back decades. They're queuing outside the cinema, he and Marjorie. The film? *It's a Wonderful Life*, maybe. He can see her now, flashing that engagement ring to all and sundry, a cheap twinkly thing but all he could afford on his clerk's wages. She had bonny brunette hair and red lipstick that tasted of petrol. He could never fathom how the other lads got all hot and bothered over lipstick; he preferred Marjorie all natural, maybe just out of the bath and smelling of Yardley's Lily of the Valley talc. It was surprising they'd had to wait so long for a baby, but you had to let nature take its course back then. Nowadays everyone is so impatient. They feel entitled to have everything. Marjorie had lost a couple of bairns, though. Miscarriages. They never talked about it. He'd never even told Sarah. You didn't always give a voice to things back then, although silence doesn't mean it hurts any less. Sarah came along in her own sweet time, named after Marjorie's sister who'd died of TB when she was a little 'un. A blessing, she is, Sarah, although he doesn't suppose he's ever told her that, either.

The printed letters swim before his eyes, but he applies himself like a third-rate Sherlock Holmes, bent over the paper with the glass poised. All he needs is a smoky old pipe and a deerstalker.

> When you have a hallucination, try making changes to the things around you and to what you are doing, to see if this will make your hallucination stop.

Some hope. This has probably been written by a medical bod who's never been in this particular boat, but he reads on anyway, tilting his head this way and that. He can only see part-sentences, but he's not daft. He can fill in the gaps.

> Putting the TV or radio on, or standing up and moving around, or going into a different room can sometimes make the hallucination disappear.

Rubbish. The bloody things appear when he goes into another room. The hall, the bedroom. What about them going through Marjorie's jewellery box? Does it explain how to deal with that?

> Some people find that looking directly at the image, or reaching out to touch it, causes it to fade. Sometimes moving your eyes or blinking rapidly can also help.

> Visions of people can be frightening, particularly if they're inside your home. If the images are of very small people or people in costumes then it may be easier to realise that they are hallucinations than if the figure looks normal. Having a good idea of when you're likely to have real people visiting you will help in making you feel secure in your home or your surroundings.

Righty-ho. He could give it a bash. Blinking rapidly. He'll try that next time. Hallucinations can be frightening, it says here. Too bloody right. He needs a new set of bloody eyes. He reaches for his stick. Grumbling, he makes his way into the hall.

He lays the magnifying glass on the table, and rolls Sarah's printed advice into a scroll, as if preparing to swat a fly. He's no longer sure how helpful this stuff is. He's prepared to take it on board, but here he is lurking outside his bedroom, and nothing is working. He's tried the rapid blinking and the refocusing your eyes, but she's still there.

He peeks around the door frame. She's sitting on the end of his bed, a tiny thing in a pale dress. Her feet are bare and she seems to be studying them. At any rate, her head is bowed, her long hair falling over her face. She's not moving. She's just sitting there like a hare in a field, stock-still, trying to be invisible.

Not quite sure what to do next, he tries to remember what else the help sheet suggested:

> If your hallucinations happen in dim light, then opening the curtains, turning on a light or the television may help. Certain lighting conditions may also mean that you see the hallucinations more often in one room than another.

That's true. He often sees the Figures in the hall, or in his bedroom. The curtains are half drawn from when he got up this morning. The sun had been bright, and Marjorie had a thing about things getting faded. Always leave the curtain half drawn until the sun moves to the front at midday, she used to say, otherwise it will fade the carpet. Probably an old wives' tale; he was pretty sure modern carpets were made of sterner stuff, but he followed her lead. He still pegs out his shirts by the tails and cleans the teacups with salt every Monday.

If he goes into the room and opens the curtains the vision should fade. Simple. He doesn't know why he feels so jittery, like his heart is punching a hole through his chest wall. This is *his* house. He's not having these – these *strangers* invading his home. The bedroom he shared with his wife! No wee girl in a white dress is going to stop him being master of his own house!

He marches into the bedroom – as much as he can march these days – and, keeping his eyes averted from the bed, he swipes the rolled-up paper – left, right, left, right, left, right. There's a definite scent in the air. A ripe muskiness, like sweaty children after they've been out playing all day in summer. Left, right, left, right. He props his walking stick against the wall and with both hands and all his might flings the curtains wide.

Daylight floods the room, turns the windowsill a dazzling white. The effort has left him beaten and breathless. Winded, he turns slowly.

The vision has gone.

Phew! He shakes his head and lets his mouth relax into a little smile. Bloody hell. Old age doesn't come itself, Marjorie used to say, and she was right. All manner of infirmities come with it. He can just about cope with the arthritis and the aches and pains, the slowness, but this vision thing scares him, and he's not a man that's ever been prone to strange fears.

Still, the advice works. That's good to know. He bats the scroll of paper against his forehead, buoyed up by this little victory. The room is pleasant and bright, with nothing out of place. Time for a nice cuppa. As he makes his way from the bedroom, his eyes stray to the foot of the bed. If he didn't know better, he would swear there's a bottom-shaped indent in the duvet. He smooths out the linen on his way past, but there's nothing to see, really. He knows now, it's just his eyes playing tricks.

When he opens the door, Grant is standing on the step.

'Here's one for you,' he says. 'Red red wi-i-ine . . . goes to my . . .'

'Hea-hea-ead,' John sings dutifully. 'Come in, son. Is it Wednesday already?'

'Wednesday it is, sir.' The lad wipes his trainers on the mat. 'What's on the agenda today?'

'Whatever. I'm not fussed.'

John slumps into his chair, leaving Grant to close the front door. He's feeling weighed down today. He's tried to follow the advice he's been given, but he's still having hallucinations. It's making him anxious, and the anxiety is making him ache – his hips, knees, skull, all over.

The lad strolls in as only the young can, irrepressible, filling the space with energy and the smell of the big wide world. It's easy to forget there's a life beyond the door, that all the important stuff is going on just out of reach. Politics, commerce: vital business transactions being brokered out of earshot, out of sight. And here he is, John, shrunk in the wash to a version of his former self. Peering out from his shell, afraid of what he might see.

Grant perches on the edge of the couch, the way Sarah does when she's itching to get away, but he's more focused, vigilant. He's glancing around like he's checking the place out.

John feels his body sag. He's come to dread talking about it. Whatever Sarah says to the contrary, she thinks he's losing the plot. The last time she'd visited had been particularly bad. He'd woken up in the night to see a grotesque face hovering over his bed. It had blind white eyes and spiral horns. He'd scrambled out of bed so quickly he'd got his foot caught in the duvet and fallen to the floor. Crawling over to the dressing table, he'd managed to haul himself upright, but then he couldn't find the light switch – he was fumbling around on the wrong wall – and got stuck behind the door in the dark for what seemed like a lifetime.

He tried to tell Sarah all this, but she just talked over him. When he mentioned the horns, she actually looked like she wanted to stick her fingers in her ears. Ever practical, she said she'd buy a night light, and that was the end of it.

But somehow there's an openness about the lad's face that invites confession.

'You remember I told you I've been seeing things, son?' John peers at Grant, trying to get a fix on his expression. He doesn't wince like Sarah does. He just listens, calmly. Takes it in his stride. 'Shadows, shapes. People that aren't there. Sarah says no one can get in, and she took me to the optician's. Did she tell you?'

There's a hesitation. 'No. No, we haven't spoken.'

'Well, it turns out I've got Charlie's Bonnets.'

'Charlie's what now?

'Bonnets. It's a thing you get in your head when you're half blind like me. Look at this, Tranter.' He picks up a sheaf of papers from the table and wafts them, creating a little breeze. 'Instructions on how to get rid of the guppy.'

That was Grant's word. He didn't know what it meant but it seemed to fit the problem.

'And is it working?'

John looks him steadily in the eye. 'No, Grant. It is not working. I'm surrounded by things that aren't here, but they feel so *real*. I'm seeing the wee girl more than the others now. She's about so high' – he indicates shoulder height – 'and I can't see much, but I can see her hair, Trant. Long and all down her back, and I can smell her.' He throws up his hand, as if he can't quite believe it himself. 'She disappears in the blink of an eye but she leaves a peculiar smell behind. She smells wild, unwashed.'

Grant starts to speak and then stops, scratches his crazy hair. 'Where did you see her last?'

'She's been in the bedroom, in the kitchen, but yesterday she was in the back garden. I saw her. Well, I thought I did. I'd just fed the birds and I was coming in and struggling with the door lock. That back door is an absolute bugger to lock these days. Anyway, I saw the flash of her dress—'

'She was wearing a dress? What colour?'

'Oh, I don't know, Trant. Maybe white. Thing is, it's not just the little girl, but lots of things! I see little people dancing on the window ledges, shapes in my hall messing with the electrics. My home is swarming with them. I . . . I'm scared. I don't know what to do.' He dashes a tear from his eye.

'First of all,' says Grant, 'let me make you a sandwich.' He hoists up a carrier bag. 'Fresh white bread and a nice custard tart for afters. How does that sound?'

John nods solemnly. He's a good lad. 'Do me a favour, son. Don't mention this to Sarah.'

'No?'

'No. If I keep banging on about this stuff, she'll have me locked up.'

'Ach, that's a bit harsh, John. She worries about you.'

'She hasn't been doing much worrying this week, then.' John humphs his way into the kitchen. 'Three times I've called her, and has she called back? Not on your nelly.'

Grant puts down his carrier bag and takes over in the kitchen. He makes it look so effortless: filling the kettle to the required volume, unpeeling that fiddly seal on the bread wrapper, locating a butter knife. The sort of things that take John twenty minutes are done in the shake of a lamb's tail. Grant reminds him of himself at that age – fit and careless, in constant motion. Without the hair, of course. He'd never have got a job in a building society with that mop. He's whistling the red wine song as he butters the bread.

'Marmalade or ham?'

'Marmalade, please.' He'd become partial to a marmalade sandwich. Sarah teases him that he's turning into Paddington Bear, whoever that is. 'I used to whistle,' he says now.

'Give us a tune, then.' Grant grins at him as he twists off the lid of the marmalade.

'I can't now. It's an age thing. Something to do with your teeth. I think you need teeth to whistle.'

Grant cuts the sandwich in half with a flourish. 'Just as well. Sarah says whistling summons up the Devil.'

John laughs. 'Oh, and Sarah would know! I'd better watch my step or she'll be accusing me of witchcraft. Not a word, mind, about any of this.'

*

'What can you see, Trant?'

John leans on the patio table. He'd considered sitting on the chair but thought better of it; without a cushion the cold iron chills him to the marrow. Grant said it would be interesting to see what was over the garden wall, and he'd gone over the top, dropping with a thud into Mrs Chalmers' flower bed. She grew dahlias in that spot. She always complained of getting earwigs on her cardigan when she brushed up against them. Dahlias are very bad for earwigs.

'Anything untoward, Trant? Are the dahlias blooming?'

A grunt was followed by: 'Dunno what a dahlia looks like, but there are some bonny yellow flowers and stones and . . . God, this place is a right mess.'

'I blame the son,' John mutters. 'Can't remember his name. Bit of a drinker, by all accounts. Mrs Chalmers was a very tidy woman.'

'She'd be turning in her grave if she saw all this.' Grant sounds quite distant and out of breath, as if he's conducting a very thorough investigation.

'She isn't dead, son. Oh no. They put her in a home.' He is just about to tell the whole story when the dark dreadlocks come into view. 'I hear a car. *Oh shit*. I'm coming back.'

John can hear it now, the faint rumble of an engine.

Grant tumbles over the wall, twists and lands on his feet like a cat. 'Jesus, that was a close shave.' He sucks in a breath. 'I reckon someone is living there, John.'

'Really?'

'The blinds are all down, but the place is piled up with old slates and concrete blocks and a wheelbarrow, scaffolding poles, that kind of thing. Either someone is living there or they're using it for storage. And I found something weird hanging on a bush.'

Grant pulls something from his pocket. John can't make out what it is; he's too perturbed about what Mrs Chalmers would say if she knew some rough types were storing scaffolding in her garden. He hopes it isn't squatters, but if it is squatters – weird dropout hippie types – Grant's theory might just make sense.

'So what should we do now? Should we tell someone?'

'Nah, could be legit.' Grant strokes his chin. 'Leave it with me, boss. I think I might have a plan. We need to think out the box. Try and see things from another angle.'

Another move, another place, another house. This house has a garden, although the dark man keeps the doors locked. He is afraid we'll run away. He is afraid we'll tell someone. Whoever lived in this house before must have been a bit like us – they had to leave without their things. Every day when the men have gone, I sneak down to the kitchen to play with what's left: a big shell, a little china horse, a pack of playing cards and an old blue teapot. Inside the teapot I find a key for the back door. I think whoever lived here before hid the key just for me. Outside, it's a different world. I can sit on an old chair in the garden, hide under the bushes. I find a stone with holes right through it, some of them so big I can wriggle my finger into them, like a worm. I stare at it for a long time, wondering how the holes got there. Maybe once, at the start of the world, the stones were soft like clay and all the children got to make shapes with them. I keep the stone with my other treasures in an old bag of my mother's. We can't keep too much stuff in case we have to move again, but I have an eagle feather, a real diamond ring and a little wooden cat. I hide the pouch in different places in case the men take it. The men come to our room when my ma's out. She wouldn't like it if she knew.

Sarah

'Charles Bonnet Syndrome.'

'Charles what? Never heard of it. Is that what they're saying?' Peggy looks flabbergasted, as if I've just announced that my father has the plague. We're having an early morning coffee in the canteen. Peggy is on another cleaning binge and the smell of bleach is so pungent my eyes are watering. Bleach is not on the approved cleaning products list, but she smuggles it in from home and we both pretend not to notice. She stifles a cough and I dab my eyes with a scrap of tissue.

'It's really common, apparently. The brain overcompensates for what you can't see.'

I've done a crash course in hallucinations since our visit to the optician's and some of the stories I've read online are pretty horrific. I'm deliberately trying to play down Dad's experiences. If I keep my cool and seem matter-of-fact, perhaps he'll take his cue from me and be more rational. Otherwise, we're both going to be emotional wrecks. Imagine seeing horned beings above your bed. When he described that, a chill descended that stayed with me all night.

'So the brain makes things up?'

'Yup. People see all sorts of things. It's fascinating. Charles Bonnet was a naturalist from Geneva. His grandfather had cataracts and imagined he saw all manner of things – people, patterns, birds.'

'Well,' says Peggy with great finality, 'now I've heard it all.

If I ever have to go down that route, please God, let me see George Clooney.'

I slip my mobile from my jacket pocket, checking my unanswered text for the hundredth time. Grant has given me up as a bad job. I'm destined to be on my own for ever. A lost cause, a missed chance.

It's now Thursday, five whole days since I rejected him. He's either taken the rejection to heart, or he just can't be bothered. There are plenty more fish in the sea. Why put any effort into one who obviously doesn't want to be caught? When I read my text it comes across as unpleasantly desperate and the emoji's frown has turned into a smirk. It's laughing at me.

'No Mai today.' Peggy drains her cup and gets stiffly to her feet. She reaches for my mug. 'Finished?'

I nod miserably. I suppose I should get up too. I've never felt less like work. 'I'll give her a few days, and if she doesn't come back I'll contact her boss.'

'Is that it?' Peggy says. 'Is that all we can do? Don't you have an address?'

'No, I don't.' I get to my feet. 'We can't get involved any further.'

Peggy makes some kind of disapproving noise as she takes the mugs away, but I don't care. I feel suddenly drained. I pick up my phone again. I've tried Hannah twice since Monday and each time it went straight to voicemail. Worry is starting to nibble away at me. I send a WhatsApp message. *Hey, Hannah. Sorry I missed your calls. What's happening over there?*

Somewhere between the canteen and the shop floor, my phone pings. I'm scared to look. I want both Hannah and Grant to get in touch so badly I feel sick. It's Hannah.

Time difference ☹ *I'll phone later.*

I send a thumbs-up, and my shredded nerves begin to settle like feathers. *Breathe.* Now you, Grant.

*

I get home about three. It was a bit of a nothing day at work. I like my shifts to be busy, to return home exhausted. You know where you are when you're exhausted. It's perfectly legitimate to lounge around in your PJs and watch *Love Island* when you're knackered. But today I feel on high alert. Anxious. Things are getting away from me. Like that red stripe in the canteen, my life seems to be on a slant.

Since Friday Grant has been growing into a symptom. Like a mole or an unexplained headache, he's alerted me to the fact that I need to shake things up. I thought I was inviting change, I really did, but maybe it will take more than a relationship to do that. It was never going to work, was it? A young guy like that? No, I'll have to write Grant off as an experiment and take my life into my own hands. I can climb out of this rut without someone holding the ladder.

I will travel. I'll get over my fear of flying and visit Hannah in India, wherever. The *real* heartbreak is staring me in the face. I need to catch up with my child. However connected we appear to be technologically, we're still at arm's length. I cannot take my daughter's hand, or hug her, or bask in the smell of her. I cannot make out the tiny inflections in her voice that alert me to problems or gauge the tiredness in her eyes.

We are not connected. The distance scares me. The thought of flying scares me. *If you never leave the nest, you'll never learn to fly.* Did I just make that up? My greatest fear is that one day something might happen to push me from the nest.

At home I can't be bothered to cook. I think about ordering a midweek takeaway, but takeaways for one are too sad. I end up pacing the sitting room like a tiger. The floorboard goes squeak, squeak. Eventually, when I can stand my own company no longer, I pull on my jacket and let myself out the front door. The stairs are slick with drizzle, water pooling in the depressions made by generations of feet. I always step down them with care, reverence, but today my brain is bogged down by my own inertia.

*

I find myself staring at Lumsdain House. My thoughts have carried me through the town and across the square and down Butter Wynd without consciously plotting a route. The place looks dark in the rain, the masonry black and gritty, and there are two, no, three people locking up. There are cheery goodbyes and a young woman breaks away. She walks past me, hands in pockets, head down, glancing obliquely at me from beneath an overlarge hood. The two figures who are left are Grant and his mother. *Oh shit.*

Mirren spots me first. She drops the keys into her sequinned knapsack and waves as she hurries towards me. 'It's you! Did you manage to catch Eric the other day? Thank goodness I brought my car. This looks like it's on for the night!' Her curls are frizzing crazily round her head; the shaved side is dark and slick. She's waiting for an answer but all I can think is: this is Grant's mother. What would Grant's mother think if she knew?

Grant steps in. 'Mrs Sutherland! You're a bit of a stranger.'

A stranger?

Mirren's curious glance flits between us. 'Do you know each other?'

'Remember the old gent I was telling you about? John? This is his daughter, Sarah.'

'Oh yes! I remember now.'

We shake hands. Hers are indoor warm; mine are cold and clammy. So, he's discussed my father with his mum. Is that all he's told her? Has he mentioned our night-time excursion with her misappropriated keys? Having drinks with an older woman? I feel obliged to communicate, so I spit out some inane remark about the rain.

'We're getting soaked here!' she says. 'Can I give you a lift anywhere?'

'No, no. I'm just out for some air, thanks. I'll be fine. Nice to meet you again.'

I manage to smile at Mirren while ignoring Grant and turning to face the way I've come. Hunching into my jacket, I set off down the road. There may be some discussion behind me. I just want to get away so I quicken my pace. I'm not entirely surprised when I hear footsteps pounding the pavement behind me.

'Wait up!'

Grant catches up with me. The rain cannot obscure his grin. Droplets cling to his hair and make his face gleam, but he is not soaked by it, not bogged down like I am. I stop in the middle of the pavement and face him. If tension was lightning it would be arcing between us.

'I'm sorry I didn't answer your text.'

'I'm sorry I let you go away.'

We speak more or less at the same time, and then laugh nervously.

I try again. 'I just don't do one night stands, and I'm too old to start now. I'm too old full stop. Too old for you.'

'Maybe it wasn't ever going to be a one night stand.'

'But you said—'

'Whoa.' He holds up a hand. 'Sometimes you just have to

seize the moment. Yes, it's a bit scary. Life is scary.'

His words needle me. 'Maybe I can't cope with that. I can't even cope with you not answering my texts. We're from different generations. Okay, we're attracted to each other. Let's just leave it at that. You're right. I'm not a risk-taker. You need to go and find someone who is.'

As I look at him, standing there dripping in the rain, I feel a crushing sense of sadness. How can you yearn for something that's never happened? Before I throw myself at him and kiss him, I turn on my heel and quick-march back into town. I don't care if he's following me. I don't even pause to listen. The rain is getting heavier, shrouding the narrow streets in a thick grey blanket. The yellow lights of the Black Bull loom out of the mist like a beacon. Having a drink now would be a huge mistake. I'd be plastered by seven, pouring out my sorrows to the indifferent barman, and in bed by nine.

My phone pings.

We can work this out. Let's talk about it over a drink.

As I read the text I know he's behind me. I turn around reluctantly. 'One drink. In the pub.'

He emerges from the shadows. 'It's a deal.' He winks and opens the door of the pub for me. As reunions go, it's not perfect. But it will do for now.

*

We sit with our heads together over pints in a dark corner of the pub. We talk about general things: Wisebuy, Peggy, the guys in the warehouse and my dad, who's now taken to having a bath most Wednesdays while Grant scoots around with the vacuum.

'He's actually just playing with the fancy seat. I can hear

it going up and down. I'm not sure if he's getting washed or just trying to go into orbit!'

I relax enough to smile. I'm aware there are more pressing things we – I – need to talk about. Important things. I want to know where I fit into Grant's life, and whether he can ever fit into mine, and does he even want to try. Despite the warm fug of the Black Bull, a chill settles in my bones. I kind of know already, don't I? I swallow my beer, working it past the lump in my throat. Grant knows too. He drops the waggishness.

'I should have called you. I'm sorry. I just wasn't sure . . .' He throws up a hand and lets it drop, plucks nervously at the bracelets on his wrist, head down. He seems suddenly young and unsure. This I can relate to.

I address the top of his head. 'It's fine. Honestly. I just don't know what the hell I'm doing. Jesus, I haven't been on a date since – since 1993!'

It's a number plucked out of thin air as a joke. What age would I have been then – about 17? As soon as Grant looks up with that mischievous glint, I know what he's going to say.

'That's the year I was born!'

I groan and he reaches for my hand across the table. 'Don't overthink it.' His thumb finds the pulse spot on my wrist, strokes. 'Let's not do numbers.'

Weakness floods through me. I feel mouldable, not like putty in his hands, but a firmer more resilient material. Flexible, yet unbreakable. Maybe I can be what he wants. A buddy, a friend, a lover. Maybe things don't have to be as cut and dried as I imagined.

'Are we okay?' His voice is so low I can barely hear him, so I have to lean in closer.

I guess we are.

Sarah

Grant does come back to mine, but things have changed. Maybe he's come to a new understanding, decided to do things my way. We have a bit of a cuddle on the couch, but despite the attraction it's all quite chaste. He doesn't push his luck, and I feel oddly disappointed. We're arrested on the borderline between friendship and something else. Friendship wins. For tonight, anyway.

'I'd better go.'

He kisses the softness in the shadow of my neck and I let my fingers graze the skin beneath his T-shirt. Everything is pulsing with possibility, but I sit back. Let him go. He has to be somewhere, he says. He's meeting a mate. I experience a contrary spurt of jealousy. I have vague memories of a time when I would have known how to keep him here, but the lines have been established. Let's leave it at that. I watch him as he stands up, shoves his feet into his flip flops. The pockets of his jeans are bulging with stuff; his phone pings somewhere in the depths. Who might that be? Unease settles in the pit of my belly. I want to trust him, but he's such an unknown quantity.

He turns to me with an angelic smile. 'I forgot! Here's a wee pressie for you. Don't say I never give you anything.'

With a flourish he produces a pendant. My initial delight turns into shock. I can't believe what I'm looking at. A smooth little hagstone on a leather thong. I take it from him, wordless. I'm so shocked my thanks have died on my tongue.

He doesn't seem to notice. 'I know how you love all this weird shit, and trust me, this is seriously weird. You wouldn't believe it.'

I don't know what to believe. It's *my* pendant on a leather thong. My hagstone. *Where the hell did he get that?*

He kisses me on the cheek. 'I really have to go,' he says. 'Later.' He winks and turns away from me and disappears back to his own life.

*

The next day, I get a message from Charlotte asking if I want to meet for lunch. We agree on a time at the Pantry, but I suspect this isn't purely a social invitation.

'I'm afraid I've had to let the journals go,' Charlotte announces over our baked potatoes. 'We ran out of time and the archive van came this morning.'

'I didn't even have time to say goodbye!' I'm half joking. Part of me is actually glad to see the back of the Reverend Wilkie's spidery script, but still I have a sense of ownership. It's not easy to let him go.

'And I mentioned the witch marks in Lumsdain House to the burgh architect,' Charlotte is saying. 'I don't think they've ever been logged, so he's going to make some notes and—'

'Just a minute.' I put down my fork. 'Why do you keep going over my head?'

'Over your head?' Charlotte dabs at her mouth with a serviette. She looks perplexed.

'Yes. As if I don't matter.'

'It's not that, Sarah. It's just that I'm in a position to make things happen. I have contacts.'

Anger starts to rise up. 'This is *my* story. I've done the groundwork. It was me who made the link between the old song and the minister. It was me who identified the witch marks. I deserve some *recognition*.'

Charlotte lowers her serviette. With that one word, things whirr and click into place. I want Charlotte to recognise that I do know my stuff. I want Grant to recognise that I'm not just a Friday night diversion. I *count*.

'Sarah, please, don't be upset,' Charlotte says quickly. There's a trace of panic in her eyes. 'I didn't mean to take it all away from you. How about I give you the email address of the council archaeologist and you can take it from there?'

'Yes.' I pick up my fork again, poke at my food. 'That would be good.'

'Right. Let's do that.' Relieved, Charlotte starts rooting through her bag. 'I have the last few pages of the journal for you.' She hands them over. 'It seems to end quite abruptly, but, well, I'm sure you'll be able to finish off the story.'

I take the papers. 'I'm going to write a book, Charlotte. Alie Gowdie's story: a new perspective.'

'Good. That's a great idea.' Charlotte nods, obviously relieved that I've recovered my equilibrium. 'You can arrange to visit the archives, and if there are any contact details you need, I'd be happy to help. You can collaborate with Eric and the archaeology department, and yes, I'm delighted, Sarah. It's about time you did something for yourself.'

'Yes. For myself.' Even I can hear the bitterness in my voice.

Charlotte looks at me with renewed interest. 'How are things with the toyboy?'

'He was never my toyboy! And anyway, it didn't get started, not really.'

'Oh.' Charlotte gives a little shrug. 'Well, it wouldn't have worked, would it?'

'Why wouldn't it?' The part of me that has always been

envious of Charlotte's smug domestic contentment bristles to attention.

'The age difference, for a start. And then the fact that the guy is from a totally different background to you—'

'Is this a race thing, Charlotte?'

'No!' She sits back, aghast. That was mean of me. Charlotte is the least bigoted person I know, but I can't stand to have her point out all the things I know myself. She is the voice of reason, while even now that insistent little devil inside me is whispering that age gaps work for other people, why not for me?

I swallow. 'I'm sorry. It's just that I'd hoped . . . I *thought* things were changing for me. Grant makes me feel young, I suppose. Takes me back to the days before I became bogged down and ancient.'

Charlotte gives a laugh. 'You are not ancient! And there's plenty more fish in the sea. Maybe he's woken you up to the possibility of having someone in your life again.'

'Yeah, maybe.' My baked potato looks suddenly cold and unappetising. I push my plate away.

Charlotte sighs. 'If he's so important to you, maybe you can fix whatever's wrong?'

My hand strays to my neck. This morning I pulled the pendant over my head, but it felt tainted, as if all the good was running out of it like a broken hourglass. I tell Charlotte my suspicions, that Grant has been seeing the supermarket cleaner. I never expected anything of him – we weren't an item, after all – but even so the betrayal is painful. I want to whip off the necklace and chuck it in the nearest bin, but only thoughts of Hannah stop me from doing so.

'And you're certain this is *the* pendant?' Charlotte peers at my throat.

'Of course.' I tilt the stone. 'There's a little chip out of it where I dropped it on the bathroom tiles. I gave it to Mai – and instantly regretted it – and then it turns up in Grant's pocket.'

'Hmmm. She could've sold it, if she needed the money. Maybe Grant picked it up cheap down the pub or something.'

I hadn't thought of that, and a fresh surge of hope presents itself. 'That does sound like Grant.'

But then so does this scenario: Grant meets Mai in some backstreet dive. He buys her a drink, they have a snog, and it leads to something else. Maybe Black Van Man finds out and starts slapping her around. The affair comes to an end, but Mai gives Grant a keepsake: a pendant. *My bloody pendant!*

'There's only one thing to do. Ask him.'

It seems so simple. Yes, I can do that. I'm just so afraid of the answer.

Sarah

Since Wednesday is now a Grant Day, flagged up on the calendar in scarlet letters, I no longer need to pop in to Dad's midweek. It just means I have more time to brood. I've barely slept since Grant gave me the gift. The irony is that I tried to protect my heart by not sleeping with him. My heart has other ideas – it's already involved. How the bloody hell did I let that happen? Could Grant really be seeing Mai? *Just ask him*. Charlotte is so practical.

On Friday, en route to my dad's, I decide to call Grant, actually speak to him, rather than allowing him to hide behind a text message.

He answers on the third ring. 'Hey! How you doing?'

'I'm fine, thanks. Grant, I need to ask you about the pendant.'

'I knew you'd like it. It's one of those hagstone things.'

'I know what it is. That's the problem. It's *my* pendant. As in *mine*. Where did you get it?'

My words are clipped. There's a pause at the other end. I imagine Grant wracking his brains for a plausible answer. In the void I hear another voice, not Grant's, but equally familiar. There's a muffled aside, as if Grant is holding his hand over the phone, and then he gets back to me.

'You got me. Hands up. I didn't buy it, I—'

'Grant, where are you?'

'Um . . .'

'You're at Dad's, aren't you? I can hear him. It's not even Wednesday. What's going on?'

Again, the pause. 'It's a wee bit complicated.'

My father's voice breaks in again, asking Grant what he takes in his tea.

'Complicated? Right.' My pace automatically picks up until I'm pounding the pavement in a fury. The last thing I need is complications, especially involving my father. 'You owe me a few explanations, Grant Tranter.'

He launches into a rambling explanation about why he's currently with Dad, but I'm only half listening. As I turn into Cornhill Crescent, the sudden rev of an engine distracts me. The street signs proclaim this is a 20 zone, but someone is obviously on a mission. I step back involuntarily from the edge of the pavement. A large black van cruises past. It's coated with dust. My eyes follow it. There on the grimy rear doors are three symbols: a simple heart, the frowning face, and my own effort, the crude drawing I added almost a week ago, just before the vehicle knocked Peggy off her feet. Only now, an unknown finger has added a downturned mouth.

I make a weird squeaky noise. 'Hold on a minute,' I whisper. Why am I whispering?

The van speeds up and veers off Cornhill Crescent into the adjacent cul-de-sac. The houses there are pre-war relatives of Dad's modern bungalow. You can tell the rented ones by the overgrown gardens and the peeling paint. I pass the end of this road almost daily but never have cause to venture further. I do know, though, that the last house at the end of the cul-de-sac belongs to Mrs Chalmers.

I speed up until I reach Dad's house. 'I don't know what's going on, Grant, but we need to talk.'

On the other end of the line, there's a pause. 'If it's about the pendant, I can explain.'

I ring the doorbell. Grant opens the front door almost immediately, his phone pressed against his ear. His jaw drops. I hang up and sweep past him into the hallway. He takes an uncertain step back as I confront him.

'So what are you doing here on a Friday?'

'It's your lucky day,' he quips, but his usual bantering tone is missing. There is an air of tension that doesn't escape me. I've interrupted something. I want to tackle Grant about Mai, but now I have a more pressing conundrum. Why is Black Van Man here, just out of sight beyond the garden wall?

Dad is lurking in the lounge, leaning on his walking stick in front of the dining table. For some unfathomable reason, there are a few pieces of Lego on the table and a small plush teddy. I glare at both men, waiting for an explanation, and I swear something furtive passes between them.

'You explain, John,' Grant says awkwardly. 'You made me promise not to tell Sarah.'

'Not to tell me what?'

Dad shakes his head sadly. 'You won't approve. You just think I'm making a fuss about nothing, but Grant understands . . . about the guppy.'

Tension bubbles through me. 'Grant is filling your head with nonsense! We've already sorted this out. You know what the optician said.' I take a deep breath and try to relax my shoulders, my clenched fists. 'I'm not trying to make light of what's happening to you, but I refuse to believe your house is filled with . . . with . . .'

What? Strange apparitions, dancing fairies and horned demons?

'See?' Dad appeals to Grant.

'Maybe we should show her the evidence.'

'What evidence?' There's an icy sensation between my shoulder blades. I suddenly want to sit down.

Dad nods, once, like a signal, and Grant takes over. 'Your dad has been seeing these visions. And you're correct!' He stalls me as I start to object. 'It's all to do with the Charles' – he twirls a hand vaguely – 'syndrome thing.'

'Bonnets,' Dad supplies.

'Exactly. Those. And he *kind of* gets that, but not quite, *because . . .*'

'Show her,' says Dad.

Grant jerks his head towards the kitchen and we troop through. I'm not sure where this is going. My mouth has gone dry. The bad feeling I got when I saw Black Van Man just now has trebled. We seem to be looking at the kitchen window, above the sink. There's a dried-up primula in a plastic pot, and a sprinkling of peat moss on the sill, as if it's been knocked over and hurriedly righted.

'Your dad has seen a little girl drinking water from the tap.'

I shudder. He'd told me things like that before, but it gave me the creeps so much I just wanted to shut him up. I've discounted his fears, in much the same way as Charlotte sometimes discounts me. Now I feel sickened. He must have felt so alone, so scared. But there's no time to dwell on it. Grant is pointing to something on the windowpane. I stoop closer.

The ghost of an impression. A child's handprint upon the glass. The breath stalls in my chest.

Grant says, 'Look closer. It's on the *inside*.'

Sarah

I take a step back. My mind takes a step back too, fails to compute.

'That's not possible. Dad's had no visitors for months, and certainly not any kids. Has someone visited you with a child, Dad?'

My father comes up close to me. His voice is low but surprisingly strong. 'I've gone along with the party line on this, Sarah. Yes, some of the Figures might be hallucinations, but I'm telling you there is SOMEONE COMING INTO MY HOUSE!'

The effort of raising his voice leaves him breathless. I've never seen him look more vulnerable. I want to reach out to him, but I don't know how. The should have's come thick and fast – I should have spent more time with him, listened to him. I take a deep breath and go to the back door. It's unlocked and apparently the key is missing. A welcome cool breeze rushes in when I open it. Stress has brought on a hot flush; I press my hands against my burning cheeks. I survey the garden. A couple of plastic planters have been knocked over and one of the patio chairs is pushed against the back wall.

Grant follows my gaze. 'Things are disappearing from the patio table. Food mainly. Crusts of bread, a fly cemetery.'

'A sausage roll, once,' Dad adds.

'And the patio chair keeps mysteriously placing itself beside the back wall. I thought it was your dad moving it.'

'And I thought it was Grant.'

'And it turns out it was neither of us.'

They pause to let this sink in. I'm just about to ask for an explanation about the Lego, when Dad says with great finality, 'We think there may be rough types in Mrs Chalmers' house. Squatters. Grant went over the wall to check things out.'

'Oh God. Black Van Man. We have a cleaner at work, Mai. You know Mai, don't you, Grant?' My voice turns waspish, but Grant looks bemused rather than busted. 'She arrives every morning in a creepy black van. The same van passed me just now and disappeared into the cul-de-sac.' I nod towards the wall.

'The place is a tip,' Grant says. 'Looks like a builder's yard. I think we should investigate.'

'Or let the authorities deal with it.'

My words are lost. Grant is already crossing the lawn.

That spectral handprint has really shaken me up. My legs wobble as I follow Grant across the grass.

'I really don't think we should be doing this.' I try to stall him but he's already climbing onto the patio chair. 'I have to warn you, Grant, if you're having a thing with Mai, you'd better back off. That guy in the black van is seriously scary.'

He stares down at me from the chair. 'What the hell are you talking about? I don't know anyone called Mai.' He turns back to whatever he's spotted over the wall. 'I can see the van parked in the driveway. A Merc. It's a builder's van. Look at the cement dust on it.'

'Can you see symbols on the back?'

'Symbols?' His voice sounds far off.

'Smiley faces, except they're not smiling. They're miserable. I think it's a cry for help.' I tell him about how I'd added a round face of my own, as an experiment, and how some unknown hand had drawn in the mouth later. Horrible new possibilities are starting to open up like a seismic crack in the fabric of this sleepy neighbourhood.

Grant swears softly. 'Maybe they're modern-day witch marks.'

The remainder of my body heat slinks away. 'We need to call someone.'

But he has already vaulted onto the top of the wall. My own ascent takes longer and is more of a struggle, but I've no intention of being left behind. For once, I'm not going to stay on the safe side. There's a lot of scrambling on my part. I pull a muscle in my arm and scrape my shin, but eventually I drop down into the flower bed where Grant is crouching beneath a shrub.

'Dahlias. Watch out for the earwigs. This is crazy – someone will see us!'

He shushes me. 'The blinds are all drawn. Unless someone comes out, they won't spot us.'

Now is not the best time, but I'm desperate to get to the bottom of the pendant mystery.

'Grant, how did you get the pendant?'

He holds up his hands and replies in a whisper, 'I found it. Did you lose it?'

'Did I lose it? No, I didn't lose it! I gave it away. I was worried about Mai, so I gave her it for protection. I know it's probably silly superstition, but . . .' Anxiously, I move aside a bunch of leaves to get a clearer view of the house. One of the upstairs windows is a blank square with no blind. There's no sign of life, no lights, no noise.

'So tell me more about this Mai.'

Even I can see he is genuinely bewildered. The thought of

Grant carrying on with Mai has been tormenting me. Now I feel utterly foolish: a jealous middle-aged woman. Relationships are really not my forte and I've fallen at the first hurdle. Taking a deep breath, I fill him in on the relevant details. 'She's Vietnamese. She's always dropped off at work by Black Van Man' – I gesture towards the silent vehicle – 'who almost mowed Peggy and me down when we tried to investigate. She had a black eye and we caught her stealing food. We were worried about her. Oh my God. It's staring us in the face, isn't it? Right under our noses.'

Grant is looking pained. 'Slave labour. They talk about it in the past tense but it's never gone away.'

Human trafficking in Cornhill Crescent.

I swallow hard. 'Here I am worrying about how many Kilgour shoppers ended up with a one-legged chicken, when all along that girl was starving. I should have alerted someone sooner!'

'Sssh.' He points to the upstairs window. A tiny moon face shimmers behind the glass. Even from here we can see it's a child's face. We remain motionless, as if it might vanish before our eyes.

'She must have been taking food home to the child. Her child.' He changes his position. It's hard on the limbs, crouching under a bush, and I'm not sure what we're still doing here. 'I had a hunch, brought some toys from the nursery. I was going to leave them on the patio table. I reckoned if the toys disappeared we'd know for sure there was a real live kid coming into the garden. Birds don't take toys.'

Under the dahlias, our eyes meet. 'What the hell do we do now?'

'We need to get that kid out of that house.'

*

I rise carefully to my feet. My knees are aching and it's a relief to straighten up. The face at the window immediately darts out of sight, only to reappear a few seconds later. I guess she's curious. Is it a girl? Only a semi-circle of face is now visible: two eyes and a mop of hair. She's peeping over the window ledge. I make an exaggerated pantomime gesture. *Come down*. From ground level, Grant urges caution, but crusader zeal is now zipping through me. I can rescue her. It's too late for Abel; too late for all the little kids that were held in Lumsdain House over the centuries, but this kid – *this* kid is almost in touching distance of safety.

Come down. Don't be afraid.

Without warning, the back door swings open. *Aw fuck*. We both go into panic mode, scrambling from cover, tripping, heading towards the back wall, but it's too late. We've been spotted. Time to talk our way out of trouble.

Black Van Man looks very, very angry. 'Who the fuck are you?' he growls in heavily accented English.

'We live in the house over the wall.' I shoot him a wide smile, which wobbles at the corners. 'We . . . we lost something.'

The man approaches. He's all in black – naturally! – but the effect is blurred with cement dust. Tattoos of thorny roses encircle giant biceps and snake under the sleeves of his T-shirt.

I scrabble around for an excuse, a reason as to why we're lurking in the back garden. 'We've lost the cat. Have you seen it? It's black.' I start to call, 'Puss, puss, puss!'

'What the fuck?' Grant hisses at me. We trade glares.

The man is suspicious and spoiling for a fight. I continue to smile idiotically at him, a harmless catless person.

'Get the *fuck* out of my property.'

His English is very good. I try to make eye contact, but the brim of his cap obscures his eyes, leaving deep clefts of shadow. Any thoughts of trying to appeal to his better nature melt away as quickly as the child's face at the now vacant bedroom window. Somehow, my brain has conflated the Reverend Wilkie with this gangmaster. I take a step forward, with Grant's low warning in my ears.

'Who's the little girl?' I jerk my head towards the window.

The guy doesn't move. He's solid, like an ox. He's weighing me up. I think of the damage to Mai's face, but I'm not going to let him intimidate me.

'She's mine,' he says eventually.

I narrow my eyes at him. His meaning is clear, but he's not going to get away with that, either. 'She's Mai's child, isn't she? Mai was stealing from the store, which suggests to me she's being kept short of food or the money to buy food.'

The guy smiles, an alligator smile, with teeth. He recognises me. 'You're the bossy cunt from the shop.'

I raise my chin, even though it's wobbling as much as my smile. 'Good to see you again. We're going to go now, but rest assured we'll be making a full report to the authorities.'

Behind me, Grant groans. 'Not now, Sarah. Let's just . . .'

I imagine the Scooby Doo gang back-pedalling over the wall at this point, accompanied by appropriate sound effects, but the only sound is Black Van Man's two-fingered whistle. The shrillness riffs through my bladder. Did I really think he'd be working alone?

'The invitation to leave is . . .' His vocabulary fails him, but I get the picture. Timed out.

The situation degenerates into a bad movie scene. Two goons come out of the house, similarly dark and threatening, muscles bulging under their shirts.

Grant grabs my arm. I turn on him in panic. 'I told you we should have called someone!'

I've never been so scared in my life; my legs have turned

to jelly. I always thought the idea of knees knocking together was a joke, but I'm not laughing now. Black Van Man mutters something in his own language and the two men lunge forward and grab a hold of Grant. I'm not expecting it. Reality slips into a slow-moving, pared-down version. My blood freezes, turning me into an observer. I see two strangers converging on Grant. One punches him in the gut, the other smacks him in the face. A single grunt, Grant's trainers skid on the grass, and he goes down with such a sickening thud that it brings me round. I hate confrontation but now is not the time to be passive. I wade in, desperately trying to haul off the nearest assailant. Clinging to his arm is like trying to control a pile of runaway logs. I end up with an elbow in the face. I fall backwards and land painfully on my backside. The fight and the breath are knocked out of me, but the attack is short and sharp, over in the blink of an eye. A warning.

Black Van Man calls off his goons with a sharp command. He doesn't come any closer, just spits out a parting shot. 'Get out and don't come back. You don't speak to *anyone*, do I make myself clear?'

They back off, leaving Grant crumpled beside the dahlias. One of them growls at me and I scuttle backwards.

I throw myself at Grant's prone body. There's blood all over his face and he's groaning and clutching at his ribs. I mop the blood from Grant's nose with my sleeve.

'Can you stand? Come on!' I try to haul him upright, but his body is rigid, clenched against the pain, his face bloodless beneath all the messy tomato-ketchup red.

'What the hell do we do now?'

I see the lady waving at me, and I want to yell at her to go back to the safe side of the wall. I come down the stairs, go out the back door while the men are arguing. They don't see me. The lady is very upset and the man with the funny hair is on the ground. I try not to look but I can see the blood. There is a plastic step on this side of the wall which I use to climb to the other side. The drop down is so high it makes my teeth rattle and my head pound.

The old man's back door is never locked. I like to think he leaves the door open specially for me, because he knows how hungry I am, how thirsty, but sometimes he can be very cross and it's best to avoid him. I push open the door. The kitchen is empty. The kettle is warm and there are three mugs laid out for tea.

I like the kitchen best. It smells of home. Not like my grand-mother's kitchen in Ninh Binh, but it smells like an old man's home should – of bread and soup and the sticky sweets he keeps in a tin by the window. The big man always says if I don't stay out of sight people will come and take me away and I will never see my mother again. If I stay still and silent they forget about me. So now I am a ghost, only moving when no one is around to see me. I don't really exist.

In his bedroom, the old man keeps a box full of jewels. I love to look at them, and once I took a ring to add to my treasures. I feel bad about that, and I know I should give it back, but we had to leave all our things in Vietnam. I just want something of my own. My mother doesn't know about the ring, but one day she came back from work and gave me a gift all wrapped up in her hand. Keep it away from the men, she said. It's special. It's our secret. It's very small and smooth, and it looks like one of the stones I found in the garden. She says it is full of luck, but I'm not so sure. My mother has been wrong before. It's full of holes and I'm afraid all the luck will drip out. Then something bad might happen. Just in case, I took the gift outside and hung it on the rose bush that grows beside the yellow flowers.

I think I was right. Our luck has run out. Bad things are happening over the wall and I need to make it stop. The thing I want is in the other room. As I creep through the kitchen doorway, I meet the old man coming towards me.

He peers at me and raises his walking stick. I'm afraid he may beat me with it so I stand very still with my eyes to the floor. I've learned to stay quiet, like a mouse, when men get cross. He says something in a sharp voice, but I don't understand. As he comes nearer I step to the side and we circle each other. I think he is afraid of me, but I don't know why. I'm not really a ghost, just a little girl. I reach out and touch his hand. His hands look like my grandmother's, all crooked and dried out, like lizard skin. I don't want to scare him. Being scared is the worst thing in the world. He pulls away, but that gives me enough space to run around him. The thing I'm looking for sits on the little table beside his chair.

Many months ago, Ma showed me what to do. They took away her mobile phone when we got to England, but in that first house there was a telephone fixed to the wall. It was dead, but she showed me what to do anyway. She'd seen it in a movie. Until now, neither of us has been brave enough to do what I'm about to do.

I pick up the handset. I press the buttons, just like she showed me. Nine. Three times. It rings and rings. Maybe this will change everything. The table is dusty. I draw a round face with two dots. A lady's voice begins to speak in the language I don't really understand. I'm not sure what to do next, but the old man is standing behind me. He has kind eyes in a wrinkly face. They don't look scared any more. I can hear the lady's voice, quite loud now, so I pass the telephone to him. Old people always know what to do. I glance down at my dust drawing and with my finger add a smile.

John

Sarah places a mug of tea on the little table beside his chair with a loud sigh. It's been a difficult few hours. She traces the path of the little girl's finger in the dust, lingering over the smiley mouth.

'Not having a cuppa? You're always on the go,' he chides gently.

'Mirren is picking Grant up from the hospital and I said I'd drop by to see him.'

'How's he doing?'

'They didn't keep him in, just long enough to patch him up. He's got a broken rib and his face is a mess. He was worried about his nose, but it isn't broken. Could've been worse.'

'Who would believe it, eh?' He shakes his head. 'In this day and age, right on your doorstep. I even have the number written down. Look.' He reaches for his notebook and turns to the back, points to the list of helpline numbers he's copied from the television: Salvation Army Appeal, Dementia Awareness and the Modern Slavery Hotline. 'If only I'd known it was a *real* little girl haunting me, I'd have called that number right away. The social worker who came to pick her up said that the little one's mother had taught her how to dial 999 in case anything happened to her. But why didn't Mai confide in you, Sarah? She must have had every opportunity to get help.'

'It's easy for us to say that, Dad, but it's all about fear, isn't it? People traffickers take everything from them: passport, money, dignity. How can they survive alone, in a strange country, with no work and no bank account? Everyone a stranger and no family support. I can't imagine it.'

He reaches over and squeezes her hand. 'We don't know how lucky we are. What will happen now?'

'The police took the three men away. Maybe there are other migrants in there, who knows? You should have seen it, Dad – police, ambulances, social workers. They didn't hang around.'

'It's just terrible.' John takes a sip of his tea. It's okay but a bit skimpy on the sugar. 'What would Mrs Chalmers think? Do you think her son knew they were in his house?'

'Maybe he did a deal with them, who knows? Good for little Chau, though, slipping over the wall like that and making the call.'

He coughs. 'It was me, actually, who told them what was going on. Doesn't speak a word of English, the wee lass. Chau, is that her name? They came in here to collect her, but she was terrified, poor little mite.'

'Mai told me her name. It means "like a pearl". They've been taken to a family centre somewhere. At least they're together and safe now.' Sarah gets to her feet. 'Hopefully someone will give us an update. At least you won't have anyone sneaking around your house any more.'

He nods, but the jury's out on that one. There's still the little people and the horned gargoyles to contend with, but he knows better than to mention them.

Sarah

The next day, I tell the whole incredible story to Peggy. We're leaning on the windowsill, watching the customers come and go. A normal Scottish Saturday morning: tired mums in leggings, whiny kids, guys buying cheap lager for the afternoon sport. I can still see the black van reversing into the entrance, the tiny figure of Mai traipsing across the tarmac. How did she feel leaving that little girl in the house every day, probably hungry and cold and with no one to mind her? Was the back of the van full of enslaved migrants en route to a building site? There's still a police presence at Mrs Chalmers' house. The neighbours will be agog. I can see the press quotes now: *It's such a quiet neighbourhood. Nothing like that ever happens here. We're just so shocked.*

A finger of fear chills my neck. I hope it works out for Mai. I hope someone helps them, shows them a bit of kindness. It could have been so different. No one ever notices the cleaner.

I turn to Peggy. 'Just as well you don't miss a trick, Peg. I didn't even spot the black eye.'

Satisfaction steals over her features. 'You might think I'm a gossip, but some things need to be talked about. Too many things get swept under the carpet because people don't want to get involved. I can't believe it. Imagine that sort of thing happening under our noses, right here in Kilgour. In Wisebuy!'

We let that settle, watch the traffic in silence. 'The wee girl was coming into Dad's house looking for food,' I tell her. 'God knows how they've been living. According to Grant, they bring Vietnamese women over here to work in nail bars. Often they have kids.'

'According to Grant?' Peggy arches her pencilled brows.

'Don't!' I move away from the window and stretch. Every muscle in my body is aching from yesterday's encounter. 'I only came in for a couple of hours today. I'm owed some time.'

I check the time on my phone, notice a couple of new messages. There's one from Grant: *Fancy a drink tonight? I'm feeling a bit better.*

I won't reply straight away. I don't want him to know how desperately worried I've been. Hannah would no doubt tell me to play it cool. I do a quick calculation. It's three here, so early evening in India. I go into Messenger and press call. The usual beeps, the typical sick anticipation in my stomach. It's so long since we've spoken face-to-face, mother and daughter.

The video screen comes to life, but it's Aisling.

'How goes it, Mrs S? How are ya?'

'Hi, Aisling. Where's Hannah? She mentioned a job last time? Where is she? I really need to speak to her. Why have you got her phone?'

'Chill, Mrs S! She's in the shower. I'll get her to call you back.'

'Okay, thanks. Have her call me back.'

My hand strays to the hollow of my throat. I'm so glad to have the hagstone back. My belief in it may be at odds with my rational self, but it's a comfort against the threats you can't see, the evils that you have no control over.

*

In my imagination, the Reverend Wilkie dresses in black and roams the countryside on a dark, mud-spattered horse. The

239

wide brim of his hat shades the deep sockets of his eyes, and children hide when he passes by, staying silent as mice. I've built a picture of him in my mind. Perhaps the picture is untrue, but it's true to me. Somewhere along the line the image has been fused with the old illustration in Hannah's book. Wee Willie Wilkie with a shock of white hair poking out from beneath his night cap. That down-turned waspish mouth. Trawling the hospital in the dead of night with a dripping candle. No hiding place.

One week on, and I'm just about done with the Reverend Wilkie. I feel obliged to go through the last few photocopies, but it's like struggling to complete a mediocre novel. I want to find out how it ends, but I'm not expecting any more surprises. The stones have all been overturned. What it's taught me is that the things that have come to light aren't always the things you expect, but what you can expect is that history will repeat itself, century after century, and we will never learn. Hungry kids, frightened women, abuse of power.

Today is the day when everything slots into place. Look at this:

I did myself travel to Edinburgh to seek a commission from the Privy Council to try the Witch Alisoune Gowdie. The trial by our magistraytes is but a formaility. The goode residents of Kilgour have made their wishes known. The woman is dangerous and a threat to Christian society.

The sayde Alisoune Gowdie was soone after araigned, condemned, and adjudged by the law to die, and then to be burned according to the lawe of the lande. Whereupon she was put into a carte, and being first strangled, was immediately put into a great fire, being readie provided for that purpose, and there burned on the Witch's Knowe on a Saterdaie in the ende of October, 1648.

It was my beleyf all along that Alisoune Gowdie was a

witch. She was born with sight in only one eye, a sure sign that she had been touched by evil in the womb. They say a sightless eye looks out into the Land of Faeries and it's only but a small step until she was gazing into the eyes of Satan himself.

I mull over that last paragraph for a very long time, and then with a great sigh I push away the papers. This is the end of the story, but not quite. Not quite. I need a coffee. Grant is coming over tonight and it's time I started thinking about the living rather than the dead.

I have a shower and wash my hair, stick on a nice floral dress I've been keeping for *an occasion*, although I'm not sure what sort of occasion it will be. Grant is still in a lot of pain. The doctor says it will take up to a month for his ribs to heal.

He arrives at half seven on the dot, with flowers, which makes me want to laugh. He looks perkier than I thought he'd be, despite the bruising to his face. His handsome nose remains intact, but his usual bouncy energy has taken a knock and he seems content to sit carefully on the sofa.

'Flowers?' I come to stand in front of him, hugging them to my chest.

'What? Isn't that what you want? Flowers and stuff?'

'What do you think I want?'

He considers this with his head on one side. 'Someone reliable and conventional. Someone who notifies you of arrangements in advance and can remember Duran Duran first time around. You know that's not me, right?'

'No, it's not, but you'll do for now.' I lean over and kiss him, very gently, on account of his injuries. 'I'll go and put these in water. Do you want a beer?'

He makes a face. 'Maybe just a coffee. I'm on really strong painkillers and my mum's picking me up in a couple of hours.'

I can't help giggling. 'How romantic. She doesn't know about . . .' I don't want to say 'us'. Is there an 'us'?

'No, not that she'd care. She's very open-minded. I don't think there'll be much romance happening tonight.'

I'm still laughing as I trot down to the kitchen. He's a bit pissed off, but I'm relieved, if I'm honest. He's not the sort of person I can leave dangling in the friend zone, and this buys me some time, before I have to make some sort of commitment.

I make two mugs of coffee. When I come back, he's resting his head against the back of the couch with his eyes closed. For a minute I think the painkillers have kicked in and he's sleeping, but he opens an eye when I place the mugs on the coffee table. I sit down beside him.

'Do you want to hear a good story?'

'You're the storyteller,' he murmurs. 'Go ahead.'

I jump up and grab my photocopies from the desk. The floorboard squeaks.

'Jesus, that floor would do my head in if I lived here. You should get someone to fix it.'

'It might be a big job and I'm always too busy. Look.' I sit down with him on the sofa and spread the pages across our knees. 'This is where he talks about her execution – poor Alie – but here' – I point to the words – 'it mentions she was blind in one eye, from birth. Do you think she had Charles Bonnet Syndrome? She told someone she saw little people. Sounds a lot like Dad's hallucinations.'

Grant raises an eyebrow. 'It's possible. They wouldn't have had a clue about sight and perception in those days. But the real reason is that she knew the minister's dirty secret. He wanted to get rid of her.'

'Of course. That's at the heart of it.' I gaze reflectively at the papers.

'Have you finished it?'

'Well, some of it might be missing. It just seems to peter out. Listen to this bit. He's actually included the costs for the execution . . . £35 for the guys who extracted the confession; £6 to George Cathie the witch brodder; £10 to the executioner. Even the wooden stake is there, which is thirteen shillings and over £2 for peat and coal for the fire.'

'God, that's gross. Costly business, burning witches.'

'It gets worse. He tries to bill Alie's husband for the money.'

'No!'

'That's what they did! You were responsible for your wife's misdeeds. But here it says that Robert Webster left the parish – upped and went, "lock, stock and barrel" – and, yay, he took Abel with him!'

'Really? The lad got away?' Grant moves cautiously so he can see the page. 'This bit?'

I point out the sentence. To be honest, I'm beginning to know the minister's handwriting as intimately as my own. '"The above monies were to be demanded of Robert Webster for the execution of his wife, but it was found that he has left this parish lock, stock and barrel and has taken the child Abel with him. Somebody must be made to pay. I have intelligence of where he is boarding, so I will ride out tomorrow and parley with him." And that's where it stops.'

I look under the page, as if something else might be lurking there.

Grant wrinkles his nose. 'Hmmm. Well, it was good knowing you, Mr Wilkie, but our acquaintance ends here. You a *bad man*. Hope you met a *bad man* end.' He collects the papers together.

I laugh. 'I've spent way too long in the seventeenth century.'

Grant eases himself out of the couch, papers in hand.

'I can do that. Are you okay?'

'So long as I don't cough or laugh. Don't make me laugh.'

'I'll try not to.' I listen to the sounds of him moving around the desk, shuffling the papers as he tidies them into a pile. The floorboard squeaks. I check my phone and read Hannah's message: *All good here, mam. I'll call you at the weekend* ☺

It makes me feel pleasantly mellow. At least I know Hannah's okay. I do miss speaking with her. Idly, I re-read the message. Something doesn't quite tally, but my attention is grabbed by a few choice words from Grant. I glance over the back of the couch. The man can't leave anything alone. He's pulled back the rug to expose the wonky floorboard.

'Grant,' I swivel around and kneel on the couch, 'leave it! It's fine. You'll hurt yourself.'

'It's annoying me.' He bounces a foot on it, just to demonstrate. 'I have a mate who could fix that for you on the cheap.'

Crack.

Oh shit.

I slam down my coffee mug. 'I told you to leave it alone.'

By the time I get to my feet, Grant has managed to hunker down and remove the broken wedge of board. He's grimacing in pain and I'm just about to protest again when I realise he's uncovered a sizeable hole under the floor.

We both peer into it, Grant with growing fascination, me hoping not to see daylight.

'Have you broken through to my downstairs ceiling?'

'No, no, it hasn't. Look, there's a gap between the joists but it's stuffed with old rags. If I can just lift the rest of this board, I can . . . Have you got a hammer?'

I sigh heavily. This is going to end in disaster, I can feel it.

The remainder of the floorboard comes away quite easily. It's pretty rotten. I make a mental note to contact a joiner in the morning, but probably not Grant's budget pal. He's staring into the hole, prodding something with the claw of the hammer.

'What is it? Buried doubloons? Seriously, maybe Robert hid the family silver!'

A frisson of excitement runs up my bare arms and I crouch beside the hole, heedless of my new dress. There's a bundle of cloth. I touch it, and my hands come away damp and soily. It's like sailcloth, heavy-duty canvas.

Grant lifts it carefully clear of the gap and sets it down. It looks heavy, but the wrappings are coming loose and it's hard to gauge the shape. I think of all the stories I've heard – all the stories I've been told – of things being buried under floors. They are rarely pleasant. Dead cats to ward off witches. Unwanted babies.

I shuffle back a notch.

Grant is unwinding the covering. He glances up to meet my eye. 'Do you want to do the honours?'

I shake my head like a scared kid. He keeps unwrapping. Someone wanted to keep this well and truly hidden.

Because the package is so bulky and clammy and old, it slips from Grant's probing fingers and rolls. It rolls clear of the cloth. Across the centuries, against all odds, we come face-to-face with the Reverend William Wilkie.

*

The mummified head of the minister had been deliberately hidden. The location of his other body parts is a riddle for another day.

Right here, right now, is the last sort of buried treasure we expected to find.

It's difficult to comprehend what we're looking at. I'm not sure how I even know this is Wilkie, but trust me, I *know*.

Even the last remnants of his hair give the game away. They are just as I imagine, thick hanks of white still clinging to the bony scalp. What remains of the skin is taut and unrecognisable, scraps of a deep reddish leather. He had good teeth, William, possibly on account of Mrs Telfer's superior cooking skills, but his mouth, frozen in fear or disbelief, is downturned, like a child's drawing of a mouth. As if, in death, he has been disappointed. The Reverend's luck appears to have run out. Cause of death is unmistakeable and the murder weapon still visible. A sharp-ended seventeenth-century weaver's shuttle, complete with red thread, juts from the empty eye socket.

'Oh my days, that's horrible!' Grant makes a face and wipes his fingers on his trousers. 'What the fuck? It's been there all that time?'

All the time I've been living here, so has he. Just out of sight. Despite my revulsion, I can't take my eyes off the skull. I have a hundred questions, but right now I can only think of that last paragraph. That abrupt ending to a false and biased account, a legacy of bile and discrimination and accusing fingers.

'Robert must have killed him and brought him back here. A weaver's shuttle! And that red thread too. A bind against spells. He was making sure he protected himself, that the real witch didn't strike back.'

'What are we going to do with it?' Grant looks at his hands as if he has blood on them. There's a rank smell present that wasn't in the room before, and I suddenly want to get this thing out of my home.

'I'll phone Charlotte. She'll know who to contact. Or the police? I bet they'll rip up the whole bloody floor. This is a listed building. They'd better get a fully qualified tradesman in if they want to do that.'

Grant holds his side and grimaces. 'Don't make me laugh.'

I glance over at the head of the man who has occupied my thoughts for too long. 'If this is him, he got what he deserved.'

'If it's him. Do you think we'll ever find out?'

'Maybe, once the experts have been let loose on him. This is going to be a fantastic final chapter to my book.'

'Your book?'

I grin. 'I'm going to write Alie's story. The new story. At last, she's going to be heard.'

*

It's the perfect ending, isn't it? History can be problematic, of course; sometimes it's hard to sift the fact from the fiction, the lies from the truth. Stories are like puzzles, charity shop jigsaws with half the pieces missing. It's up to you to fill in the blanks, let your mind form a version of the true picture. We all have different versions – it's a matter of perspective – and even when you think you know the ending, prepare to be surprised. Other, bigger stories are unfolding just out of sight. You need to know how to read the clues.

TO BE CONTINUED ...

A Note from the Author

The town of Kilgour is a fictional one, although it could easily be any small town on the east coast of Scotland. Equally, the imaginary Alie Gowdie could be any one of the hundreds of women and men who were accused of witchcraft in the sixteenth and seventeenth centuries. Alie could be your ancestor, or mine.

Like Sarah Sutherland, I am very much an enthusiastic amateur in the history stakes, so I am deeply indebted to experts in the field, such as Julian Goodare, Director of the Survey of Scottish Witchcraft project, whose writings on the subject fired my imagination. The survey (Julian Goodare, Lauren Martin, Joyce Miller and Louise Yeoman) is an amazing resource and can be accessed online at www.shca. ed.ac.uk/Research/witches/.

Thanks also to the National Library of Scotland, a treasure trove of actual and virtual books. As I browsed its fascinating collection of digitised journals, the words of men such as Sir Archibald Wariston spoke to me across the centuries and gave me an insight into how the Reverend Wilkie might have put his thoughts into words.

I'm the first to admit that I like to make things up, but when writing about Alie's life and death, I've tried to be historically accurate and remain faithful to the language and ideology of the time. Any mistakes are all mine, and I apologise to the real historians! I have stitched together Alie's story from trial notes, actual confessions and contemporary accounts. Alie is an amalgam of several 'witches' from various parts of Scotland. She is an 'every-witch'; my humble attempt to give a face to the faceless and a voice to those who need to be heard.

As bizarre as it may seem, Charles Bonnet Syndrome is very real. My experience of caring for my late dad, who was diagnosed with the condition in his final years, has crept into this book. His optician explained that it often goes undiagnosed, with sufferers and their families assuming that dementia is the only possible explanation for such frightening visions. If this affects you or your loved one, please don't suffer in silence. There is information here: www.nhs.uk/conditions/charles-bonnet-syndrome.

Acknowledgements

As ever, I'm grateful to a whole family of people who helped bring this book into the world. Thank you to everyone at Polygon: Alison Rae, my editor, for her patience and good humour; Lucy Mertekis for organising me and being so helpful; the dream team of Jan, Kristian and Kathryn. Also Jamie and everyone else I don't always get to see, but I know are there, especially Neville and Hugh. Thanks so much for your continued support for my writing.

A huge thank you, as always, to the fabulous Jenny Brown, agent extraordinaire, always calm, always cheerful. I'm so lucky to be working with you.

Thank you to the members of the Angus Writers' Circle for their continued friendship and support, especially Gillian, Ann, Margaret and Suzanne. Thank you to my 'splinter group', Novellers – Dawn, Elizabeth, Kerry and Richard – for always being there, with inspirational words, wordsprints and endless lattes!

A big shout out to my family and friends. Thank you for all your support, for reading my books and badgering other people to read them! Thanks to June, Kenny and Fiona (Fobel Shop, Carnoustie) for putting up with my frequent absences in book festival season.

I'm so grateful to my 'virtual' friends on Twitter, all the writers, readers, reviewers and book bloggers who have been so generous and supportive.

I couldn't do it without you all!